Between
Earth and Sky

Also by Alan Morris
in Large Print:

By Honor Bound
Heart of Valor
Bright Sword of Justice

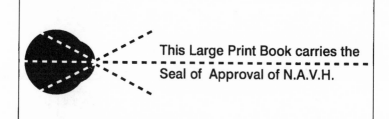

This Large Print Book carries the
Seal of Approval of N.A.V.H.

Guardians of the North

Between Earth and Sky

ALAN MORRIS

Thorndike Press • Thorndike, Maine

Published in 1999 by arrangement with
Bethany House Publishers.

Thorndike Large Print® Christian Fiction Series.

The tree indicium is a trademark of Thorndike Press.

The text of this Large Print edition is unabridged.
Other aspects of the book may vary from the original edition.

Set in 16 pt. Plantin.

Printed in the United States on permanent paper.

Library of Congress Cataloging in Publication Data

Morris, Alan, 1959–
    Between earth and sky / Alan Morris.
       p.   cm .
    Originally published in series: Guardians of the north,
Book 4
    ISBN 0-7862-1692-1 (lg. print : hc : alk. paper)
    1. Custer, George Armstrong, 1839–1876 —
Fiction. 2. Little Bighorn, Battle of the, Mont., 1876 —
Fiction. 3. Indians of North America — Wars —
Great Plains — Fiction. 4. Indians of North America —
Wars — 1866–1895 — Fiction. 5. Oglala Indians —
Kings and rulers — Fiction. 6. Crazy Horse, ca.
1842–1877 — Fiction. 7. Large type books. I. Title.
II. Series: Morris, Alan, 1959–   Guardians of the north.
[PS3563.O87395B48   1999]
813′.54—dc21   98-42037

To Stacy,
my big sister with real class,
who also happens to possess
a wicked left hook.

Contents

Part Four: Brave Hearts to the Front

Part One

May 1876

AMBITION

In years long-numbered with the past, when I was verging upon manhood, my every thought was ambitious — not to be wealthy, not to be learned, but to be great. I desired to link my name with acts & men, and in such a manner as to be a mark of honor — not only to the present, but to future generations.

George Armstrong Custer

Chapter One

Reception

Outside the chapel at Fort Macleod, a bank of ominous thunderheads scudded across the sky, tumbling over the late afternoon sun like gunsmoke. Lightning pulsed through the dark clouds in flashes and sparks. The resulting thunder was low and threatening as it rolled across the plains to the ears of the spectators gathered outside the chapel.

The people formed two long lines, extending all the way from the chapel to the mess hall. Every once in a while some of them would tear their eyes away from the approaching storm clouds to glance at the door of the chapel in anticipation.

Dressed in a fine cotton suit of deep blue and feeling quite self-conscious, Del Dekko eyed the black clouds and muttered, "Headed this way, too."

"What did you say, Del?" Hunter Stone asked. Well over six feet tall, Stone sometimes had trouble hearing the man who barely came to his shoulder. Hunter thought his hearing was going at times, even at the age of twenty-eight, and the thought disturbed him when he took the time to think about it, which didn't happen very often.

"I said that storm's headin' right toward us," Del declared.

"How do you know?"

Del had an unfortunate wandering eye, but he fixed the steady one on Stone in exasperation. "Hunter, when you gonna learn that I know the prairies? I know when it's gonna snow, and I know when it's gonna rain." He nodded toward the cloud bank. "It's comin' this way. Count on it."

"If you say so, Del," Stone said as he smiled and looked over at the huge sign that hung over the mess hall door. In neat large letters and bright red paint, it read:

CONGRATULATIONS
VIC AND MEGAN!!!

Hunter glanced across the path created by the two lines of people to the one responsible for the sign. His grin widened when he found her looking back at him. "It looks great, Reena."

"Thank you, sir," Reena O'Donnell replied demurely. Her black hair, normally long and flowing, was parted in the middle and arranged in intricate clusters of soft curls that framed her forehead and the sides of her face.

Hunter's breath caught as he gazed at her delicate high cheekbones, fine straight nose, and sky-blue eyes. "You look beautiful today, Reena."

"And you're very handsome."

Reena wore a lilac and beige calico dress with fitted bodice and narrow collar. The waist was slightly high, and the sleeves were long and tight with a slit, flared at elbow length. The oversleeves were trimmed with lilac silk.

Stone was dressed in his finest uniform, complete with saber and spotless white gauntlets. He glanced around at the other Mounties in the line who were indeed handsome in their dress uniforms. The heat and humidity of the May afternoon, however, caused sweat to roll down his well-dressed back. Suddenly impatient, he glanced at the door to the chapel just in time to see Jaye Eliot Vickersham and his brand-new bride, Mrs. Vickersham, appear, looking impossibly happy.

Vic, as his friends called him, had the eye and nose and jaw of England. His face reflected the personality inside of him: open, honest, and noble. The son of an earl, he was unfailingly polite, regal in bearing, and the best friend Hunter had ever known. Now, as Stone watched the couple pause at the top of the steps, he felt a rush of affection and admiration for his friend.

Vic's bride, Megan, was Reena's sister, though their resemblance to each other was negligible. Megan only came to Reena's shoulder in height, with honey-blond hair and a shapely figure. Standing on the stoop with her new husband, she beamed with pleasure.

The gathered crowd applauded the couple, then the Mounties in the line withdrew their sabers and lifted them high, forming an arch over the path to the mess hall for the reception. Vic, with a self-conscious grin at Hunter over all the pomp and circumstance, took Megan's arm and guided her through the throng of friends and wellwishers. Some of the ladies threw tiny violets over them as they walked beneath the shiny canopy of swords.

"Well, well, well," Del drawled as he, Reena, and Stone turned to follow the couple.

"What is it, Del?" Stone asked, though

14

he knew what was coming.

"I'm afraid my old friend Vic is now among the league of frightened men." He shook his head sadly. "Sure is a shame. He was such a good man."

"Del!" Reena cried.

"Oh, sorry, Miss Reena. I didn't know you was behind me."

"It doesn't matter! Today's supposed to be a happy day for Vic."

Del pulled at the waistline of his trousers uncomfortably and again eyed the menacing storm looming ever closer. "I guess I'm happy for him — if he's happy. You really think he is?"

"Of course! Just look at him."

"Mmm."

"Del, why are you so down on marriage?" Hunter asked.

"Years ago I had a best friend break us up by gettin' married. Ruined his life. He never knew what happiness was 'til he married that gal — then it was too late."

"What happened to them?" Reena asked, with a wink at Stone.

"She might as well of just shot him on their wedding day. Would've saved him ten years of misery. When she put her finger through that wedding ring, it was the last thing she ever did by hand. Straightaway

15

she had him washing dishes, clothes, kids — then he'd have his own chores to tend to." Del shook his head and grunted. "Poor ol' Richie. Died nearly ten years to the day he married that hag."

"His heart give out or something?" Stone asked.

"Nope. He fell down a well. She prob'ly wouldn't have even missed him, except for the dirty dishes piling up in the sink. Poor ol' Richie," Del repeated.

Reena slipped her arm through Hunter's and said, "Somehow I don't think Megan will have Vic washing dishes and clothes, Del."

"Are you sure, Miss Reena?"

"Yes, I'm quite sure."

"That's good. She'd miss him if he fell down a well, though, wouldn't she?"

Reena laughed, and Hunter smiled, admiring the musical sound of her soft voice.

"Yes," Reena assured their friend, "Megan would definitely miss her husband if he fell down a well."

As Del entered the mess hall, Stone paused at the door. The wedding reception had already begun inside, and the sound of singing and the tapping of dancing feet on the wooden floor flowed outdoors. The noise of approaching horses made Stone

16

turn toward the large gate of the fort just as two teams of oxen came through, straining at their yokes from the heavily ladened wagons they pulled. Behind them, a troop of fifty Mounties followed. When they were all inside the gate, the interior of the fort seemed to have shrunk considerably.

Standing beside Stone, Reena followed his gaze toward the new men. "Did someone start a war I don't know about?"

Stone grinned without humor. "As a matter of fact, they did. The Sioux in Montana and Dakota Territory have become more powerful and skilled than the U.S. Army had counted on. Our own Secretary of State Scott is very nervous and sent us those field guns and extra men."

"Those guns are very ugly," Reena observed with obvious distaste.

"Mmm . . . and extremely deadly. They're nine-pounders."

"They look like they weigh quite a bit more than that."

Laughing, Stone told her, "No, that means they fire nine-pound shells and create quite a mess."

They watched as two men led the oxen to the quartermaster's office. The barrels of the cannons gleamed a dull, ash-colored gray beneath the sunless sky. During Stone's training at Dufferin, he'd seen the damage the field guns were capable of inflicting, and it had been impressive in a frightening sort of way. He hoped that he wouldn't find himself on the receiving end of a barrage from them anytime in the future.

"Come on," Reena said, taking his arm. "Let's not think about cannons today. This is a day to enjoy the festivities."

"All right . . . but I've got to inform Colonel Macleod that the reinforcements have arrived." He heard a deep roll of thunder come from the storm bank and cast a wary eye at the dark sky before following Reena inside.

The aroma of roasted venison permeated the air, and Hunter felt his mouth watering. He'd barely gotten through the door when an arm was thrown around his shoulders.

"There's my best man." Vickersham grinned. "I was beginning to wonder if you'd even attend my reception."

"Where's Megan?"

Vickersham shrugged, looking around the crowded room. "I don't know . . . somewhere in that mass of humanity."

"Shouldn't you be hovering over her, giving her every bit of your attention, throwing lovesick looks her way?"

Laughing, Vickersham replied, "Hunter, have you forgotten? We're married now. Married people don't act that way."

"You sound like you've been talking to Del."

"What was that?" Del asked, appearing in front of them. He held a cup of punch in one hand and a pastry in the other. Crumbs from the pastry were scattered in his bushy gray beard. "I heard my name, and ordinarily I wouldn't worry about it, but when it's you two doing the talkin' I get worried."

Beside Del stood Constable Dirk Becker, a huge, solidly built young man of twenty. Becker's passion since childhood was knives — any kind and any size — and that love had directly contributed to the long scar that ran down the left side of his face from cheek to jawline. The pale line gave a hardness to his innocent young face that often disturbed those who didn't know him. To those who did, it was merely accepted as part of Dirk — unfortunate, to be sure, yet just as much a feature as his bright, inquisitive blue eyes or his short-cropped brown hair.

His companion was Jenny Sweet, a shy, introspective girl who was the daughter of a dead whiskey trader. She was short, barely coming to Becker's shoulder, with light brown hair and hazel eyes.

Becker thrust out his hand to Vickersham. "Congratulations, Vic. Megan is a wonderful woman."

"Thank you, Dirk. Maybe you'll be fortunate enough to find one someday." He didn't glance pointedly at Jenny, but everyone knew what he was implying.

"Now, Vic," Del complained, "don't go wishin' a wife on that boy. Maybe he's like me — a confirmed bachelor."

Stone raised an eyebrow at Becker. "How about that, Dirk? Are you going to follow in Del's footsteps?"

Becker, every bit as tall as Stone's six foot three, glanced down at Del. "That's . . . um . . . *scary* is the only word that comes to mind."

"Now, listen here, you big —"

Stone cleared his throat loudly. "Well, if it isn't the radiant bride."

Megan strode up to them, unable to conceal her confidence and happiness on her wedding day. "Gentlemen."

Stone leaned over and planted a gentle kiss on her cheek.

"Thank you, Hunter."

"Congratulations." With a wink at

Becker, he added, "I sure don't admire your future, though."

"What do you mean?"

Stone threw an arm around Vickersham's shoulders and said, "Megan, don't you realize the responsibility you took on when you married this limey? I know, because I've lived in the same room with him for too long. In the future you will have to endure years and years of impossible cleanliness — verging on prissiness, mind you — unfailing, sickening politeness, and that clipped aristocratic accent to listen to."

Megan pushed Stone's arm off of Vickersham and kissed her husband on the cheek. "Sounds glorious."

"Quite," Vic agreed with a grin.

"I think I'm gonna be sick," Del muttered.

"Del, why are you eating a pastry before dinner?" Vickersham asked.

Defiantly drawing himself up to his full height, Del said, "I expect I can eat what I want, when I want. Comes with being unattached, you see, though you wouldn't know anything about that anymore."

"What's all that commotion outside?" Becker asked, craning his neck to see around Stone.

21

Snapping his fingers, Stone said, "I forgot . . . it's the reinforcements and nine-pounder cannons. I've got to go tell the colonel."

Megan and Vickersham drifted over to a window to see all the excitement outside. They were silent for a moment, then Megan said, "There's no possibility of any of you going down to Montana to fight, is there?"

"Of course not, darling. That Indian unrest is not Canada's problem."

Megan sighed. "I still remember the day a company from our neighborhood in Chicago went off to fight in the War of Secession. The town held a big parade, and all the young men were handsome in their new uniforms as they marched by, but . . ."

"But what?"

"A good many of those boys didn't come back." She nodded out the window at the scarlet-clad men milling around, inspecting the cannon like boys with a new play toy. "That sight reminds me of that day."

"Horrible business, that war. Any war, for that matter."

Megan suddenly turned to him, her face intense. "Promise me something, Vic."

Attempting to make light of it, though he

knew what was coming, Vickersham said lightly, "Anything, my dear, anything. Today's the day for promises."

"I'm glad you feel that way," Megan returned, the serious tone still in her voice. "I want you to promise me that you won't fight in a war."

"Megan —"

"Promise me," she insisted.

Vic took her in his arms and gazed directly into her eyes. "Darling, there are no guarantees in Police work. You know that as well as —"

"You could guarantee me if you wanted to. Please, Vic?"

Vickersham saw the pleading look in her eyes and knew how important the promise would be to her. Visions of Indian uprisings in the North-West Territory filled his thoughts, though there were no signs in sight of any problems from the tribes. The Canadian Indians — Blackfoot, Sarcee, Assiniboine, Blood — all were a peaceful people whose chiefs had welcomed the Mounties onto their land with open arms. There was the occasional renegade who broke the law, but nothing close to an armed rebellion by a whole tribe. It could be worse in the Territory — it could be the rampaging Sioux on Canada's soil, instead of America's.

Grinning suddenly, Vic kissed Megan full on the mouth quickly, then said, "I promise."

"Thank you. Oh, and by the way — I love you."

"I love you, too."

Colonel James Macleod passed by them on the way to the door, hardly able to control his excitement about the newly arrived reinforcements. He was a tall man, with piercing blue eyes and the air of complete authority about him. He held the title of Assistant Commissioner of the North-West Mounted Police, and no one doubted that the "Assistant" part of his title would disappear one day.

"Do you see them, Vickersham?" Macleod asked as he hurried by.

"I see them, sir."

"They're beautiful, aren't they?"

Before Vickersham could answer, the colonel was out the door, hurrying toward the new men and cannons.

"His day has been made, hasn't it?" Megan commented.

Vickersham gently wrapped his arm around her shoulders. "Not like mine has."

"May I have your attention?" Stone called from the dais at the far end of the mess hall. Reena stood beside him, and both of them were grinning at Vic and Megan.

"Oh no," Vic muttered.

"It's been brought to my attention," Stone went on, "that the best man and" — he bowed to Reena beside him — "the best lady —"

"Thank you." Reena smiled.

"Hear, hear!" Del Dekko called.

"— are to propose toasts to the honorable couple, even if it is just cherry punch in these glasses. Vic, would you and Megan please come forward?"

"I was hoping they'd forget this part," Vic whispered to her as they walked arm in arm to the front. On the way he received even more slaps on the back from his fellow Mounties. When he reached the dais, he spread his hands wide and said, "Here I am, Hunter — unarmed, and ready for the verbal fusillade."

"Oh, that's too rich." Stone grinned, then raised his glass of punch for the toast. "If Vic's appearance were as impressive as his vocabulary, he'd be prettier than his wife. Alas, old friend, that's not the case." When the laughter subsided, Stone continued. "I'm not much on speeches, and when I was informed that I'd have this duty, I was less than pleased. However, after thinking about it, I can't think of a better honor." He raised himself up to his full height. "To Jaye Eliot Vickersham — the best friend, finest Christian man, and most capable officer that I've ever had the honor to know and serve with. Every life in this room has been touched and blessed by knowing you, Vic. Congratulations!"

Many "Hear, hears" were uttered, and the whole room raised their glasses to honor Vic. Blushing, he lifted a hand to acknowledge them and reached out to shake Stone's hand. "Thank you, Hunter."

Reena waited while Vickersham received more congratulations from the people around him, then gazed down at Megan. "I don't have to tell you —"

She was interrupted by a huge clash of thunder, and as if on cue, a hard rain began to pelt the roof and blow against the windows with alarming ferocity. Uneasy glances were passed around the room.

"Told you so," Del called to Stone, who nodded and frowned.

Just then the door burst open and Dirk Becker came through it with a yearling antelope in tow, both already soaking wet. Becker led the yearling by a rope, but the shivering animal needed no urging to come inside. Looking up sheepishly, Becker shouted, "Sorry, Hunter!"

"It's all right. Come forward."

"What's this?" Vickersham asked.

"A surprise spoiled, Vic."

Reena looked at Megan with a gleam in her eye and said, "May we present you with your wedding present?"

"What?" Megan replied, staring at the animal being led directly toward her. The yearling was brownish-gray colored, with a white chest and tail. It stopped in front of Megan and looked at her expectantly.

"You'll have to name her, Megan," Reena said. "She's as tame as a lamb."

"Name her? It's a deer, Reena!"

"Antelope."

"Whatever. How can we have an antelope for a pet?"

"Now, darling —" Vickersham began.

"Vic, this isn't a dog or a cat! This is —" Megan broke off when the yearling began licking her hand. The large, liquid brown eyes looked up at her trustingly.

The onlookers uttered soft "Awws!" almost in unison.

The mild consternation on Megan's face vanished instantly, and she knelt down in front of the antelope and petted its neck, while speaking softly to it.

Vickersham glanced at Hunter and

Reena and said lightly, "You know, I was hoping for a new addition to the family, but I didn't plan on it being quite so soon — or have fur, for that matter."

A new crash of thunder rent the air, and the baby antelope jerked and moved closer to Megan. "Poor baby!" Megan said, placing an arm protectively across its back, heedless of soiling her pretty dress. "Reena, where did you find her?"

"Hunter found her. She was wandering around by herself, so he thought her mother had been killed."

"She's adorable . . . thank you!"

Vickersham gave Stone a look and said, "Yes, thanks, old chap . . . I think."

"Ladies and gentlemen!" Reena called to the gathering over the pounding rain. "May I present my wonderful big sister — the one who beat me up, teased me, pulled my hair, and, incidentally, loved me without question — the proud mother of an antelope and wife of a Mountie, Mrs. Jaye Eliot Vickersham!"

Megan's face glowed with pleasure as she took her arms from around the yearling and wrapped them around her husband.

Chapter Two
Night Thoughts

The storm continued for two hours, eventually raining hail down on the fort. Those enjoying the party inside weren't bothered by it at all, except for the occasional peal of thunder that made everyone jerk, then laugh at their own nervousness. Sometimes the band was affected by the booming, causing sour notes to come forth and thereby generating more merriness. By dusk the clouds had passed over, leaving a spectacular orange-red sunset over the mountain peaks of the Rockies.

In an uncharacteristic show of rule-bending, Colonel Macleod had allowed Vickersham to build a house just outside the town and close to the fort. Vickersham had had all the help he'd needed from his fellow Mounties, and the structure was built in one month. Just before Megan and Vic left the mess hall to go to their new home, Reena gave her sister a big hug at the door.

"Don't worry," Reena told her, "I'll take

care of Twinkle tonight." Twinkle was the yearling antelope, so named by Megan because of the twinkle in her eye.

"Thanks."

"Aren't you excited?" Reena gushed, grabbing her sister's arm. "Isn't it a wonderful day?"

"I'm so happy, Reena! I feel like I've wasted so many years with . . . well, never mind. Louis won't be mentioned today again."

Her first husband, Louis Goldsen, had been a successful banker used to getting what he wanted. He was a smooth man in all his business deals and made his fortune selling whiskey illegally to the Indians in the Territories. Though he was an influential and respected man in Chicago society, he had turned out to be an immoral scoundrel, and had abused Megan with his fists a number of times. When a deal went bad, he'd been killed on the prairie, alone, fittingly enough by another whiskey runner more ruthless than he. Megan had never loved Louis and had only married him to rise further in society. After Louis' death, she'd had to come to terms with the way she was. Through those difficult times, she had come to faith and grown from the ordeal. But it was too late for Louis. Even now, Megan sometimes felt sad about that.

"I understand," Reena assured her. "But Vic's a wonderful man — I'm so happy for you."

"Thank you, Reena," Megan said as she gave her sister a hug.

Behind them, Stone, Becker, and Del were shaking Vickersham's hand.

"Congratulations, Vic," Del said.

Vickersham's eyebrows raised. "I thought you were against marriage, Del."

"Awww — I just like to give you a hard time. You know that. I can see how she makes you feel. Never had that feeling before."

"Maybe you will someday."

Jack Sheffield appeared and patted Vickersham on the back. "I hope you didn't mind my stumbling around the wedding vows, Vic."

"Not at all. I know it was your first time, but then again it was the first time for me, too."

Sheffield grinned. "I guess it still worked, though, right? How does it feel to be a married man?"

Vickersham pursed his lips as he thought about it. "Obligatory." The men laughed, then Vic added, "But in a very good way, you know."

"Ask him again in a week," Del chided.

Right then Megan, Reena, and Jenny joined them.

"Ask him what?" Megan wanted to know.

"Nothin'," Del muttered.

Sheffield's face lit up. "That may not be a bad idea. Why don't we all get together in a week for dinner and see how the newlyweds are doing?"

Everyone thought a dinner was a good idea, so they all agreed to meet at Vickersham's house the following Saturday. None of them could know it, but the get-together would never take place. The next time they would all be together would be a long time, and one of them would never make that future meeting.

Stone and Becker walked Reena and Jenny back to the boardinghouse in town. Reena would spend the night there, then return to the Blackfoot tribe the next day, where she was a missionary.

Reena held the rope that led Twinkle, but she thought that the lead was just a formality. The antelope walked beside her, perfectly content to keep pace with them, sometimes actually moving ahead of them so that Reena had to gently pull her back.

"What a wonderful wedding," Jenny sighed. "Are they all like that, Reena?"

"Not really. It means much more when the people who are getting married are close to you."

"I can't imagine what it would be like if it was your own." Jenny suddenly glanced over at Stone. "I'm sorry, Hunter."

Stone looked surprised. "It's all right."

"How was yours, Hunter?" Becker asked, casting a cautious glance at Reena.

Stone, too, considered her reaction before answering. Her face didn't change as she walked along, absently petting the yearling. When the silence dragged on awkwardly, she looked over at him expectantly.

"How was it, Hunter?" she asked, puzzled at his hesitation. Then it dawned on her, and she smiled at him. "You can talk about Betsy — I don't mind."

His wife had been killed over two years ago at the hands of Red Wolf, a renegade Indian. Hunter had gone through a terrible time afterward, blaming himself for her death, and for a long time was obsessed with revenge. Reena knew he was out of the mourning stage and was only reluctant to answer Becker's question because of his deep feelings for her.

"It was a small wedding, by our choice," Stone said as he remembered that day. "Betsy's father was a minister and performed the ceremony." He took a deep breath, smiled, then murmured, "She wore white and purple asters in her hair."

Reena looked up at him and saw that he was totally lost in his reminiscence. A stab of jealousy rose up in her over the woman she'd never known, but she immediately quelled it. Betsy had obviously made Hunter very happy. Reena's mood quickly changed and she felt sympathy for the young girl whose happy, simple life had been tragically cut short.

Noticing that Becker and Jenny were casting uncomfortable glances at her over Stone's heartfelt answer, Reena broke into his silent reverie. "So, you had one of those wonderful weddings, too?"

Stone shook his head and seemed to be surprised by his surroundings and the three people with him. "Yes, it was."

Darkness was almost upon them, but they walked along in companionable silence. The air was crisp and clean after the hard rain, almost sweet. They'd almost reached the white, ivy-strewn fence in front of the boardinghouse when Stone suddenly asked Reena, "Have you heard from Liam?"

"Yes, as a matter of fact. He's back in West Point, studying furiously to catch up on what he missed."

"Good for him," Stone nodded.

Liam O'Donnell had left West Point the previous December, come to the Territories, and unknowingly fallen in with a very bad outlaw and his men. Following a skirmish in which a Mountie had been killed, Liam had been captured by Hunter and sentenced to ten years imprisonment by Colonel Macleod. At the urging of Stone and Vickersham, after learning all the facts, Macleod had traded Liam's co-operation in bringing the outlaws to the Mounties in exchange for his freedom and a clean record. Liam had cooperated fully and won his pardon.

"I hope he learned something from all that," Becker commented as he opened the front gate for them.

"Oh, he learned something, all right." Reena smiled. "He learned the value of a good education, and not to get on the wrong side of the North-West Mounted Police. I don't think he'll ever step foot over the border again."

"That's a shame," Stone said. "I liked the kid."

Reena glanced at him sideways. "You

almost killed the kid."

"Just because —"

"I know, Hunter. I'm only teasing."

He looked at her as if unsure whether she was telling the truth. When she gave him a brilliant smile, he relaxed.

Reena let Twinkle loose in the fenced yard, and they went inside. The ladies left Stone and Becker in the parlor while they went to make coffee. Stone sat down heavily on the sofa, letting out a sigh.

"Tired, Hunter?" Becker asked as he picked up a small porcelain figure of a horse and rider sitting on the fireplace mantel.

"No . . . exhausted. I need a vacation."

"You don't have to do *everything* around the fort, you know. You don't have to ride out on every patrol, train every recruit personally —"

"I know, I know."

"But you do it anyway. Why?"

Stone shrugged. "I don't have anything better to do, I guess." He slowly rubbed his face, then dropped his hands into his lap. "Why are you looking at me like that, Dirk?"

"You amuse me sometimes," Becker grinned.

"I'm glad I provide you with free entertainment. What do you find so amusing?"

Becker carefully replaced the figurine on the mantel and sat down across from Stone, the smile still playing at the edges of his full mouth. "You mean besides the fact that you want everyone to think that you don't have any feelings?"

"I don't know what —"

"Or the aforementioned drive to do everything yourself, or die trying?"

"That's not —"

"Or how about the way you try so hard to keep Reena wondering how you feel about her?"

Stone sat up straight. "She knows I love her!"

At that moment, Reena and Jenny entered the parlor, with Jenny carrying a silver coffee tray. Reena smiled brightly and asked, "Who do you love, Hunter?"

"Oh . . . um . . . you're back." He glared at Becker accusingly. "You saw them coming, didn't you?"

Becker's eyes grew wide and innocent. "What do you mean?"

Reena seated herself beside Stone, who immediately rose to his feet. "Don't sit down."

"Why not?"

"Because . . . we're . . . going for a walk."

"But we just walked here! What about the coffee?" Despite her protests, Reena stood also.

Stone reached down to the coffee tray Jenny had placed on the table in front of the sofa. He quickly poured two steaming cups of coffee, then turned back to Reena. "We'll go sit on the porch with Twinkle, then."

Reena glanced at Becker curiously, but he only grinned and shrugged his broad shoulders. To Stone she said, "All right. It sure isn't boring when you're around. I have to give you that."

Becker and Jenny watched them as they left the parlor and went out to the porch. Jenny poured coffee for herself and Dirk, then sat back in her chair and sipped silently.

Becker grinned at her. "You're even more quiet than usual, Jenny. Something bothering you?"

"No. Just a little tired, I guess." Her voice held the down-country twang of the mountain folk, which only endeared her to Becker even more.

"Seems to be catching."

"What do you mean?" she asked, looking up from her cup.

"Being tired. Everyone's tired tonight."

"I wonder why?" Jenny pondered. "Is it because of the wedding, do you think?"

"Probably." Becker watched in amusement as she added more sugar to her already sugar-laden coffee. "Why don't you just spoon that stuff directly into your mouth? There's hardly any coffee left in that cup anyway."

"Mind your own business, Dirk Becker," Jenny warned playfully. "I ain't — I mean, I'm not hurting anyone with the way I drink my coffee."

"No one but you."

"What's the matter with a little sugar?"

"Nothing . . . let's change the subject."

"I'm not through with the sugar one yet."

Impulsively, Becker leaned over and kissed her softly on the mouth. Jenny stiffened, then wouldn't meet his eyes, choosing to stir her coffee even more. Becker sat back in his chair, surprised at himself. He'd never kissed her before.

"I suppose I could get slapped for doing that," he mused.

"No."

He saw that she was blushing now. "I'm sorry, Jenny, I —"

"Don't apologize, Dirk, please. I just . . . wasn't expecting it, that's all."

39

Becker didn't know what to say to that, so he remained silent. He watched her take a sip — or rather, a gulp — of the hot coffee, sputter, and almost spill the whole cup on her dress.

"Oh!"

Deftly Becker caught the cup and moved it away from her.

"That's hot!" she exclaimed, standing up and examining her dress for any stains. Embarrassed once again, she avoided his eyes and sat back down. To cover her discomfort, Jenny stretched her arms straight in front of her, down between her knees and into her dress, and groaned.

Becker smiled inwardly at the movement. He doubted she'd worn a dress more than three or four times in her life, and she thought nothing of the unladylike motion. Her innocence only made him care for her all the more.

Softly, Jenny said, "I'll bet you've kissed a hundred girls in your life."

"Well, I'd say you give me more credit than is due. More like fifty." Her round-eyed glance caused him to quickly say, "I'm only joking, Jenny. I . . . haven't had much experience with women."

"That's not true."

"It is. I was always . . . shy."

She searched his face for the truth and plainly saw the honesty in his eyes. Her arms were still stretched between her knees, and with horror she realized how silly she must look. Jerking her arms back to her sides, she cast a furtive look at him, but he carefully acted casual and sipped his coffee with only the hint of a smile playing at the corners of his mouth.

After a moment, she said, "I've never had a man kiss me like that before."

"How did they kiss you?" Becker asked, then bit his tongue. The first time he'd laid eyes on her, a man named Sad Sid had been pawing at her inside a stable. Becker had gotten into a fight with Sid and ended up wounding him with a knife. Disturbingly, Jenny had shaken off the traumatic encounter too easily. Being the daughter of a whiskey trader, Becker was sure that she'd had to fight off aggressive men many times before.

Now, as he realized his slip, he found himself apologizing again. "I'm sorry, Jenny. I shouldn't have said that."

"It's all right, Dirk," Jenny reassured him. "It's all in the past now. I've managed to forget most of it."

"You didn't deserve to be treated that way, Jenny." Her smile warmed him.

"Thank you. It just happened, that's all.

What's there to do about it now?"

Despite her nonchalance, Becker sensed a sadness that only time and God could heal. "You know, Jenny — God can help heal you inside, too. He did it for me."

She stood and moved restlessly to the fireplace mantel. With her small delicate hands, she picked up the same horse and rider figurine that Becker had toyed with earlier. So softly that he could barely hear her, Jenny asked, "Then where was He when I was growing up? Why did He let all those horrible things happen to me?"

Becker moved over to her and placed his hands on her shoulders from behind. "He was there, Jenny. It's just —"

"I didn't know about no — any God! How could I have asked for help if I didn't know? The only time I heard His name was when someone was cussin'." She spun around and faced him, and the hurt on her face showed that she hadn't come close to facing her wretched past. "How was I supposed to know, Dirk? How?"

Becker took her in his arms, and a small sob escaped from her trembling lips. She clung to him hard, and he could feel her small fingers digging into his back. The top of her head smelled like roses. He held her, knowing he should only be feeling sympathy and concern, but his growing attraction toward her overpowered every other emotion.

Pulling away slightly, Jenny looked up at him with wet eyes and whispered, "Kiss me again, Dirk. Please?"

Gently, he took her face in his strong hands and kissed her again.

As soon as Stone and Reena had seated themselves on the porch steps, Twinkle trotted over to them from across the yard, where she'd been carefully sniffing out singing crickets. She had a look of pure euphoria, as if they had come outside to only see her. Stone scratched the top of her ridged head absentmindedly as he unfastened the top two buttons on his dress tunic. The night had turned steamy with the falling darkness.

"Look at her," Reena observed. "She's afraid to move, in case you'll stop scratching her."

Twinkle held herself perfectly still under Stone's attentions. Stone grinned and playfully pulled his hand back a few inches. Twinkle immediately moved her head beneath his hand again.

"I think you have a friend for life, Hunter."

"Looks that way, doesn't it?"

"Have you ever had any pets?"

"I had a dog when I was a boy, but not since then."

Reena looked up at the ebony sky, remembering. "We had a dog, too, when I was a girl. She was a beagle, with long floppy ears and endless energy. Megan and I would throw a ball for her on the back lawn for what seemed like hours at a time, and Flopsy never got tired of it."

"Flopsy?"

"What's wrong with that?"

Stone grinned and looked away. "Oh, nothing."

Reena nudged him with her arm playfully. "Well, what was your dog's name?"

"I don't remember," he mumbled.

"Come on — tell me."

"Doodles."

"Doodles?"

"What's wrong with that?"

Reena mimicked his earlier action of grinning, avoiding his eyes, and repeating, "Oh, nothing."

"He could draw."

"What!"

"He could draw. He'd take a stick in his mouth sometimes and draw in the dirt with it. It was amazing."

"What did he draw?"

"Reena, he wasn't Michelangelo. He was a dog. But I still think he was trying to sketch something in his head at those times."

"And what happened to this talented Doodles?" A shadow passed over Stone's face that Reena could clearly see despite the darkness.

"A constable shot him."

"What for?" Reena asked, horrified.

Stone was scratching Twinkle's neck now. The antelope had its nose straight up in the air, allowing him to scratch the full length of it. Stone's voice was strangely devoid of emotion as he answered. "A city councilman who was extremely drunk and stumbling passed too close to our house. Doodles was startled by the way he was acting and began to bark at him viciously. The councilman found a constable and apparently convinced him that Doodles was some sort of dangerous threat to the community. So Doodles died, no questions asked."

Reena said nothing but suddenly felt terribly sad.

"My father raised a complaint at the next councilmen's meeting, but what could be done? Doodles was gone."

"That must have been terrible for you. How old were you?"

"About twelve or thirteen."

Reena watched him closely, but his face was a mask, carefully covering up whatever pain he felt at the dreadful memory. She wondered if Hunter had seen the constable actually shoot his dog, then realized that she didn't *want* to have knowledge of that particular fact. The tragedy he'd described at such a tender age must have affected him deeply. She reached up and placed her hand on the back of his neck. He turned to her and gave her his I'm-all-right-it's-in-the-past smile that she knew so well. For a year or two after his wife's death, Reena had often seen the same look whenever his wife, Betsy, would surface in a conversation.

"What about Flopsy?" Stone asked. "I hope she had a better demise."

"She died peacefully at the ripe old age of ten. Megan and I cried for days. Our father got us a cat to try to ease the pain, but cats are just different, you know?"

"No. Never been around them."

"Sometimes they look at you like . . . if they were bigger than you, you'd be their next meal."

Stone grunted and said, "Some pet."

Twinkle suddenly moved over to Reena,

seemingly to accept equal amounts of affection from each of them. Reena patted her head and continued to scratch her neck as Hunter had done. They sat together in silence for a while, enjoying the night and each other's company.

"You know something?" Hunter asked in a quiet voice. "I feel great. I used to be so . . . so *serious* about everything. And now that I've accepted Christ I know that I don't have to control everything. I've got Him for that."

"It's wonderful, isn't it?" Reena said.

Then she remembered the words that were spoken in the parlor.

"Who do you love, Hunter?"

He turned to her, surprised, then actually blushed. "You know the answer to that."

Reena waited for him to say more, but when he didn't, she felt a pinch of disappointment. One of the qualities she loved about Hunter was his inner strength. However, when it came to hiding his affection or deep feelings, he was unfortunately quite adept at that, too. Her disappointment quickly turned to frustration, and all at once she became irritated with the noisy crickets. *They never shut up, and he never talks,* she thought, knowing how silly and petulant it sounded, but not caring.

Turning to him, she placed both hands on each side of his face and pulled him close to hers. "I *do* know the answer, Hunter. It's just nice to hear you say it sometimes."

He looked at her intently, his eyes caressing every inch of her face before answering. "You're so beautiful."

It wasn't exactly what Reena was looking for, but she felt the tenseness inside her vanish instantly. Just as she opened her mouth to thank him, he spoke again.

"I *do* love you, Reena. With all my heart."

He leaned forward and pressed his lips against hers softly . . . oh, so softly . . . and something inside Reena let loose. With a fierceness that almost frightened her, she threw her arms around his neck and submitted to the feeling of love that swept her.

After a few moments, they both felt an urgent nudge against their sides that soon turned into outright burrowing. When she'd succeeded in parting them, Twinkle placed her chin on Reena's knees and looked up at them with expressive eyes.

Deep in the night, Megan Vickersham

awoke and held her new husband close. They'd fallen asleep together nearly simultaneously hours earlier, with Megan enjoying his strong arms wrapped around her. She remembered sighing with comfort and security and pure happiness at the thought of being married to such a loving man.

Now, with Vic's head cradled comfortably in the crook of her shoulder and silver moonbeams flowing through the window, Megan reached up and gently swept aside a lock of dark brown hair from his forehead. He stirred the tiniest bit, then settled back in and began to snore lightly.

Megan smiled and thought of how much she loved him. Implicitly. Utterly. Without reservation. *What would I do without him, Lord?* she questioned in her mind. The thought stunned her; why would she even think such a thing?

Louis.

To think of her first husband while lying next to her second one on her bridal bed was obscene. There was no comparison between the two men. Louis had been brutal. Vic was gentle and caring. Louis had been a snake, while Vic was the finest, most caring man she'd ever known. But she knew why her mind had conjured up the earlier thought — Louis had died violently and suddenly, leaving her a widow in the blink of an eye. She felt a sudden twinge of fear as she thought of the dangerous job Vic held. He often had to deal with cruel, sometimes savage, men. Any day, he could come across a particularly ruthless man who . . .

Stop it.

Megan suddenly wanted to wake him, to hear his soothing voice telling her that she was silly and everything would be fine. Instead, she squeezed him and nestled down farther so that his face was against hers. He stopped snoring, moaned softly, then went right back to sleep again.

Megan didn't mind. The uncomfortable, sinister feeling left her, and she smiled again as she became aware of his warm breath against her neck.

He wasn't going to die prematurely.

Absolutely not.

Not if Mrs. Megan Vickersham had any say in the matter.

Chapter Three

Campaign Beginnings

What in the name of my beloved Ireland am I doing here? Faron O'Donnell questioned himself for perhaps the thousandth time in the past two weeks. He rolled his bright blue eyes up to the fog-shrouded morning sky as if he really expected an answer from the heavens. His build was bold and stocky, sitting evenly in the saddle. A trim gray beard framed his face, but from underneath the battered Stetson he wore sprang some of his hair's original color streaked with white — a fiery red.

Faron watched the gaudy, noisy spectacle before him from the back of his horse at the gate of Fort Abraham Lincoln in Dakota Territory. At the base of a bluff beside the fort, the yellow Missouri River offered its fishy, dark scent to the morning. The Seventh Cavalry paraded around the parade ground of the fort like gods of war embarking on a holy mission. The wives of the Ree scouts wailed mournfully at the top of their lungs. The sons of the cavalry-men proudly marched beside their fathers' horses, waving flags and beating tin pans in pure joy.

Above all this din came the clear tunes of a song dear to Faron O'Donnell's old Irish heart, played perfectly by the regimental band. Barely able to hear his own voice over the noise, he sang along with the first stanza:

Let Bacchus' sons be not dismayed
But join with me each jovial blade;
Come booze and sing and lend your aid
To help me with the chorus.

Before he could get to the beloved chorus, Faron heard a voice from behind him. "Not joining in with the festivities, scout?"

Faron turned and saw an officer of the Seventh coming up beside him. Since he was new to the regiment, Faron recognized the man's insignia as a captain, but he couldn't recall his name. "Good morning, sir. No, I think I'll just spectate, if'n ye don't mind, sir."

The man shrugged his shoulders. "It's none of my affair. The man you'll have to take it up with is the glorious gentleman at the head of the Seventh." He nodded at the parade, a sardonic smile on his soft, almost feminine, lips.

At the head of the Seventh's column, in the center of the wild send-off — indeed, *glowing* amid the celebration — Lieutenant Colonel George Armstrong Custer sat atop his mount, waving his hat and grinning at all those around him. Faron was shocked to discover that the legendary long, curly blond locks Custer had sported had been shorn off for the campaign. The colonel's sweeping tawny dragoon's mustache sharpened the bony, hawkish nose and accented the depth of his eye sockets. Though his build was sinuous and muscular, there was an ill-concealed restlessness about it. He looked down at the people around him with a bright light glowing from his piercing light blue eyes that Faron could see even from a distance. As Faron watched, Custer suddenly leaned down and kissed a beautiful, petite woman who'd appeared at his horse's side. Bess, Custer's beloved wife. Custer whispered something in her ear, then straightened up and favored her a lofty look of love and affection. Then he turned the troop toward the gate.

The officer beside Faron grunted with an unmistakable combination of disgust

and derision. Then he mumbled something under his breath.

"What was that, sir?" Faron asked politely.

"What? Oh, nothing. Just expressing my
humble opinion to no one but myself." He
turned to Faron, and his baby blue eyes
locked on him as if noticing him for the
first time. "What's your name, scout?"

"Faron O'Donnell, sir."

"Captain Benteen, H Company," the
man returned cordially, offering his hand.
His moon face was open and magnani-
mous now, much different from the dark
visage Faron had seen while Benteen had
observed Custer. All at once his face
changed yet again. "That blasted song —
do you know the words to that chorus?"

"Of course . . ." Faron waited until the
appropriate time, then sang in a surprisingly sweet voice that contrasted with his
look.

Instead of Spa we'll drink down ale.
And pay the reck'ning on the nail;
No man for debt shall go to gaol
From Garry Owen in glory.

Benteen's face shifted again, brightening
up like a child's on Christmas morning.

"Ah, sung like a true Irishman. So those are the famous words to 'Garry Owen.' "

The regimental band, as if on cue, shifted to "The Girl I Left Behind Me," rumored to be Custer's personal favorite. Benteen rolled his eyes. "I hate these sentimental songs."

Faron had to stop himself from defending the song of his native land. He was a scout in the military now — by necessity more than want, to be sure — so he would have to recognize the chain of command and accept the fact that he was among the lowest rank in the regiment.

As the Seventh approached them, the wives and children followed, as if unwilling for the celebration to end. Custer's favorite scouts — a Ree Indian named Bloody Knife, and "Lonesome Charley" Reynolds — moved to the head of the column. Faron's lip curled slightly as he observed Bloody Knife. The Irishman had developed a quick and strong dislike for the man in a very short period of time. Bloody Knife knew he was Custer's favorite scout and carried himself with an arrogance and haughtiness that Faron, and more than a few others, despised. Lonesome Charley had told Faron that Custer indulged the Ree so much that Bloody Knife was the only one able to chide the colonel about his marksmanship with a rifle and pistol. Custer often gave Bloody Knife rewards as a king does a court jester. Bloody Knife wore one now — a black neckerchief with blue stars.

Lonesome Charley was so named because he always lived alone and possessed a very subdued character. The information he'd conveyed to Faron about Bloody Knife was one of the few things Faron had heard him say to anyone. Because of his few words, no one knew much about Charley. He seemed a good sort to Faron, though, and he liked Lonesome Charley.

"How did you come to be with the Seventh, O'Donnell?" Benteen asked, breaking into Faron's thoughts.

"I'm on my way to the northern Rockies. Thought I'd fall in with you good fellows part of the way."

"Crazy Horse got you spooked, too?" Benteen asked, not unkindly.

"Let's just say I've got a healthy respect for the man, Captain."

Benteen snorted. "Most all of us do." He again looked at Custer pointedly.

Faron considered him. "What do ye mean, sir?"

"You'll find out, O'Donnell. Believe me, you'll find out." Benteen whirled his horse and rode to the head of his company of men.

Faron watched him ride off, baffled by his remark. He'd never been around Custer personally, except for four days previous when Custer had hired him as a scout. In that short time, Faron had sensed the brash arrogance of Custer, but he decided that so great a soldier and leader deserved more than a five-minute assessment.

As Bloody Knife and Lonesome Charley rode up beside him, Faron nodded to Charley, who returned the greeting. Bloody Knife didn't so much as look at him.

All at once, for apparently no reason whatsoever, Faron wondered if joining Custer's troops had been a good idea after all. He could very well have traveled to the Canadian Rockies alone — after all, he'd ridden down here by himself despite the rumors of Crazy Horse and the Sioux raiding at will — but this time had been different. The news of a gathering of thousands of Indians on the warpath had made him nervous, so he'd decided to increase his chances of safety with numbers. Despite the festive atmosphere of the place, he sensed something else beneath it all — an intangible foreboding that was entirely un-explainable.

Faron shrugged his broad shoulders and fell in beside Charley. His instincts had saved his life a few times in the mountains, and he had no reason to believe that they wouldn't now. If something was wrong, Faron was sure that he would eventually know it somewhere inside him.

On May 17, 1876, the Seventh Cavalry, under the command of General Alfred Terry, had orders to move to the Bighorn Mountains and subdue what was called "a large gathering of Sioux." The movement was to be coordinated with two other branches of the army, Colonel John Gibbon's column from Fort Ellis in the west, and General George Crook from Fort Laramie, south of the Little Bighorn.

Though the overall command was in the hands of General Terry, the nation's eyes were on the flamboyant "boy general Custer" and his famous cavalry unit. Many believed that no force of Indians, however amassed, could stand up to the irresistible force of the Seventh.

The army's soldiers, artillery, and white-hooded supply wagons extended in a serpentine line for almost two miles. When

Faron judged that the whole train had fallen in line behind them, he glanced back to admire the sight. The morning fog was beginning to dissipate, and the sun broke through at one area, reflecting brightly on the weapons of the soldiers. Faron's attention was caught by something up in the sky, and when he looked, his eyes widened. "Hey, Charley . . . look at that."

Lonesome Charley glanced at Faron curiously, then turned slowly in the saddle. "What?"

"Up in the sky, man! Do ye see it?"

"No, I — oh, yeah, now I do. What is that?"

"I've never seen nothin' like it in all me days."

Above the supply wagons with their white canopied beds was an ethereal reflection against the web-silver fog of the wagon train itself.

In awe, Lonesome Charley Reynolds murmured, "It looks like we're riding across the sky."

Bloody Knife noticed they were distracted and turned in his saddle to look. His face, normally dark and coppery, seemed to pale. At the same time, Custer saw his scouts' gaping looks and looked back himself.

Faron didn't think the colonel would be able to see the reflection since he was farther back in line than the scouts, but Custer kept looking. Finally the sun burned through the fog cloud, and the image dispersed into harmless white against the blue sky behind it. When Custer turned back to the front, his eyes locked with Bloody Knife's. A forbidding, troubled look passed between them. *He doesn't look so arrogant now,* Faron thought, which for some reason brought back the uneasy feeling he'd noticed before.

"Bad omen," Bloody Knife muttered, his face still showing distress.

"What did you say?" Charley asked the Ree.

Bloody Knife only looked at him.

"Why is that a bad omen?" Faron asked.

The Indian refused to look at the Irishman but gave his explanation to Charley. "We ride in the great sky."

"So?" Charley prompted.

"Bad omen." Bloody Knife again looked behind them, as if to make sure the reflection hadn't returned. When he saw that it was truly gone, he brought his coal-black eyes back to Custer, frowned slightly, then turned back to the front.

"Is that all you're going to say?" Charley

asked, obviously scared now.

Bloody Knife didn't answer.

"Bah!" Faron growled. "Just a mirage, like you see in the desert."

The Ree's ebony eyes fixed on Faron steadily. After a moment he said, "You will know."

"Know what?" Faron was tiring of what seemed a self-styled mysteriousness in Bloody Knife, and they'd only just begun their journey. When the Indian again chose not to answer a direct question, Faron felt his temper rise. Defiantly, he said clearly to no one in particular, "Mirage."

The regiment rode all day across the green, rolling sea of prairie. Toward dusk, Faron and Charley were joined by Mitch Bouyer, a man famed for his expert knowledge of the Great Plains. He had a round, indifferent face, with a neatly trimmed gray beard. Faron liked him a lot.

"Hello, gents," Bouyer called out.

"Mitch," Charley nodded.

Faron touched the brim of his hat. "Evenin'."

"Oh, it's not evening, O'Donnell."

Faron pointedly looked at the red-orange clouds hovering above the western horizon where the sun had gone down an hour before. "Have I lost me wits, or aren't those beautiful clouds about to turn blue with the fallin' o' the sun?"

"Ah, you've got a lot to learn, Faron," Mitch said loftily, then winked at Charley. Both men laughed heartily.

"And what would be so funny, me lads?" Faron wondered.

Mitch slapped him on the back resoundingly, sending a cloud of dust into the air from Faron's shirt. "You are, my friend. To General Custer, this might as well be midday." He produced a small bag of hardtack from his saddlebags and promptly popped a biscuit in his mouth. Around the mouthful he explained, "The general ain't like any man you've met, I don't think. He ain't built like the rest of us."

"How do ye mean?" Faron asked, curious about Bouyer's knowledge of the general.

Bouyer tapped his chest with the palm of his hand. "The man's gotta clock inside him that goes on its own time. I've seen the man go for days without sleep, and he can ride farther without a rest than anyone I ever saw."

Charley added, "He only stops because he figured out in the war that the rest of us poor souls need some rest every night. Really grates on him, too."

Faron considered the two men and decided they weren't serious. "So why doesn't he sleep while we do?"

Mitch moved the hardtack from one jaw to the other before answering. "Writes letters."

"All night?"

"All night. Oh, he might catch an hour or two of winks, but never more than that."

"Who does he write to?"

"His wife. I've seen him write letters that were twenty pages long. Tells her everything."

Faron had always considered himself to have a solid constitution when it came to physical stamina. He needed only a few hours sleep a night and could keep up with a man half as young as his sixty-six years. But what he was hearing about Custer went beyond anything he'd ever seen. As he thought about the man's indomitable stamina, something else occurred to him. "What's this 'general' business? I thought Custer was only a lieutenant colonel."

Mitch said, "He was breveted to general in the war, then returned to his regular rank of lieutenant colonel when it was over. It's customary to refer to a man by the highest rank he's ever held."

"So I should call him general?"

Bouyer eyed him squarely. "If you don't want a blistering look that'll take the hide off you, you do."

Faron's new friends were right. They traveled until well after dark into the quavering whistles of screech owls and the mournful moans of coyotes. Faron estimated it was about one o'clock in the morning when they finally stopped and made camp. He was surprised at the weariness he felt in his bones as he made his bunk with the other scouts.

"Don't get too comfortable," Bouyer advised. "Remember what I told you — we could be saddling up in an hour."

Faron wasn't sure if the man was joking or not, so he quickly threw himself down and tried to make sleep come as soon as possible. Bouyer, however, wasn't ready to let an opportunity for good conversation drop for the night.

"What are you doing in these parts, O'Donnell?"

"Sad to say, but I was one o' the ones who came to look for Black Hills gold." Faron himself could hear the sourness in his voice.

"A little late, weren't you?"

"Aye. Hearst has all the good mines locked up in his Homestake Mining Company. As if he needs the money after producin' the richest mine in the Comstock Lode."

"Should have shared his wealth with you by bowing out of the Black Hills, eh?" Bouyer asked with amusement.

"I wouldn't have minded one bit." Faron took a deep breath, and then a yawn came over him. "But, alas . . . it wasn't to be."

"What about the luck of the Irish?"

Faron glanced over at Bouyer but could only see a murky shape against the tawny light of a few fires from the army's camp. "I suppose I was in the wrong county the day they handed that out."

Bouyer chuckled deep in his throat. "Maybe you should go back and ask for your portion."

"Ye just met me, Mitch. Already tryin' to get rid o' me?" Bouyer was silent for so long that Faron thought he'd fallen asleep.

Finally Bouyer murmured, "I wish I was there."

Faron was startled by the wistfulness in his tone. Remembering the foreboding feeling he'd felt pass through him that morning, Faron wondered if Bouyer was feeling the same thing. Softly, nonchalantly, he asked, "What's wrong with where ye are now, Mitch?"

Another long pause. When he spoke again, his tone was light and the melancholy gone. "I've never seen Ireland. I hear it's a grand sight."

"Aye, that it is."

Bouyer ended the conversation by rolling over with his back to Faron, who was left with an unanswered question to ponder. Sleep had been difficult since he'd joined the troops. After spending the last three years almost totally alone, the restless sounds of men around him — snoring, murmuring, movement — caused him to jerk fully awake time after time when he'd almost drifted off. On this night, the popping and hissing of numerous dying fires was the culprit. The popping reminded him of far-off gunfire.

The night was warm, but Faron felt a bone-deep chill spread through him. He buried himself deeper into his blanket and forced his gritty eyes to stay shut, despite the gunfirelike rattling throughout the camp.

Faron dreamed of his nieces, Reena and Megan.

It wasn't uncommon. In fact, it was happening more and more often. The last he'd heard of Megan, she'd stolen Reena's fiance out from under her sister's fine little nose. It was the breaking point for Reena. Wanting to get away and begin a new life, Reena had asked her uncle to take her back with him. Faron had finally agreed to let her accompany him to the North-West Territories, where she planned on beginning a mission work among the Indians. Faron had thought her daft at the time. The roughest time Reena had ever experienced to that point in the great outdoors was camping in her lush backyard in Chicago.

Faron often wondered if Reena had succeeded. On his way to the Black Hills he'd tried to find her Indian village, but he had no way of knowing what tribe she was with, or in what part of the vast prairie they lived. He could have stopped by the Mountie post he'd seen and enquired, but — and he hated to admit it even to himself — the gold fever had bitten him really hard and he was afraid the Mounties would tell him that Reena was two hundred miles north of the post, which was the way he'd come. It disgusted him to think that he'd placed his favorite niece on one side of a set of scales, the brilliant, shining gold on the other, and his own kin had come up short with alarmingly little conscience giving him trouble.

He was dreaming of the time he took the girls to a small country fair in a bean field outside of Chicago. That day had been warm and breezy, filled with all the sunshine imaginable. In the dream Faron couldn't see the sky because everything immediately around the three of them was cobalt shadow and murky images. Reena and Megan were fighting over who'd pitched a beanbag the farthest, though the beanbags were lost in the eerie grayness enveloping them. Faron knew that there *had* been some sort of contest in real life, but Megan had heaved her beanbag twenty feet farther than the smaller Reena, and there had been no argument. Faron was about to perform his kindly uncle duty and separate the girls, when Reena whirled on him before he could say a word.

"You stay away from us! You're not in the family!" the rail-thin girl with ebony hair had shouted.

Faron was stunned. He looked into the blazing blue eyes so much like his and realized that she'd spoken her razor-sharp words in the Irish tongue, of which Reena knew not a word.

"You stay away!" Reena repeated, and

then she and Megan vanished into the steely mist.

"Hold there, lasses!" Faron called in desperation. "Wait for me, don't ye be runnin' off!" He charged into the mist after them and soon became disoriented and lost.

At that point, Faron felt someone nudging him awake. He didn't want to wake up. He wanted to find his nieces, but the nudging soon turned into a kick.

"Wake up!"

Faron opened his eyes to the blackness of deep night and a figure standing over him. He started to reach for his gun, but then he recognized the man's hat — Bloody Knife.

"The general wants you. Wake up."

"What time is it?" Faron asked irritably.

"No matter . . . the general wants you now."

Chapter Four

A Meeting in the Woods

Outside Custer's tent two of the largest dogs Faron had ever seen were guarding the entrance. He had been hesitant to approach them, but Bloody Knife had walked right up to the tent, ignoring the dogs, so Faron had followed suit. The tent was large but only furnished with a small desk, a chair, and a medium-sized trunk. When Faron entered, the general was sitting with his back to Faron. On the desk was paper, quill and inkwell, an oil lamp, and a photograph of a beautiful woman. *Elizabeth, his wife,* Faron thought. *But I've heard say that he calls her "Libby."* Two more hounds of the same size lounged close to their master. They were big of bone and muscle, with tawny, tangled coats.

Bloody Knife hadn't entered the tent with Faron. Custer was in the process of writing and didn't stop, even though Faron was sure the general had heard him enter. The scratching of the pen on the paper was the only noise in the tent for a full minute. Faron waited patiently — and stubbornly — the whole time, refusing to give in to the temptation to clear his throat or try to catch Custer's attention.

Finally Custer placed the pen on the desk, sat back, and stretched with a groan. He was fully dressed in his usual outfit of fringed buckskin shirt, tan trousers with a yellow stripe down both sides, and red neckerchief. His boots were saddle-brown and shiny. He turned his chair around, and Faron noticed he was growing a beard much the same cinnamon color that Faron's had been before gray had crept in over the years.

"Good morning, scout," Custer allowed.

"Mornin', sir."

"Would that be Irish in your voice?"

"Yes, sir . . . all over my voice."

"Mmm. I come from Teutonic stock myself. My ancestors' original name was K-ü-s-t-e-r. Küster." The name reverberated in the tent like the clang of a sword. He paused, obviously pleased with the sound of it himself, then his pale blue eyes fell back on Faron. Looking him up and down, he took in Faron's stocky frame with a slightly critical eye, then said, "You have the look more of a Scot than an Irishman. I could envision you sweeping down on the English with a bloody clan, screaming until your lungs felt they would burst. Ha!"

Faron burned inside at being told he looked like one of Ireland's natural rivals. His lips drawn taut, he said, "We *Irish* swept down on the English a few times ourselves."

Custer hesitated, hearing the heavy sarcastic emphasis with the absence of "sir" at the end. Rubbing his whiskers thoughtfully, he answered, "That you did, scout, that you did."

"The name's O'Donnell, sir."

The flush that spread over Custer's face radiated scarlet storm signals. "Insolence is not required here, scout. I am your commander, and there's nothing you can do about that." Pleased with himself, Custer leaned over and began stroking the flank of one of the hounds. "My dogs desire a hunt today. In all the preparations for embarking on our campaign, I had no time to exercise them properly. You'll find us some antelope or other game this morning?"

"Do me best, sir," Faron replied, still seething over the general's lofty arrogance.

Again the long, gauging inspection. "I'll be forced to hope that's enough, scout. We leave within the hour. Dismissed."

Faron spun and reached for the tent flap.
"O'Donnell."

"Yes, sir?"

"You're in the army now . . . or rather, attached to it. It's considered customary to salute a superior officer before leaving his presence."

Through wooden lips Faron said, "Yes, sir," and saluted for the first time in his life.

"That's the British style. In the United States we salute with palm turned down, not out."

Seething inside, Faron complied and began to wonder if the hunt would happen after all, or if Custer would simply sit in his tent belittling him all day.

Custer nodded. "Now you're dismissed."

On his way to gather his blankets and saddle his horse, Faron growled, "Beast! How can the man speak of *my* insolence? If he weren't who he was, I'd bash his head for him!"

The black mood followed him through all his preparations for the early morning hunt.

Mornings were usually Faron's favorite part of the day, but not this particular one.

He enjoyed seeing the sun rise on the prairie, not stumbling about in the darkness before dawn. That was the time for nocturnals, the predators that ruled the night. He didn't wish to be riding about during their hunting times.

Riding behind Custer's entourage and navigating a fair-sized dry gulch, Faron muttered, "This is a time for sleep and dreams and snugglin' with your wife, if you're fortunate enough to have one." His own wife, Margaret, had died in 1867, and he'd loved her achingly. Following his devastating loss, Faron had left his beloved Ireland and come to America, where he roamed until he eventually wound up in Canada. He could still picture Margaret's sweet face to that day — every soft and gentle facet. When she died, his interest in women had died with her, as surely as if a surgeon had cut it directly out of the essence that made him a man.

"Did you say something, sir?" a raw-faced boy of the Seventh asked him.

Custer always took a few of his men with him on hunts, more for what he thought of as their enjoyment than for protection. This young lad seemed out of place and nervous to Faron. He looked no more than twenty and stayed well back from the general who rode at the head of the column.

"I said," Faron returned in a low voice, "that we should all be sleeping in our blankets rather than prancin' around in the middle of the night. *I* should be, anyways."

"Me, too." The statement was uttered so quietly that Faron barely heard him.

"Then what are ye doin' out here, boy?" Though it was still dark, enough light had invaded the early morning for Faron to see the youngster's pained look.

"I didn't have a choice. The general thinks this is good for morale and handpicks a few of us for every hunt."

"Can't ye say no?"

"Are you crazy? General Custer probably hasn't heard that word since he was a child."

Faron chuckled lightly. "Where ye from, lad?"

"Ohio . . . the general's home state. He tries to pick one of us every time, thinking he's doing us a favor. It sure would be more favorable to me to let me sleep. It's going to be hard to come by for the next month."

"So I've heard," Faron said as he rubbed his neck and yawned.

On they rode through the breaking dawn, over the prairie broken by uncountable gullies, ditches, and riverbeds, both dry and wet. Occasionally the landscape was dotted with stands of trees, and Faron figured that Custer was headed for one of them to find antelope. Why Custer hadn't sent Faron ahead — since he *was* a scout — the Irishman didn't know, but he was glad of it.

An imaginary boundary existed around Fort Abraham Lincoln. East of the fort, the Indians lived in sulky peace, sitting in silent rows along sidewalks of towns and in front of Indian agencies — white men could sleep at night in safety. But west of the fort, the Indians were a free and intractable people with an indomitable spirit. They remained at peace if it pleased them, and at war if it served their purpose. The memory of evils done on them by white people made them hostile and insolent, warlike by nature. By day they sometimes came to the post for a council, heard the empty promises of the general, and made feigned gestures of friendship. But by night, these same braves waited in the darkness outside the guard line to cut down any foolish trooper who strayed too far from safety. Despite being invaded by army troops, this territory was still hostile Indian country. Faron had no desire to blunder into a Sioux war party encampment all by himself and wake them from *their* sleep. That wouldn't do at all.

Faron could already tell the day was going to be hot and muggy, as the sun's bright orange rays began to creep over the horizon. When he took a deep breath, he could smell the prairie fragrances of plum, crabapple, and wild roses, with the ever present scent of sage beneath it all. He began to feel a little better about being up for the dawn after all.

The hunting party began to ascend a high hill with a large stand of cottonwoods at the crown. Halfway up, Custer turned and signaled Faron forward.

"Here we go, lad," Faron said to the nameless private. "The hunt is about to be on."

"Good luck, sir."

When Faron reached the front of the small column, Custer wasted no time in giving his instructions. Pointing to the forest, he ordered, "Ride into that stand of trees and see if you can find some game. Try to flush them this way. I'll keep the dogs with me and wait for your success."

"Yes, sir." Faron spurred his gelding up the slope toward the trees with one thought in mind. *This is my test. That's why he chose me to lead this outing, to see if I could back up my title as scout. Not much room for failure here after his comment on "success."*

Faron guided the horse down a draw, then back up again, and rode along the ridge to the crest and the blank wall of trees. A light wind sprang up, and he heard the leaves sighing their pleasure, as if sensing the steamy day ahead and soaking up whatever breeze they could to store against the blazing sun sure to come. He hesitated a moment and looked back down the hill to Custer and the men waiting below. White faces like tiny moons stared back at him. Even the dogs, standing beside their master's horse, watched him expectantly.

With a shake of his head, Faron plunged into the forest.

The leafy canopy overhead produced gloomy dark shadows beneath that startled him at first. He trusted the gelding to keep from falling into a hole, or sniffing out any beast that might take an interest in having them for breakfast. "Now, how am I supposed to see any deer, I ask you?" Faron queried the horse. "I can barely see your head in front of me!" As the horse moved farther into the trees, he had to duck low branches and try to avoid any large ones that would dismount him. The gelding seemed confident anyway, so Faron grimly hung on.

As he rode down a small ravine and up the other side, a strange thought occurred to Faron. "Now, wouldn't it be somethin' if I get lost in here?" he mused to himself. "Our Almighty Custer would have a day with that one, eh?" He reached down and patted the horse's neck just as they reached the top of the ravine and broke out into a clearing.

Faron blinked against the sudden light that shone down from the branchless sky overhead, unexpected because he'd been looking down at the ground. The gelding stopped suddenly and began backing up. Faron looked up, still blinking, then his eyes widened.

On the other side of the small clearing stood three Indians. They, too, were blinking against the bright light because apparently Faron's surprise entrance had awakened them. They all stared at one another for the briefest of moments. In that time, Faron's eyes were drawn to the brave on the left, dressed simply in breechcloth and leggings. His hair and skin were lighter than the other two — much lighter — and his golden brown eyes glowed with fierce intelligence.

It was him.

Him.

Faron was so stunned he froze in the saddle, even as he saw the other two braves raise their pistols toward him. His mind registered the scene slowly, as if time had stood still. Yellow sunlight flashed along one of the pistol barrels, jolting him out of his shock, and he fumbled for his rifle, knowing he was already too late. The light-skinned Indian reached out toward the other two as if to stop them from firing, but the clearing erupted with explosions.

Faron felt sharp stings and muscles tearing as a brutal force knocked him backward over the gelding's haunches.

When he hit the ground, he didn't feel it.

Crazy Horse cursed and slammed his hand down on the braves' arms. Both men turned and looked at him in surprise.

"What is it?" Bad Moon asked.

Crazy Horse looked over at the fallen white man who'd been shot, knowing he was probably a scout for the army. To his companions he growled, "Don't you remember why we're here?" Hastily he began rolling up the blanket he'd been sleeping on, motioning the other two to do the same. Within seconds, they were atop their horses and ready to ride.

"What about him?" Bad Moon asked, nodding at the crumpled form across the clearing.

"We have no time," Crazy Horse muttered. "We move now!"

The other man, Big Tree, leaped on the back of his pony, rode across the opening, and grabbed the reins of the gelding. When he looked down at the white man, his face registered no concern or compassion.

Crazy Horse decided to ignore Big Tree's rebellion for the moment as he turned his horse west, in the direction away from where the white man had appeared. Out of all the Sioux nation, no one knew Big Tree's impetuous nature more than Crazy Horse. Also, he was aware that his two companions had reacted solely out of instinct when the man had burst into the clearing. Crazy Horse himself, when he'd been their brash age, would probably have reacted the same way.

They moved swiftly and deftly through the woods, finally breaking out into the clear and running their ponies for all they were worth. Sioux horses were renowned for their endurance. He glanced behind him, half expecting to see a regiment of mounted cavalry riding down on them, but there was only the forest and open prairie. He let out a sigh of relief and cast stern glances at Bad Moon and Big Tree. His sleep had been deep and undisturbed — the first of that kind in a long while — and he was angry at the white scout for blundering into them. He was more enraged over having to leap on the back of a horse and ride twenty miles before being fully awake. They could have killed the man quietly, or even let him go and flee.

No, I could not let him go, Crazy Horse grimly realized. *He recognized me . . . I could see it in his eyes.*

All his life Crazy Horse had been a mere shadow to his enemies, an apparition that appeared out of nowhere, dealt out his revenge, then vanished in thin air. Despite having no ego to speak of, Crazy Horse did enjoy that factor about his fame. The element of surprise was very important on the barren plains, and any rumor that enhanced the reputation of being able to wield that advantage in devastating fashion was more than welcome to him.

Even as he pondered this, he wished he'd taken the time to be sure that the man in the clearing was indeed dead. He reassured himself with the knowledge that the bluecoats could do nothing about it, since he would have put many miles between them and their slow-moving wagons by nightfall. But as the Master of Surprise, it grated and chafed when the advantage was suddenly turned on him.

After about eight miles, Crazy Horse slowed his pony to a walk — not because he was tired, but because the white man's gelding was sweating and breathing heavily. There was no telling how far it had been ridden before coming upon them. It was a good-looking, steady mount, and Crazy Horse didn't want it to die. When he begrudgingly told Big Tree of this, the younger brave grinned.

"So you are glad I took the horse," Big Tree stated proudly.

"Since there are no bluecoats following . . . yes. If there were, I would shoot you myself."

Big Tree laughed and brandished the white man's rifle. "Then I would have to shoot you back many times with this rifle. It is one of those that fire many times, and I don't miss with them."

Bad Moon reached out to inspect the rifle, but Big Tree jerked it away and cradled it protectively in the crook of his arm. "No one touches my new rifle. My good medicine is all over it, and anyone else would stain it."

"Bah!" Bad Moon snorted. "It still has the white man's spirit all over it — it is no good!"

Black eyes narrowing, Big Tree fixed his friend with a withering glare. "I say it is good. Maybe I will shoot *you* with it, Bad Moon!" When Bad Moon waved him off contemptuously, Big Tree reached toward him. "Or . . . maybe I take back the gift necklace I gave you —"

"No!" Bad Moon cried out in genuine fear. His hand quickly reached up and covered the necklace protectively. It was made of bear claws and tiny brass bells — the bear Big Tree had killed himself, while the bells had been taken from one of the many settlers they had raided. "If you take it back, I will die in battle!"

"That's right," Big Tree nodded. "So don't touch my gun."

Bad Moon, still clutching the necklace as if afraid Big Tree would reach out and snatch it, moved his horse away to the other side of Crazy Horse. "I won't touch your gun."

"I know you won't . . . now!" Big Tree grinned.

"That's enough," Crazy Horse told

them. "You fight all the time." He knew that Bad Moon was serious when speaking about his imminent death should he lose the necklace. He believed that it was part of his spirit now, and to lose your spirit is to lose your life. Big Tree was sometimes cruel with his teasing, but he quickly grew tired of mocking his friend because Bad Moon never put up much of a fight.

"How did you know that white face was an army scout?" Big Tree asked.

"I don't know it, but why else would a white man be traveling alone in our country?"

"Maybe because he was a fool?"

Crazy Horse shook his head. "No. He was a scout. The bluecoats are coming, as the elders have warned us."

"They will not be enough," Big Tree announced grandly and waved his hand. "Our numbers are as the blades of grass on the prairie. We will grind them into dust."

Crazy Horse didn't answer. His people were very confident right now and spoiling for a fight. Most of them thought as his brother, that mere numbers alone would turn the tide. True, it was the first time so many had been gathered together in one place along with their Cheyenne brothers. But Crazy Horse knew the bluecoats were just as courageous in battle as any Sioux brave, and they were better equipped with their repeating rifles and cannons. Because of that, he hated to admit, one bluecoat could probably count for ten Indians.

The thought caused him to turn and look behind them again. Seeing that no bluecoats were trailing them didn't make him feel much better.

Faron woke to searing, blinding pain, and in his mind's eye, the face of the most feared Indian in the land continued to stare at him. The features of Crazy Horse were familiar to him only by the words of those who'd seen him and lived to tell about it. Light skinned for an Indian. Narrow face. Golden eyes, full of intelligence. Faron would never forget that face as long as he lived.

Opening his eyes, he saw that he was lying on blankets, bouncing along in the bed of a wagon. Where the wagon had come from he didn't know, because the hunting party hadn't had one. Custer must have sent one of the men back to the camp for it. Beside the wagon rode the young private Faron had ridden with earlier on the hunt. "Why ain't I dead?" Faron croaked, his voice so weak and full of pain that it shocked him.

"What?" said the young soldier.

Faron repeated his question, though it caused him to wince.

The kid shrugged. "Too tough, I guess."

Faron saw a flash of distaste cross the boy's face when he looked down on his wounds.

"Is he awake?" Custer asked, appearing beside the kid. His eyes considered Faron's wounds impassively. "You've been severely wounded, scout," he commented needlessly.

"Don't I know it," Faron groaned.

"You took three bullets, one of which is still inside you."

"Feels more like thirty." Faron didn't have the energy to raise his head and look down at his wounds. *Be too depressing, anyway.* He did, however, notice that he couldn't move his left arm.

"I'm surprised you're still alive," Custer commented matter-of-factly. "A man your age . . . very impressive, I might add."

"Thank you," Faron returned dryly. "Am I gonna live?"

"Depends."

"On what?"

"On the skills of our usually drunken regimental doctor and your stamina. We can't just leave you out here in the middle of Indian country, so you'll have to travel with us."

"I was suspectin' that," Faron moaned.

"I take it that Indians shot you."

"You take it right. What you probably *won't* take is which Indian."

Custer had been lazily brushing the sleeve of his buckskin shirt, but his head whipped around at once. "What do you mean? Who was it?"

"Crazy Horse himself . . . or, two fellas with him, rather." Faron shifted, cried out, then tried to settle into some sort of position where the fiery wounds wouldn't hurt quite so badly. It was impossible, he discovered. Black waves washed over his vision, and he knew he was close to passing out again.

Custer fixed him with his intense blue gaze. "Crazy Horse . . . are you sure?"

"Yep."

The kid and Custer both glanced behind them at the same time, anxious looks plainly on their faces.

Faron grimaced and said, "Don't ye fear, sir. There was only three of 'em." The image of a maniacal surgeon suddenly came to him, standing over him ghoulishly with bloodshot eyes and a gory scalpel held in unsteady hand. "I'll not stand for it," he mumbled, feeling feverish and cold at the same time. "I'll not."

"What's that, O'Donnell?"

Faron stared off in the distance, thinking of time lost, time gained, and time left. Then he looked at Custer and said, "General?"

"Yes?"

"I don't relish the thought of dyin' at the hands of some drunk surgeon." Very close to unconsciousness now, Faron managed to whisper, "I need you to send a telegram."

Chapter Five

The Messenger

Reena watched Jack Sheffield as he worked in the bean field with the Blackfoot Indians. The bare backs of the braves glistened with sweat in the summer's heat, but they didn't seem to mind it. Jack wore black pants and a sodden white shirt with the sleeves rolled up above his elbows. Occasionally, he would remove his straw hat and wipe his brow with a blue kerchief, revealing his striking red hair, which at the moment was wet and flat on his head.

Reena's eyes went to the small corn field and the watermelon patch beside it. The Indians loved the melons and ate some every day. Across from the corn field, which billowed in the breeze with fat stalks, grazed the cattle and goats, with a small group of pigs farrowing for food. Children moved among the goats, laughing gleefully when one of the billys lowered his head and pushed against them.

The whole tribe was now fully self-sustaining, except for the sugar they accepted from the Canadian government. Plenty Trees, the tribe's chief, would often walk among the fields with an unmistakable look of self-satisfaction over his people's triumph.

But the success was all due to Reverend Jack Sheffield, and everyone in the village knew it.

As Reena watched from outside her tepee, Jack turned and spotted her attention on him. Reena quickly averted her gaze. From the corner of her eye she could see him begin to make his way toward her, and she shifted nervously. Jack had professed his love for her only a month or two after his arrival, and she still wasn't completely comfortable around him because of that. The way he looked at her was . . . disturbing sometimes. He could no more hide his feelings for her than fly to the moon. Hunter noticed it — everyone noticed it, even the Blackfoot.

Jack plopped himself down beside her on the ground by her blanket and handed her a purple prairie violet that he'd apparently just picked in the field on his way over.

"Why, thank you, Jack!" Reena exclaimed, delighted.

"A prairie violet for your thoughts." He

grinned at her, revealing even white teeth in an extremely handsome face.

Reena could feel herself blushing, and it only made her more unsettled. *Why should he make me act like a schoolgirl?* "Oh, I wasn't . . . I mean . . . I wasn't thinking anything, really."

"Could have fooled me." He wrapped his arms around his knees and looked at her in his disturbingly direct way. "Reena, may I ask you something?"

"Of course."

"You don't have to answer if you don't want to."

"Jack, ask me." She twirled the violet in her hand nervously, dreading what was coming. Besides having a direct gaze, his questions could sometimes be pointed also.

"Something's been on my mind for a while, and I know it's probably foolish, but . . ."

"Go on."

"Well, you've been talking to Hunter about God for years, then suddenly he's saved in one of my services a few months ago. Does that bother you? That he wasn't converted while you were . . . um . . . trying to share your faith with him?"

Reena didn't know what she'd expected

him to ask, but it certainly wasn't this. "Why, Jack, that's preposterous! Of course I don't mind."

He looked at her uncertainly.

"Jack, Hunter was saved in the presence of all his friends and God. It doesn't matter *where* it was. It just matters that he did it."

"That's the way I feel about it, but I wasn't sure —"

"You're silly sometimes," she teased.

He looked at her. "I like being silly around you. As a matter of fact, it's the *only* time I'm silly."

Reena didn't answer and couldn't meet his eyes. He must have sensed her discomfort, because he changed the subject at once.

"Have you seen your sister since the wedding?"

"The day after, before I left town. She was . . . radiant. I suppose that's the only way to put it."

"Good for her. Megan deserves a little happiness after what she's been through."

"Yes, she does," Reena said softly.

They sat in silence for a while, watching the Indians work the fields. Reena knew in her heart that she couldn't encourage Jack's affections. She loved Hunter, and though she suspected that many women would relish and even promote the attentions of two handsome men, she found that sort of behavior childish and insulting. While growing up, she had watched Megan's coquettish expertise as she jockeyed for three or four boys' affections at a time, playing them against one another unmercifully. Appalled, Reena had vowed to herself that she would never behave that way.

Secretly, Reena glanced over to Sheffield's fine profile. He was a devoted man of God. He was extremely handsome. Kind, thoughtful, and sincere in everything he did, Jack always put others' well-being before his own. He was everything a woman could ever long for in a husband. . . .

Suddenly, her eyes were drawn beyond Jack to an Indian rider riding into the camp surrounded by a Blackfoot guard. The Indian wasn't Blackfoot, Reena could see. He was short, but powerful, dressed only in buckskin leggings with a breastplate of bone hairpipes and blue and green glass beads. A single hawk feather hung loosely from his long black hair. On the legs of his White Plains pony were painted red crooked slashes — obviously some sort of symbol of his prowess as a warrior.

Plenty Trees had spotted the brave before Reena and appeared in front of them with a challenging look. "What do you want?" he asked in Blackfoot.

Surprisingly, the warrior from another tribe spoke in the same language. "I am Bad Weasel, of the Sioux. I bring great news."

Plenty Trees' eyes widened. The Sioux were not known as roamers, and their land was far to the south. Plenty Trees had never even seen a Sioux. "What do you want?" he repeated.

Bad Weasel's gaze swept over Reena and Jack haughtily. "We do not speak in front of *them*."

"I will say where we speak," Plenty Trees returned. "They are our friends, and we speak here."

Bad Weasel shrugged, but a contemptuous smile played at his lips. "Very well. I bring news of a great gathering of my people in the mountains to the south. We wish the Blackfoot to join us."

"For what reason?"

"Brotherhood . . . getting to know one another."

"And?" Plenty Trees asked suspiciously.

"What is wrong with that?"

Plenty Trees crossed his arms. "When have the Sioux —"

"And Cheyenne. The *brave* Cheyenne are with us."

Bad Weasel's meaning was not lost on Plenty Trees, but he ignored it.

"When have the Sioux *or* the Cheyenne invited the Blackfoot for feasting? We are not enemies, but we are not friends, either. What else are you planning? What do you want from us?"

An ugly smile spread across Bad Weasel's mouth, revealing blackened teeth. "We make war on the white eyes once and for all. We will drive them from our land, never to return." His disdainful look came around to Reena and Jack again, but he spoke to Plenty Trees. "If you were smart, Blackfoot, you would drive them away, too."

"My name is Chief Plenty Trees, and the white man has only helped the Blackfoot here. We do not need your war."

"Then you are a coward," Bad Weasel sneered.

Plenty Trees charged the Sioux on the pony, but his braves restrained him. Struggling in their arms, Plenty Trees shouted, "You will leave my village! Before I kill you!"

Bad Weasel didn't flinch, but his pony became nervous because of the sudden movement all around him. Reena had met many Indians in her time on the frontier, but never one like Bad Weasel. The arrogance in his bearing was almost palpable, and as she looked at him closer, she saw many scars crisscrossing his naked torso. This warrior had seen much violence in his life, and Reena somehow knew that he had come to like it.

Calmly Bad Weasel turned his pony, looking over the gathering of Blackfoot with extreme arrogance. "You will see — the white man will take your land and cage you on a reservation. You will be sorry you did not join our fight." Chest swelling as he straightened up, he growled, "You are slaves, and I spit on you!" His spittle barely missed Plenty Trees, then he turned the pony and galloped out of the village.

Plenty Trees shook off the arms that held him and turned to Reena and Jack. "I am sorry . . . I should not have been angry like that."

"It's all right, Plenty Trees," Jack said. "We aren't perfect, and we all sin. God understands that, too."

Plenty Trees nodded and went back to the bean field with the others.

Jack looked in the direction where the Sioux had disappeared and murmured to Reena, "I wonder if what he says is true?"

"You mean about an upcoming battle?"

His gaze came around to her. "No, I mean about putting the Blackfoot on a reservation. Do you think that could really happen?"

Reena shrugged. "It's already happening in the United States."

"But those Indians are hostile. The Blackfoot don't want to hurt anyone. They just want to be left alone."

Reena bit her lip thoughtfully. "Jack, have you ever heard of a tribe called the Cherokee?"

"Cherokee? I don't think so."

"They were native to Tennessee, Alabama, and other southern states. They were a peaceful tribe and didn't want to hurt anybody, either. But their land was taken from them during wars in the 1830s because of the white man's expansion."

"What happened to them?"

"The government rounded most of them up and forced them to move to Oklahoma Territory. The government tried to keep the whole thing quiet, but my father learned the truth of what is now called the 'Trail of Tears.' Thousands of them died along the way, mostly infants, children, and old people."

Jack fully faced her, horrified. "What? How . . . how?"

"Measles, whooping cough, pneumonia . . . you name it." Reena's eyes were haunted and she barely spoke above a whisper. She could remember hearing her father tell her uncle Faron about it in his office one night when Reena was only a teenager. For days afterward, Reena had nightmares about babies dying horribly.

Jack was silent for a long time, gazing off in the distance. Finally he said, "I told Plenty Trees that God understands our nature. Reena, if He does, He must be very sad sometimes. Do you think He cries?"

Reena met his strange look of concern squarely and answered, "I don't know. But if He does, He cried a lot during the Trail of Tears."

Hunter Stone sat on the front step of his quarters and watched the sun go down. It had blazed bright and full all day, and now it settled westward and melted into a shapeless bed of gold flame as it touched the Rockies.

The ceremony for striking the flag had already occurred, and Stone had eaten a large supper of beef, potatoes, and field peas. He felt full and warm. From the blacksmith shop came the *tink! tink!* of a hammer on anvil, ringing through the air with metallic shrillness. He wasn't the only one outside. A number of men were sitting in chairs around the parade ground, passing the time chatting and playing cards until lights out.

Surprisingly, Hunter found himself missing his friend Vic. When he'd teased Megan on their wedding day about Vic's obsession with tidiness, it had been with a sense of true relief that Stone was passing Vic over to her, to let her deal with his sometimes irritating habits. Now, inside his quarters, he could already see dust beginning to gather on the floor, window sills, wood-burning stove, and small desk. Sometimes he thought he could smell that strange odor that had been absent since he and Vic had moved in, hanging in the air like a den-dwelling beast. After all of that, he still couldn't bring himself to sweep and dust. Though Vic could be annoying at times, Hunter missed the good talks they'd shared in that cabin.

With the falling of the sun came no relief from the heat. The smell of grass and greenery hung in the air, rich and fragrant, just beneath the lingering aroma of supper from the mess hall. Summer crouched on the horizon, waiting to blaze down on the earth and men fourteen hours a day with gusto. Hunter dreaded the hot months because he felt the most alive in the cool falls and early springs in the land. The scorching, parched summers made him feel lazy and irritable, though he overcame it by working extra duties and details on the longer days, enduring the burden by sheer will.

The only consolation to summer, he thought lazily, swatting at a fly, *is that I get to see Reena more often in the long summer days.* The thought made him smile, and he let his head fall back with his eyes closed. Renegades, both white and red, thrived on the opportunities that presented themselves during the summer months — wagon trains, payroll shipments that ran at disturbingly regular times — and Hunter found himself checking on Reena more than ever during those sun-drenched months. At least that's what he told himself the reason was.

"You certainly look relaxed, sir."

Stone jerked and looked up to find Sergeant Preston Stride gazing down on him with what passed for amusement on his hard, stern countenance. He had once been British regular army. He brought across the Atlantic with him the famous discipline and organization that had made that fine army proud and inflicted it on the men of "C" Troop, North-West Mounted Police. Stone was glad to have him and trusted him with his life. "Hello, Stride. Yes, I suppose one would get that impression."

"Some papers for you to sign, sir." Stride handed over a clipboard with an unmistakable formal military flourish.

"What's this?"

"The day's sick call, sir."

"Hmmm . . . fever . . . fractured finger . . . cold . . . *cold?*"

Stride stared straight ahead, at attention, noncommittal about the contents of the report.

"Are you telling me," Stone asked slowly, "that someone missed a day's work because of a *cold?*"

"I only deliver the surgeon's papers, sir."

Stone jumped to his feet, still staring at the report. "Now, wait a minute . . . a headache? A lousy headache? How long has this been going on, Sergeant?"

"I normally take this report to Inspector Willingham, sir. The inspector, who is on patrol as we speak, is usually too busy to read every case."

"Follow me, Stride. I'm going to have a word with this . . . *surgeon*."

Stride followed Hunter's long pace to the surgeon's clinic, walking to the left and a bit behind him. Inside, he was smiling. Sub-Inspector Stone was his favorite officer — a man given to no nonsense when it came to the men, but also a man in whom they were more than comfortable to confide. Stride knew that Stone considered him a capable non-commissioned officer, and Stride took pride in the fact. Though he knew Stone had no prior military service, his exemplary record spoke for itself and revealed a natural born leader of men. Stride actually looked forward to the coming storm in the surgeon's clinic.

Stone burst through the door of the clinic, rattling the sign hanging from a string on the door claiming, "Dr. Thomas Stillwell, Chief Surgeon." Inside to the right, along the wall, stood four chairs. Three of them were occupied — one by a pale, sickly-looking man, another by a constable with a swollen jaw with a cloth wrapped around his chin to the back of his head, and in the third chair was none other than Del Dekko. Stone stopped abruptly. "Del, are you sick?"

"'Course not! I ain't never been sick a day of my life."

"Then what are you doing here?"

"Watchin'."

"Watching?"

"Yep."

"Watching what?"

Del cackled. "These poor sick men."

"Don't you have something better to do?"

Shrugging and crossing his legs, Del looked not the least bit guilty. "Best entertainment around most days." He glanced over at the pitiful men beside him. "Present company excluded, o' course, gents. I can see you boys are in real pain."

Behind a desk halfway into the room stood two men. Stone immediately recognized Dr. Thomas Stillwell, Chief Surgeon, by his casual shirtsleeves rolled up and his present examination of the other man's neck.

Stillwell gave the officers a perfunctory glance, then said to the patient, "This might swell with fluid again, but come see me again tomorrow after some bed rest."

Stone strode purposefully over to the men, moving behind the patient to see what the problem was. On the back of his neck, to the right, was a small boil that had recently been lanced.

"Can I help you, sir?" Stillwell asked, obviously miffed that his professional space had been invaded.

"Yes, you can, *Doctor*," Stone returned. "What's this?"

"That's a boil, sir."

"I can see that. What I don't understand is your treatment for it."

Stillwell looked surprised. "I lanced it, of course."

Stone heard Del desperately try to cover a cackle and fail. He was beginning to understand why Del found the infirmary so entertaining. "Yes, I can see that you lanced it. Is this man too weak from the horrible needle surgery on his neck to go back to work tomorrow?"

"The sun is becoming cruel, sir," Stillwell said defensively. "The blistering heat from the sun could cause —"

"So put a patch on it!" Stone roared. "You don't prescribe bed rest for a *boil!*"

Stillwell's eyes rounded, but he could find no words.

"Look at those men over there," Stone snapped, pointing to the waiting patients. "I'd say they're a bit more uncomfortable than this man." He glared accusingly at the man with the boil, who shrank back.

"I was . . . I just . . . I took the examination when the doctor told me to, sir! He goes in order —"

Stone whipped the clipboard up in front of Stillwell's face. "A cold . . . two days' rest? Two?"

Sergeant Stride watched the doctor visibly squirm and couldn't keep a smile from touching his lips.

After a moment, Stillwell managed to brace himself defensively against Stone's onslaught and answer matter-of-factly, "I was afraid it was near going to his chest, and when that happens —"

"Then when it's in his chest, give him two days' rest, Doctor. Next one . . . a headache? One day's rest?" Stone heard Del stifle a laugh again and glared at him. Del abruptly covered his mouth but couldn't hide the amusement dancing in his eyes.

"Migraines are very painful, Sub-Inspector. If you've never experienced one, then you wouldn't know —"

"It doesn't say migraine here, Doctor. Get your terms straight."

The policeman with the wrapped jaw moaned painfully.

Stone said, "Give this man a patch for that boil — I think he's capable of putting it on himself. And see to those men who are really hurting —"

The door slammed open and in charged a young sub-constable with rumpled clothes and wild red hair. "Hey, Doc, how about that —" He stopped cold when he saw Stone and Stride and snapped to attention.

Stone looked him up and down, searching for some sort of wound or affliction.

Stillwell suddenly busied himself in his desk drawer, fumbled out a patch and piece of tape, and handed it to the man with the boil. "See that this stays on tomorrow on your . . . rounds." He turned to the constable with the wrapped jaw. "Now, Constable, let's see to that —"

"Hold there, Doctor," Stone said, placing a hand on his arm and motioning to the new arrival. "This youngster seems to be in a big hurry. Don't I know you, son?"

The sub-constable looked terrified. "I . . . don't know, sir."

"He's one of the buglers, sir," Stride said smugly.

"You're gonna love this one, Hunter," Del grinned, hardly able to contain his excitement.

"What are you here for, bugler?" Stone demanded.

The boy glanced nervously to Stillwell, hoping the doctor would save him with his professional analysis, but Stillwell didn't say a word.

"And why are your clothes so wrinkled?" Stone added, then realization dawned on his face. "Did you just get out of *bed?*"

"Um . . . yes, sir."

"Are you sick?"

"Well, not exactly, I —"

"How long have you been off-duty?"

"Two days, sir."

Stone gave Stillwell a burning look, then asked the bugler, "And what is your affliction?"

One of the boy's legs visibly began shaking with the effort of trying to keep it ramrod straight. He licked his lips, then pulled them in with a look of pain. "I have . . . sore lips, sir."

Del Dekko howled and nearly fell out of his chair.

"Sore lips?" Stone asked, beyond disbelief.

Sergeant Stride suddenly spun and began examining the doctor's credentials on the wall, his hand held to his mouth.

Stillwell went back to his desk drawer and produced a small jar of clear gel. "Yes, Morton, here's your salve."

Stone snatched the jar from his hand and tossed it to the bugler. "You will sound wake-up in the morning, Morton. Tomorrow morning and every day after that until I say so. Is that clear?"

"Absolutely, sir!" Morton replied and scrambled for the door handle, missed, dropped the jar of salve, gave a quick, "Sorry, sir," and hastily made his exit.

His face red, Stone almost touched noses with Stillwell. "A word with you, Doctor, if you please."

"Of course, sir." Stillwell was visibly sweating and motioned to a closed door at the back of the room. "In my office, all right?"

Stone's big hands closed. "That will be fine."

After the door closed and the tongue-lashing began, Sergeant Stride turned to Del and asked, "How about some coffee, Mr. Dekko?"

Del cast an ear in the direction of the office, listened for a moment, then chuckled. "But the fun's just beginning, Stride!"

The sergeant cocked his head. "Not for the good doctor, I don't believe."

"You go on ahead, Stride. Soon as the doctor sees to these poor boys, I've got a callous on my toe that needs lookin' at."

Del's homely face registered pure amusement. "Who knows, I may be out of commission for a couple of days, and you'll have to bring coffee to me!"

Even after he closed the door, Stride could hear Del's hoots of laughter.

Chapter Six

The Absence of Reality

Jaye Eliot Vickersham was having a hard time concentrating on his job as he rode along. His mind . . . his heart . . . his whole *being* was filled with thoughts of Megan. Every moment spent away from her he considered a wasted moment, devoid of meaning and empty. Though a severe pragmatist by nature, his common sense couldn't quite reach through to his brain that he was being silly, obsessed, turning into an absent-minded man without a compass.

Of course he'd thought about Megan before their marriage. His dreams for them had often kept him lying awake at night. But after spending only a few weeks with her as a husband, those lofty dreams seemed puny now.

As he rode into the mountains, Vic knew his companion, Constable Edouard D'Artigue, was throwing curious looks his way, but Vic didn't care. He was thinking about the shipment of fine silk that needed fetching from I. G. Baker's store as soon as he returned to Fort Macleod. Megan loved rich, deep green colors, and Vic was going to surprise her with the material for a new dress. She would look wondrous, lovely . . .

"Excuse me, sir," D'Artigue said, clearing his throat.

"What is it?" Vic asked sharply. He had been imagining seeing Megan in her new dress, and the interruption irritated him.

"Aren't we supposed to take ze trail back there?"

"Where?"

"Ze one we just passed, sir. Ze one that led toward ze crest of this knoll."

D'Artigue's speech was much better now. When he'd first come to the Mounties, almost no one had been able to understand him through his thick accent. He had a light complexion, with pleasant features and a pencil-thin mustache above his squarely centered mouth.

Vickersham stopped his mount abruptly and turned. Sure enough, about fifty feet back he saw the upward trail Del had told him to take to the cabin. Vic hung his head. He'd skirted right past it without even seeing it. "You're right, Constable. Back we go."

"Sir?"

"Yes?"

"Ees there . . . anything I can do?"

"Concerning what, D'Artigue?"

"Nothing."

"Go on, old chap! What?"

"May I speak frankly, sir?"

Vic was losing his patience quickly. "Of course . . . now, what is it, man!"

"Er . . . well, you see, sir, it's just that ze men and I, we've noticed a change in you since you've returned. You seem more . . . um . . . oh, what is ze word? Preintro . . . spect—"

"Close your mouth, D'Artigue, before you fall all over your tongue. I think you're combining two words — preoccupied and introspective. Did you memorize this speech?"

The Frenchman looked embarrassed. "I had some help, sir. All ze men are worried about you."

"Well, tell them not to worry, my good man. I haven't changed a bit, except for the fact that I'm happier than I've ever been in my life."

"Pardon me, sir, but you don't seem it."

"Well, I am," Vickersham snapped. "And why is everyone so worried about me all of a sudden?" They rounded a bend in the thick aspens and began to ascend a rocky path. Their horses picked their way

113

through the sharp, jutted rocks carefully, and the riders swayed with their sure-footed decisions. Sorry for his sharp tone, Vic said, "D'Artigue . . . ?"

"You are right, sir. It ees none of our business."

Vickersham almost let it go at that. Sometimes he forgot that a police or army barracks was more skilled and intuitive than a ladies' quilting circle when it came to gossip. The men had nothing more to do at night than sit around and discuss the officers — their moods, their habits, even their families. The men had sensed that Vickersham's heart was not in his job, and when they felt that way about one of the men who could lead them into a scrape or battle, it understandably made them nervous. The pressure must have been great on D'Artigue to mention something to him when the men found out the Frenchman had been assigned to this patrol. D'Artigue, by nature, was a friendly, reliable man, but by no means inquisitive into other's habits. Vickersham realized the man must have hated what he'd just done.

"Listen, Edouard," Vic began slowly. He'd never called the man by his Christian name, and it felt foreign on his tongue, making him lose his concentration. "I don't mean to be quarrelsome, and I do appreciate your concern, but I'm fine. Really."

"Of course, sir." Feeling uncomfortable, D'Artigue quickly changed the subject. "Do you think that whiskey-making still is really up here?"

Vic shrugged. "The information came from a supposedly reliable source. We'll just have to see when we get there."

They rode in silence for a while, and the grade became steeper as they went. The sun blazing through the canopy of trees above them began to heat things up in earnest, but Vic barely noticed. Left alone with his thoughts again, he mused, *How else can I surprise Megan? A bonnet? A necklace? Pearls! She would positively glow in pearls! Now, where would I find —*

"Um . . . sir . . ." D'Artigue muttered. "Is this the place?"

Vickersham looked up and saw a shabby cabin. The clearing around it was strewn with trash and debris, and over by a small shed stood a horse hooked up to a wagon. Tracks around the area revealed a crisscross of wheel lines, as if the horse had moved about the yard restlessly for some time.

"The horse, sir," D'Artigue noted.

"I see it," Vic returned grimly. He dismounted and walked slowly over to the spooked horse, which threw its head when Vic reached for the bridle. "Easy, boy," Vic crooned soothingly and managed to grab hold of the harness on his shoulder. "Easy . . ."

D'Artigue appeared beside him and produced a kerchief from his back pocket. Placing it over his nose and mouth, his accented voice was dulled as he muttered, "Zat smell. Is it . . . ?"

Vic inspected underneath the leather harness lead and saw the beginnings of sores. "This horse has been harnessed for quite some time." It was only then that D'Artigue's question hit him, and his nose wrinkled. "Oh no."

Both men looked to the silent cabin. The tattered curtains were drawn fully closed, and all about the place rested the pall of deathly silence. Unmarked crates were stacked against one wall, stained and damp from recent rain showers. Beside the front door was a crudely carved child's play rifle with part of the barrel broken off.

A hawk screamed overhead as it soared deeper into the mountains, startling both men.

"D'Artigue, check around back for the

still." As he watched the Frenchman cautiously tread to the back of the house, Vic drew his Adams revolver. The back of his neck prickled. He spun and looked deep into the shadowy forest of aspen and firs but saw no movement.

"It is there, sir," D'Artigue informed him when he returned. "The coals are cold — it hasn't been used in a few days. And, sir . . . the aroma is worse by the house."

They both glanced at the cabin, and dread showed plainly on their faces. The wind had shifted to the north, carrying the horrible odor with it, but Vic thought he could still smell it in his hair and clothes. "Arm yourself, D'Artigue."

Vickersham moved to the door with his eyes steady on the windows, feeling D'Artigue close behind him. Nothing moved. No birds sang. The only sound was the soft whispering of the aspen leaves in the gentle wind.

Vic tapped lightly on the solid oak with the butt of the Adams. "North-West Mounted! Open the door, please!" His voice rang clear and sharp, sounding more confident than he felt, and he imagined that he could be heard for miles.

Nothing. Absolute silence.

He took another glance at the window.

At his shoulder, D'Artigue whispered, "The door is open, I believe."

Vic looked down and saw that he was right. Gently, he pushed open the door, hearing a rusted hasp groan noisily. The fetid stench assaulted his senses, and he quickly brought his arm up and placed his nose and mouth in the crook of his elbow. It didn't help much.

The room was untidy and heavily used. Vic had hoped the smell would be from spoiled food left out, but he could spot none in the sparse kitchen. Some moldy bread was on a cutting board, but other than an empty tin of beans and a few dishes lying around, the room was bare. A worn couch with stuffing sprouting from various holes sat forlornly in the middle of the living room. In front of the fireplace was an old quilt with many burn marks marking it. A faded daguerreotype of a stern-looking man sat on the small mantel, the lone impractical item in the room. Beyond the fireplace was a closed door.

Vic nodded toward the door, noting the sweat that glistened on D'Artigue's upper lip and forehead. D'Artigue nodded, swallowed, and followed Vic to the door, glancing back once to the open front door.

Stepping up to the door, Vickersham

again tapped lightly. "Anyone home? Police!"

The last thing he wanted to do was open that door. The stench was stronger than ever.

Vic turned the knob and let the door swing open of its own accord. For a moment, he stood there stunned, his mind numbed at what he saw. Then he heard the sound of violent retching behind him.

Vickersham stared and stared, but the whole room seemed as if it were some sort of nightmare from which he was unable to disentangle himself. A word kept tugging at the corners of his frozen brain to describe the scene, but he couldn't quite grasp it. It didn't matter. He realized that words had no meaning in this place of death.

D'Artigue was still retching behind him, and in a surprisingly calm tone, he heard himself say, "Go outside if you need to, D'Artigue."

Needing no further invitation, D'Artigue crossed to the door, half bent over and stumbling a bit.

Vic went back into the kitchen to find a towel, since holding his arm across his face was proving to be uncomfortable. He found one that had hand-holding gingerbread men stitched across it and remembered the child's toy gun outside the cabin. "Thank you, God," he whispered. "No child here." He placed the towel against his face and wished he really were smelling gingerbread rather than the stench of the dead.

Returning to the bedroom, he steeled his nerves and forced himself to look around, careful to keep everything exactly as it was when they walked in. Vic knew that his subconscious mind was soaking up details he could draw on later. He'd been blessed — or cursed, according to the situation — with a keen memory that could recall most things down to the minutiae. He studiously avoided the woman's body for a moment. He didn't know how long he was in there — his mind was still numb, and time meant nothing — when D'Artigue appeared in the doorway, pale and his face drawn.

"What do we do here, sir? What do we do?"

"Go unharness that horse and feed and water him."

"I already have."

"How do you feel, D'Artigue? Can you . . . come in here?"

His eyes flickered over the body on the

bed, then came back to Vic with a show of confidence. "I think so."

Vic studied him, then nodded. "Very well. I'm looking for the murder weapon, but I doubt we'll find it in here. Would you look under the bed on that other side, please? And tell me if you find anything unusual. Anything at all."

"Yes, sir."

Vickersham took a deep breath and leaned over the body to study it closer. Then he drew back in shock, gasping for breath.

D'Artigue's head popped up from the other side of the bed. "What is it, sir?" His eyes focused on the body, then quickly he avoided the sight by looking back at Vickersham.

"Nothing, I . . . nothing . . . go on with your search." After D'Artigue's head reluctantly disappeared again, Vic turned to the window with the gingerbread man cloth pressed tightly over his mouth — whether out of trauma or to stifle a scream, he wasn't sure. His free hand was trembling violently.

The blazing sunshine outside seemed to stop at the glass, as if light weren't allowed to enter this room.

Excitedly, D'Artigue announced, "Found

something!" In his hand was a colorfully beaded armlet that some Indians wore.

"Is that all?" Vic asked.

"Yes. Except for . . . more dried blood."

Vic closed his eyes. *This can't be happening.* "Search the rest of the cabin, will you? Then wait for me outside."

D'Artigue gave him a strange look. "Are you sure you're all right, sir?"

"Yes, I'm fine. Now go." After D'Artigue left the room, Vickersham braced himself, swallowed, and again leaned over the body. Carefully avoiding looking at the victim's face, he managed to block out his feelings and meticulously explore the wounds. It meant shifting the body and removing some clothing, but he steeled his nerves and concentrated on the search for evidence rather than on the distasteful act itself. He didn't know how he did it, but he forced himself to finish.

When he was done, he gazed out the tiny window for a moment, then went to the battered dresser against the far wall. Vic felt as if he were moving through deep sludge, that his body seemed to be answering his brain's commands with gargantuan effort. He didn't want to search through the dresser for evidence. He didn't want to find out the truth about her death. He only wanted to run outside, jump on his horse, and ride as far away from this place as he could.

From somewhere, the duty that was so deeply ingrained within forced him to look. Undergarments, old, well-worn clothes, a rusty knife beneath tattered socks, a pair of well-worn shoes, and a diary.

With trembling fingers he opened the diary, and what he read inside changed his life forever.

They buried the woman beside the shed and placed a crude cross at the head of the grave.

Silently, they stared down at the rust-colored mound of dirt for a long while. D'Artigue finally said, "We don't even know her name, sir."

Fran, Vickersham thought, with a wrench in his chest. *Her name was Fran, short for Francine.*

Vic prayed a short prayer and then put on his jacket.

As they readied to leave, D'Artigue asked, "Should we wait here for the man to return?"

"No. It could be days before he comes back — if he comes back at all." Vic scribbled a note on his notepad and nailed it on the cabin door.

D'Artigue read it, then looked at him. "Sort of simple, isn't it?"

"Well, what would you have me to say?" Vickersham snapped. He swung up on his horse and took the reins of the horse that had been harnessed.

All the way down the mountain, they didn't talk. It was only when they were two miles over the plains that D'Artigue finally broke the silence.

"What do you think happened, sir? Do you think the man went berserk and killed her?"

Vickersham didn't answer. His eyes stared straight ahead, empty of emotion. He remembered his mood on the trip to the cabin, so full of joy over his new bride, the future before him full of promise and happiness.

D'Artigue didn't press the questions and was surprised when Vickersham finally spoke, so low he could barely hear him.

"Surreal."

"What was that, sir?"

Vic swung around and gazed back up at the still-visible foothill, then faced forward to look back no more. "I said, the word was surreal."

Part Two

THE FIRST STEP

La distance n'y fait rien; il n'y a que le premier pas qui coûte.

The distance is nothing; it is only the first step that is difficult.

Mme Du Deffand

Chapter Seven

A Journey Planned

Faron awoke with a throbbing headache. However, his right arm began to hurt worse as the effect of the morphine faded away. He opened his eyes to what seemed like endless blurry white clouds.

"He's awake," someone whispered.

The white clouds weren't clouds, Faron discovered after focusing. It was the roof of a tent. "Where am I?" he croaked through parched lips, suddenly aware of a desert thirst.

"In my tent, at the moment," announced a man with a bulbous nose, shining dark eyes, and heavy, beetled brows.

The man's white apron was blood-spattered, and Faron stared at his own life essence in momentary fascination. Right then the man leaned over him and shined a light in his eyes.

"I'm Doctor Denton."

Faron clearly smelled the whiskey fumes on the man's breath. "Been partakin' of your own medicine, Doc?" he asked sarcastically. It hurt even to smile.

Denton turned to his assistant. "I'd say he's feeling fine, wouldn't you, Foster?"

"Yes, sir."

Turning back to Faron, Denton wasted no words. "I removed one bullet from your left side. Another went clean through your upper shoulder, glancing off the clavicle. The third —"

"Off the what?"

"The clavicle . . . the collarbone."

"Oh. Well, if you mean collarbone, say collarbone."

Antagonistic light flashed in Denton's eyes, but he continued on in his droning, matter-of-fact voice. "The third bullet struck your arm above the elbow in the humerus . . . um . . . upper arm bone. It shattered part of that bone and lodged itself inside. I cannot remove it. The only choice is to amputate."

The word pounded through Faron's aching head like a hammer. "You try that, sawbones, and I'll have *your* arm."

"Now, see here —" Denton stopped and consulted a clipboard by the bed on a battered oak stand. He had to squeeze one eye shut and squint with the other to read. "O'Donnell. I only have your best interests at heart, so you could show a little respect for —"

"Give me some more o' that sleepin' medicine, and I'll have a think on the matter."

Denton shook his head firmly. "That's morphine. It's dangerous and addictive."

"Look, Doc, you're allowed to partake o' your liquid painkiller, so why don't ye just let me name my own poison, too?"

"It's not the same thing —"

"Some water, then. My mouth's as dry as salt."

Denton nodded to Foster, who gave Faron a drink.

"Now, about that arm," Denton began again.

Faron savored the cool water, sloshing it around in his mouth before swallowing. "More, Foster. Keep it comin', lad." After another healthy gulp, Faron asked, "Where's that Ohio boy?"

Doctor and assistant looked at each other blankly.

"The Ohio boy! The one what was on the hunt with us."

Foster brightened. "Oh yes. He came by to check on you earlier, but we had to turn him away."

"Turn him away! *Why*, in the name

o' leprechauns?"

Denton rolled his eyes in exasperation. "We were *operating*, O'Donnell. We can't just have anyone stroll in here."

"He's my friend," Faron returned, hearing the sulkiness in his own tone. "You should have let him in."

"You're avoiding the subject, O'Donnell," Denton said roughly. "Your arm has to come off."

"Nope. Forget about it, Doc. If I leave this world, it'll be with all the parts I came into it with."

"That's foolish thinking," Denton declared. "If we don't remove it soon, gangrene will most certainly set in, and when it does —"

"Listen, Doc. You nor anybody else is gonna take a saw to this arm. And that's final," Faron said, wincing.

Denton turned to Foster. "Go find that Ohio boy. Maybe he can talk some sense into him."

Foster left, and Denton pulled up a chair beside Faron's bed. From the oak desk he produced a bottle filled with amber liquid, uncorked it, and took some deep dregs from it.

Faron watched him, still feeling drowsy and antagonistic. "That stuff help?"

130

Denton looked at him before corking the bottle and returning it to the drawer. He crossed his legs, massaged his neck, and said nothing.

Faron glanced down at the bloody bandages on his arm and torso. He could smell his own sweat and fear. To be half a man, unable to cock a rifle, unable to chop wood, unable to hunt for wild game for a good meal . . .

The tent flap opened right then and in marched the kid who'd ridden on the hunt. His pale brown eyes looked down on Faron, who attempted a grin. "There he is. What's your name, lad?"

"Private Norton, sir."

"Don't ye be sirrin' me. I ain't none o' your superiors. Now what's your *name?*"

The boy grinned, but it faded quickly when he saw Faron's bandages. "Josh. My name's Josh Norton."

"You ain't joshin' me, are ye?"

The boy smiled, but it was more out of politeness than humor.

"Bet you've only heard that one a thousand times, eh?"

"Yes, sir."

Denton cleared his throat. "Private, you're here to convince this man that his arm should come off."

"Don't ye be tellin' the lad what he ought and ought not say," Faron warned. "He gets enough o' that out there with the sergeants and lieutenants and generals. In here he can say what he wants."

Totally ignoring Faron's interruption, Denton told Norton, "Tell him the consequences will be dire."

"And what consequences aren't?" Faron croaked. He felt anger wash over him; anger at the calm tone of the doctor who spoke so easily about removing a man's arm, anger over his wretched condition, anger at the braves who had shot him. Dizziness fastened itself upon his vision, then passed. The pain in his body was increasing each second with the passing of the morphine's soothing effect. He locked eyes with Josh Norton. "That's the secret o' life, lad — avoidin' consequences. If ye do somethin' and the result is dire, it's a consequence. If the result is *good*, it's a reward. Remember that — consequences is bad, rewards is good."

Josh nodded solemnly.

"What are ye lookin' so gloomy about, boy? I ain't dead yet!" A pain coursed through his side so bad that he cried out in surprise.

"I think it's time for another dose of

morphine," Denton said, rising from the chair.

"Hold there a minute, Doc," Faron told him, then asked Josh, "Did that telegram get sent?"

"Yes, sir, I made sure of that myself."

"Good lad. Be off with ye, then, and let me know if we get an answer." To Denton he said, "Hurry up with that morphine, Doc. I *know* this'll be a reward!"

Hunter Stone busied himself in his quarters preparing to take out a patrol of raw recruits when the fresh-faced sub-constable knocked on his door.

"Sir, Colonel Macleod wishes to see you in his office."

"What for?" Stone asked curtly, though he knew the boy probably had no idea. Stone had spent too much time confined to the fort and needed the upcoming patrol to get out in the fresh, open air and revitalize his system. This messenger might be altering that plan.

"I don't know, sir. He also said to come at once."

Turning to his bunk to slip on his boots, Stone grumbled, "It's always 'at once' with the colonel."

"What was that, sir?"

"Never mind. Dismissed."

On his way to Macleod's office, he passed the new cannons on the parade ground, running a hand over the gleaming iron as he walked by. The training had yet to begin with the field guns, but it was scheduled for the next day. The previous four days had been used solely for teaching the men the characteristics of the cannon and how to load it. Stone knew the recruits were anxious to see what kind of action the nine-pounders could do.

He came across Del Dekko sitting on an anvil outside the stables, whittling a stick. "Don't you have *anything* to do, Del?"

"Sure I do." He held up the creation he was working on, which apparently was as yet undecided. "I'm whittlin'. Where you goin' all dressed up?"

"The colonel wants to see me right now."

" 'Bout what?"

Hunter shrugged.

"I'll go with you," Del said excitedly, casting aside the chunk of wood.

"What about your masterpiece?"

"I'll make another even more spectac'lar tomorrow. That was just a warm-up."

They passed the blacksmith shop and the laundry, then the hospital. Stone asked, "Why aren't you in Dr. Stillwell's office being entertained?"

Del threw him a sullen glance. " 'Cause of you."

"Me?"

"Yeah. You scared the Doc so bad the other day that he won't see no one unless they've had an accidental amputation or something. You went and took all the fun out of it."

"Sorry," Stone grinned.

"You should be. It was the only form of decent fun I could find on this post. Now I'm bored again."

They stepped through the door to the courtroom, which was empty. Macleod's office was in the back past the library room. "Say, where's Vic today?" Stone asked. "I haven't seen much of him since the wedding."

"He's gone after a stiller with that French feller — what's his name?"

"D'Artigue."

"Yeah, that one. They ain't got back yet."

When they reached Macleod's office, Stone knocked and they entered. The colonel was sitting on the edge of his desk, a half-smoked cigar in his hand. He wore no hat, and the top button of his tunic was unbuttoned in a casual fashion, but his face revealed a certain strain.

"Gentlemen."

"You wanted to see me, sir?" Stone asked as he saluted.

"Sit down."

Stone and Del each took a chair. Stone was worried about Macleod's demeanor because he was usually buoyant and full of energy. Now he seemed worried and pre-occupied.

Macleod reached onto his desk and lifted a telegram. Holding it out well before him since he hated donning his reading glasses, he read: " 'To: North-West Mounted, From: Custer Command, Seventh Cavalry. Have seriously —' "

"Excuse me, sir," Stone interrupted. "*The* Custer?"

"Have you ever heard that name any-where else, Stone? Yes, *the* Custer. Now listen up. 'Have seriously wounded scout in troop named Faron O'Donnell Stop Requests presence of niece Reena O'Donnell for aid Stop Will meet where the Powder River joins the Yellowstone in Montana Territory Stop.' "

Stone watched him, momentarily con-fused. Reena had mentioned her uncle only once or twice that he could remember. Faron O'Donnell had initially guided her to the Territories when she left Chicago, but as far as Stone knew, the last she'd seen of him was when he'd disappeared into the Rockies in search of gold. How had he come to be with Custer in the States?

"What do you think, Stone?"

"Um . . . I don't know, sir. What should I think?"

"Do you know how far away this meeting place is? If we tell Miss O'Donnell about this, knowing her as we know her, she'll be packed and ready to leave within the hour."

Del nodded in agreement. "That's Miss Reena, all right. Prob'ly leave a whirlwind in her wake, she'd leave so fast."

Stone shook his head. "We can't let her go."

"*Let?*" Macleod asked, eyebrows raised into arches. "Stone, you of all people should know that you can't stop a woman from doing what she sets her mind to. Especially Miss O'Donnell, when it comes to someone she cares about."

Stone set his lips. "I'll stop her."

"No, you won't, Hunter," Del chimed in. "Miss Reena's done everything she's ever set her cap to do all her life. And she'll set her cap on going to help her uncle. And you know it."

Stone looked at him. "Don't you have something you need to be doing?"

"Nope."

"Stone," Macleod said mildly, "are you suggesting we don't even *tell* her about this?"

Hunter thought about it for a moment, then said, "Maybe."

"Why, that's nothing short of dishonorable, and I won't —"

"Colonel, that man may be dead already if his wounds were as serious as this telegram says."

"*May* be, Hunter . . . *may* be dead. But we don't know that for sure."

"Still . . ."

Macleod waved a hand impatiently. "Enough of this. I've already decided what to do."

"Sir?" Stone said, studying him.

"You will take this telegram to Miss O'Donnell immediately, and after she insists that she's going down there and you've lost the argument, you will escort her."

"But . . . I . . ." Stone didn't know where to even start an argument.

"And you," Macleod continued, turning the force of his presence on Del, "will guide them. I'm tired of seeing you skulking around this fort trying to look like you're performing some important task whenever I come into view."

"Me?" Del asked, a look of innocence sparkling in his eyes.

"Yes, you."

"But I . . . I have duties," he stated defensively.

"Such as?"

"Well, I, um . . ." Del had to stop and really put his mind to work. Suddenly, his face brightened. "I help in the kitchen sometimes! Yeah, I help the cook a lot. Just ask him."

"I don't have to. He came to *me* and complained about your healthy appetite. Seems he can't cook fast enough to prepare enough food for the men with your fingers in the pie at the same time."

Del was incensed. "Why, that's nothin' short of treachery! As much as I've helped that man prepare meals . . . I'll stick his head in his own oven, I will!"

"You'll do nothing of the kind," Macleod retorted. "You'll go prepare a wagon and horses for the trip at once. Take an extra mount in case one of them breaks down."

"Yes, sir." Del saluted and left grumbling.

Stone, who'd barely heard the exchange between them, locked eyes with Macleod. "Sir, if I may say so —"

"No, you may not, Stone." Macleod sat down heavily in his chair and ground out the already-dead cigar in a brass ashtray. "You may listen. When was the last time you had a day off, Hunter? There, see, you can't even remember. You're due for some vacation time, my friend."

"I don't *need* a vacation, sir."

Macleod reached behind him, plucked his beret off a hook on the wall, and tossed it to Stone. On it, front and center, was the official badge of the Assistant Commissioner of the Mounted Police. "Try that on, Stone, see how it fits."

"Sir?"

"You seem to know this post better than me — the men, the right decisions. Maybe the wrong man's in charge here."

"With all due respect, Colonel, that's preposterous."

"Is it?"

"Yes, sir."

"I agree wholeheartedly. When do you leave?"

Stone packed what few civilian clothes he owned, made arrangements with the

140

quartermaster for extra firearms, ammunition, and food, then went to the stables, where he found Del.

Throwing his bag in the back of the wagon, Stone said, "I'll finish this, Del. You go pack."

"I *am* packed."

"Where are your things?"

Del pointed to the bed of the wagon. "You just threw yours on top of them."

Stone leaned over and shifted his bag. Beneath the wagon seat was a small cloth sack tied at the opening with hay string. "That's it?"

"What else do I need?"

"You only have one change of clothing?"

"One and a half. There's an extra pair of pants and two shirts."

Stone shook his head but said nothing.

Del finished harnessing the team while Stone saddled his horse, Buck. The palomino sensed a long ride was forthcoming, as evidenced by his prancing feet and the throwing of his blond-maned head.

It was midafternoon before they left the fort. The ride to Reena's Blackfoot camp was about fifteen miles, so Stone knew they wouldn't get there until dusk. As they crossed the Old Man's River that flowed beside the fort, they agreed that Stone should ride ahead of the slower wagon and give Reena the telegram, thereby allowing her time to absorb the news and prepare to go. Before they split, Vickersham and D'Artigue appeared on the plain to the west riding toward the fort.

"Hunter, what about Megan?" Del asked. "Shouldn't she know about this? It's her uncle, too."

Stone hung his head. "I forgot about Megan."

They waited for Vic and D'Artigue to reach them, though Hunter was as anxious as Buck to be on their way. As his friend neared, Stone saw a weariness in Vic's slumped shoulders that was very uncommon. When he drew up before them, Vic nodded curtly.

"Where are you fellows headed so loaded down?" Vic asked.

Stone briefly explained the situation.

"Oh my," Vic sighed. "I don't know how Megan will take this. I don't know if she's close to her uncle or not."

"Reena can take care of him," Stone said. "Besides, Megan just got married — she's not likely to want to dash off hundreds of miles across hostile Indian country."

"I don't know . . ." Vic said uncertainly.

"If you have to, *make* her stay, Vic."

"That's easy for you to say, old chap." He turned to D'Artigue. "Go get some dinner. I'll report to the colonel."

"What's the matter?" Del asked.

"Some very bad business, I'm afraid. We found a murdered woman at the cabin."

"Murdered?"

Vickersham nodded tiredly. "In a very bad way."

"Any leads?" Stone asked.

"We'll have to find her husband and go from there." He sensed Stone's anxiety to ride out and said, "Go on. You've got a long trip ahead of you."

"Are you all right, Vic?"

Smiling sardonically, Vickersham answered, "If I had a pound for every time I was asked that . . ." He stopped and shook his head. "I'm fine . . . go. Del, steer them where the Sioux aren't."

Del grinned. "Don't worry, I value my scalp as much as the next man."

Hating to leave his friend looking and acting so depressed, Stone nevertheless waved and turned to the east.

Chapter Eight

Questions Asked

"Uncle Faron?" Megan asked softly. "*My* uncle Faron?"

"Yes," Vickersham replied as he unbuttoned his tunic. His undershirt was damp from sweat, yet all he could smell was the horrific odor of the cabin.

Megan sat down on their bed and clasped her hands in her lap, her eyes far away. "But how . . . ? What's Faron doing down there? How did it happen?"

"I don't know. Hunter was in a hurry, and I only heard a sketch of the details before he rode out. We don't know any more than what was in the telegram."

Megan shook her head slowly. "Custer! Uncle Faron despised the army and hated war even more. That's why he went off into the mountains in the first place, to avoid the War of Secession — now he's with Custer?"

Vic shrugged helplessly as he sat down beside her.

"I should go," Megan murmured.

"Reena's going."

"But I should go, too — he's my uncle."

Vic placed his hands on her shoulders and began gently massaging. "Whatever needs doing, Reena can do it."

Standing abruptly, Megan moved to their mahogany dresser and turned to face him. "Of course . . . let Reena do it. There's *nothing* that *Reena* can't do!" Suddenly ashamed at her outburst, she stalked to the window and stared outside, trying to calm the stir of emotions she felt.

Vic got up and left the room without another word.

"Vic?" When she turned from the window, the door was already closing behind him.

In the kitchen he poured himself a cup of the fresh coffee Megan had made and took a chair at the dining room table. After a moment, Megan appeared in the doorway.

"Vic, I'm sorry. That was selfish and uncalled for."

"Don't apologize, darling. It's some pretty upsetting news."

Megan took a chair beside him and sat down. The dying sunlight outside the window beside her cast a soft shade of gold on her pleasant features, and Vic smiled for the first time that day.

But suddenly, the horrible black memories of what he had seen in the cabin filled his thoughts. To his horror, he saw Megan's face on the woman at the cabin — mouth distended, swollen cheeks — and he physically drew back. Megan didn't notice.

Who could have done such a thing? he thought to himself as he had countless times that day. *The husband? But how could a man do that to his wife? How could anyone do that to Fran . . . sweet, innocent Fran. . . . And the discovery that —*

"What about the dinner tomorrow night?" Megan asked.

"What?"

"The dinner."

Vic cleared his throat and tried to force grisly visions from his head, but he was still confused.

"You know, the get-together we planned on our wedding day. Jack, Hunter, Reena, Dirk, and Jenny. It was supposed to be here tomorrow night."

"Well, we can still have Dirk and Jenny, I suppose. And Reverend Sheffield."

"Vic, what's wrong? You're sweating."

"Well . . . it's hot," he answered weakly.

"No, I mean your palms. Look at them."

She peered closely at him. "Are you feeling all right?"

He rubbed his hands together, didn't like the hot, wet feeling, and wiped them on his shirt. *What if some maniac is out there loose, and this is just the beginning? What if I come home one day and find Megan —*

A firm knock pounded the front door, making him jump. He was on his feet at once, already pulling the Adams from the holster as he made his way to the door.

"Vic, what are you doing?" Megan cried from behind him.

"Go in the bedroom, Megan."

"I'll do nothing of the kind! What's the matter with you?"

Vic parted the curtains of the window by the front door with the barrel of the pistol, then relaxed visibly and holstered the weapon. He opened the door. "Hello, Dirk."

"Vic," Becker returned. "You look terrible."

"Thanks. Come in."

Becker stepped inside, removing his white helmet and nodding to Megan.

"Hello, Dirk. What brings you around?"

Becker glanced at Vickersham uncertainly, and Vic had another uncomfortable feeling. *Now what's happened?*

"I just needed to talk to Vic a moment."

"How about some coffee?" Megan asked.

"I really don't have time, Megan. But thanks." He turned to Vic. "I heard about what happened today, and —"

Vic cut him off with an unmistakable warning look. Both men looked at Megan at the same time.

"What is it?" Megan asked. "Something too important for me to hear?"

"Do you mind, darling?" Vic asked.

"Yes, I mind. I have a feeling it has to do with whatever it is that's got you so upset, Jaye Eliot Vickersham, and I intend to find out what it is."

Vic, all at once too tired to argue, nodded to Becker. "It was ghastly, Dirk, and I fully intend to track down that poor woman's husband at first light."

"You don't have to."

"What do you mean?"

"I mean he's at the fort right now. I don't think I've ever seen a man as upset and hysterical as he is right now."

Tobias Pate was a mess. His long hair trailed over his shoulders, unkempt and greasy. His fingernails were black with dirt, and his clothes held an unclean smell.

Tears had left straight clean lines through the grime on his drawn, homely face.

He sat in the officers' mess, surrounded by Vic, Becker, and Macleod. Vickersham and Becker stood on either side of Pate, while Macleod was seated opposite him. From the nearby kitchen rang the clatter of dinner dishes and pans being washed. Pate had been offered a meal, but it sat untouched before him.

Colonel Macleod's hands were clasped in front of him on the table, and his direct stare was fixed on Pate. "So, Mr. Pate, you claim to have no knowledge of your wife's death, and —"

"She wasn't my wife," Pate corrected, his voice thick with emotion. "I already told you that."

"Yes, well," was all the colonel could answer.

"Tell us your story one more time," Becker urged gently. He noticed that Vic was gripping the back of a chair tightly, watching Pate with a hawklike interest.

"How many times do I have to tell it?" Pate asked, his eyes cast downward.

"Sub-Inspector Vickersham hasn't heard it. He's the one who found your . . . woman."

Pate's bloodshot eyes looked up at Vic.

"You found her?"

Vickersham nodded, and his jaw clenched.

"It should have been me."

"No," Vic said, speaking for the first time, "it shouldn't have."

Pate watched him a moment, then his eyes dropped again to the table as he spoke in the monotonous way of one who had told a story many times. "I was going to get some supplies for my still — yeah, I've got a still, and you can arrest me if you want to, I don't care — and Frannie didn't want to go."

"Start at the beginning," Vickersham interrupted. "When did you meet . . . Frannie?"

"About two or three months ago. She just . . . showed up at my front door one day. She was half-starved and feverish, so I had to take her in. Turns out I'm glad I did, though, 'cause she was good to me. Took real good care of me." Pate's voice broke, and tears welled up in his dark brown eyes. "She wouldn't have hurt a fly. Why would someone do that to her?"

"Go on," Vic urged tightly.

Becker and Macleod glanced at him. Becker had never seen Vic so intense and his tone so emotionless.

Pate continued. "Like I said, I had to get supplies and Frannie didn't want to go. I guess she was still wore out from all the traveling she'd done to get to my place."

"Did she say where she was from?" Becker asked.

"Nope. Never did. I tried to get her to talk about her past, but she always brushed me off. Said it wasn't important. Said what was important was just that me and her were together."

"Did she want marriage?" Macleod asked.

"I offered, but she told me it was just a piece of paper, didn't mean anything. Said the stars didn't care."

Vic took a seat in the chair he'd been leaning on, moving it close to Pate. "What do you mean?"

Pate measured his close proximity and moved to the edge of his seat away from him. "She was always talking about the stars, like they were gods or something."

"Stars?"

"Yeah." Pate paused and shook his head. "Strange."

"So when did you leave the cabin?" Becker asked.

Pate thought about it. "What's today — Friday? I left on Monday."

151

"And where was *she* going?" Vic asked suddenly.

"Huh?"

"The buckboard was ready to go, horse attached, when she was . . . when we got there."

Pate looked confused. "I don't know."

"Did you have a fight?"

"No!"

Vickersham gave him a long look.

"We never had a fight, I swear! Why are you looking at me like that?"

"Why are you so defensive?" Vic demanded.

"I'm not defensive, I —"

"Where's the child?" Vic asked.

"Child? What child?"

Vic leaned in. "The little owner of the toys in the front of your cabin."

"Oh. That stuff was there when I took it over. I just haven't thrown them away."

Vic gave him a skeptical stare, then asked in a quiet, dangerous tone, "Why don't you tell us what *really* happened?"

Pate stared at him, confused. "What?"

"You killed her, didn't you? She —"

"Vickersham!" Macleod roared.

"— burned your supper, or forgot to darn your socks —"

"No!" Pate whispered, looking horrified.

152

"Vickersham, that's enough!"

"— or maybe you just couldn't stand the thought of her leaving you?"

Becker reached under Vickersham's armpits and dragged him out of the chair.

Macleod got to his feet. "Get him out of here, Becker!"

"Yes, sir," Becker said.

Vic didn't put up much resistance as Becker moved him toward the door.

Pate eyed Vic like a rat views a poisonous snake.

"You're not innocent," Vickersham whispered harshly, jabbing a finger at Pate as Becker pushed him through the door. "No one's innocent!"

Outside in the muggy night air, Vickersham shrugged off Becker's hands. "Unhand me, Constable!"

"Vic, what's the matter with you?"

"Leave me alone."

Other men were out and about in the parade area, and they all stopped to witness the fracas. Their faces shone like yellow moons in the lamplit yard.

"Why did you ask Pate those questions, Vic? I thought Indians killed her."

Vickersham strode purposefully away, head down and arms swinging.

Becker watched him until he faded from

the lights of the parade ground into the murky night.

Megan watched Vic push the food around on his plate. She'd worked hard to prepare the beef marinated in a special mixture Mrs. Howe at the boardinghouse had given her, along with the potatoes and cheese sauce and beans that had taken all day to boil. Megan had noticed that dishes took longer to cook than she was accustomed to in Chicago. Mrs. Howe had told her that it was because the air was thinner, and Megan had nodded as if she understood, but she hadn't. Anyway, for the first time Megan had somehow managed to have all the dishes come out fully cooked and delicious simultaneously, and Vic had barely touched anything. No, that was wrong — he'd touched plenty of it with his fork, but none had reached his mouth.

"You don't like it?" she asked.

"What?"

"The food. You don't like it?"

"Yes, it's wonderful, darling." He dutifully speared a beef tip and chewed it with false gusto. "Very good."

Instead of making her feel better as she was sure he intended, Megan perceived the action as condescending. She took out her frustration on the meat, cutting and sawing a chunk of it until it was divided into minuscule pieces.

Vic watched her, still chewing. "What did that poor cow do to you?"

"It's not funny, Vic!"

"I was just . . ."

Megan hastily put down her knife and fork and clasped her hands together under her chin. "I know I'm supposed to be the patient little wife and wait until you're ready to talk, but I'm not built that way, and you know it. You walked in the door tonight a different man — a changed man — and I believe I have the right to know what's got you so upset. What happened today?"

"I don't want to talk about it."

"Well, I do!"

"Megan —"

"What do you want me to do, just sit around and knit while you brood?"

His clear eyes came around to her in a surprisingly direct gaze. "Yes. If that's how you choose to bide your time."

Her face twisted with hurt, Megan half ran to their bedroom, slamming the door behind her.

Vic placed his elbows on the table and his face in his hands as the meal in front of him grew cold. The day had been nothing short of shocking. How could he tell her about the horrible way the woman had died, or what he'd discovered in that diary?

". . . so he just walked away. Just like that."

Jenny considered Becker's fine profile as he talked. They were sitting on the porch swing of the boardinghouse, swaying idly. Down the street she could hear a piano playing and dogs barking.

Lydia Meecham played with a deck of cards on the steps a few yards away. She was a bright, pretty young girl of seven, with blond hair and an insatiable appetite for knowledge. Becker had shown her a solitaire game only half an hour before, and from the looks of it, Lydia had already mastered the game.

Bringing her attention back to Becker, Jenny asked, "So what do you think's wrong with Vic?"

"I don't know."

"He's seen dead bodies before, hasn't he?"

"Yes."

"But you said this one was . . . cut up pretty bad."

Becker stretched out his long legs, and his boots landed on the wooden porch with a hollow thump. The swing stopped swaying with the grounding of his feet. "They found an Indian armband, so I guess that's where we start."

"You don't think that man didn't do it? The one she was living with?"

"I don't think so. He was so devastated when the colonel questioned him about it that it couldn't have been an act. I'm going to the cabin with Pate in the morning to see if anything's missing. Maybe it was just a raid, but I don't see why that woman had to die like that if that's all it was."

Lydia suddenly stood up, the playing cards a mess in her hands as if she'd just picked them up haphazardly. "Like what?"

They both looked at her blankly.

"A woman died like what?"

Jenny thought they were talking in low enough tones so that Lydia couldn't hear. Apparently she'd been wrong.

With a quick glance at Jenny, Becker said, "Never mind, sweetheart. Just business stuff, you know? Boring."

"Some woman died and that's boring?"

"No, not that —" Becker broke off and gave Jenny a help-me-here look.

Jenny didn't know what to say. Lydia's

father had been a ruthless killer who'd met his own death at the hands of the Mounties — Hunter specifically. For months afterward, Lydia had withdrawn from everyone and even resorted to the childish habit of sucking her thumb. Jenny had worked patiently with her, knowing what she was going through because of her own sordid adolescence and father's death. At one point Jenny had felt like throwing her hands up in frustration over Lydia's stubborn refusal to let anybody in. Then Jenny had realized that when her own father had died, she'd been an adult. Lydia was only seven years old.

Finally Lydia had begun talking again — first to her brother, Timmy, then her mother and Jenny. Never once had she made mention of her father, as far as Jenny was aware. Maybe she'd just rubbed him from her memory, the same as if she would erase something from her school lapboard.

Lydia tapped the cards on the porch railing to straighten them, then carefully set them down. Even though she wasn't looking at Jenny, she was obviously waiting for an explanation.

"Bad things happen on the prairie, Lydia," Jenny said. "Dirk has to see those things sometimes, and it helps him to talk about them. Today Mr. Vic saw something very disturbing and we're worried about him. But those things aren't for little girls to hear. Unfortunately, you'll hear about them enough when you're grown."

Lydia's eyes followed a dog across the street and seemed not to hear. Then she asked, "Why do bad things have to happen? Why doesn't God take care of everybody and nobody get hurt?"

It was Jenny's turn to look to Becker for help, since he had been a Christian for years and possessed a maturity she admired. Since she lacked his faith, she often wondered about that very thing — what kind of future did Dirk think they had when they were different in that way?

"God lets people decide their own destinies by giving them free choice, Lydia. Some people choose the bad way, and innocent people get hurt."

"I don't understand."

Becker sighed and smiled at Lydia through the late-evening gloom. "Well, believe me — sometimes I don't, either." He stood, towering over the little girl, and said lightly, "It's way past somebody's bedtime."

"Whose?" Lydia asked brightly, the serious discussion already gone from her head.

Becker scooped her up in his arms, making her squeal. "A gorgeous girl I know."

"Jenny?" Lydia giggled.

"Nope. You." He turned to Jenny and nodded.

Many times Lydia would spend the night with Jenny on Fridays because of no school the next day. Lydia's mother trusted Jenny completely, since she'd seen the improvement Jenny had accomplished with her daughter, both at the school and on her off time.

As Becker carried Lydia through the door on the way to bed, Jenny called, "I'll be up to kiss you good-night, Lydia."

"Okay!" she called out over Dirk's shoulder.

Jenny heard another squeal and knew that Becker had thrown Lydia over his shoulder like a sack of grain for the trip up the stairs. He was so good with her. He had a natural ease around children that was rare in a man. Jenny would have thought that the brutal scar on his face would make him self-conscious about the direct questions children had a habit of asking — which they invariably did on first seeing him — but their curiosity never seemed to bother him. He would answer

160

their questions honestly about receiving the wound in a silly knife fight when he was too young to know better. Then he would work his mouth sideways and stretch the muscles tight against the side of his face the wound was on, making it glow almost white, and ask, "How would you like to carry that around on your face for the rest of your life?"

Without exception, the child would shake his or her head with a mixture of revulsion and fascination. "Uh-uh."

"Then don't get into fights, with or without knives," Becker would tell them.

That the children weren't frightened of the scar in the first place was just another example of how Dirk's face had an honesty and openness about it that put people at ease.

Especially me, Jenny sighed, remembering how he'd managed to draw her out of her lonely shell.

He was a special man, of that there was no doubt.

Jenny stood and leaned against the railing, looking up at the winking stars. "Why did he choose me?" she murmured to herself. "I don't understand, when he could have any woman in the world."

Most times when she asked that —

161

which she found herself doing more and more often — she would end up counting her faults and feeling unworthy of his love. Tonight, she was content with it. She wasn't going to point out to herself that she was homely, poor, not educated, and all that. Dirk Becker found something interesting about her, and at the moment that was enough.

With a secret smile she quietly went through the door and up the stairs.

Chapter Nine

Introspection

The mountain peaks were smoldering with orange and purple from the sun's dying rays as Stone rode into the Blackfoot camp. The people came to him through the indigo twilight and greeted him warmly, touching Buck with gentle hands. He nodded to them and greeted the ones he knew by name. All the while his eyes searched the village for signs of Reena, but she didn't appear. The telegram in his breast pocket was like a lead weight, reminding him that his mission this time wasn't for pleasure, but to impart bad news.

When his gaze came upon Plenty Trees and his wife, Raindrop, Stone smiled. "Good evening, Plenty Trees."

"Stone Man, you honor us with your presence, as usual."

"Thank you. I trust all is well?"

"Very much."

"Good." Stone dismounted and had another quick look around. "Where's Reena?"

They exchanged glances quickly, then Raindrop smiled. She was a plump woman with dark, intelligent eyes. "She go for walk."

"Which way, I'll join her." He noticed the briefest of hesitations in the woman and wondered why they were acting so strange, but he waited patiently.

"That way," she pointed, "toward the stream."

"Thanks." He handed Buck's reins over to an Indian boy named Little Beaver who loved taking care of the palomino. The boy nodded and grinned. "Don't unsaddle him yet, Little Beaver."

"I will water him, Stone Man," Little Beaver said as he led the horse away.

Stone nodded to Plenty Trees and Raindrop, then headed toward the small stream that ran beside the camp. He hadn't gone very far when through the lodgepole pines and aspens emerged Reena and Jack Sheffield. Her arm was laced through his, and his hand covered her elbow.

Stone stopped abruptly. They hadn't seen him yet, and he stood frozen, only able to observe for the moment.

They were both smiling and talking in low voices. Reena wore a simple purple-and-white gingham dress with lace adorning the collar and sleeves. She was barefoot. The hem of the long dress was wet, as if she'd been wading. In her hand she carried a pinkish-purple blossom of the shooting star. Sheffield carried her moccasins in his free hand.

Hunter had the sudden urge to bolt — to hide behind something. Their demeanor was one of easy companionship, of intimacy, of . . . fun. The jealous stab in his belly was intense.

He looked behind him for someplace to go so that he wouldn't be caught staring. Instead, his eyes found Raindrop's. No sad smile touched her lips, but she nodded slightly, and the movement seemed to carry with it a combination of understanding, empathy, and reassurance.

When he turned back, Reena was watching him, her arm no longer through Sheffield's, but at her side. He saw a look of surprise written plainly on her delicate features, and something else — guilt? Stone couldn't be sure.

"Hunter! What are you doing here?"

Sheffield handed Reena her moccasins and stepped forward with hand extended. "Hello, Hunter."

"Reverend." He took the offered hand, though his initial impulse had been to slap it away.

"Come on, Hunter . . . call me Jack. We're all friends here."

Some of us are friendlier than others, Stone thought dryly. If his face reflected the cold hostility he felt inside, Sheffield did not seem to sense it or acknowledge it.

"You haven't been here since our tomato plants have come in, have you? Would you like to see them? Some of them are as big as —"

"I didn't come here to see tomatoes," Stone said curtly.

Sheffield's face lost most of its good cheer. He definitely sensed animosity in Stone's voice now. "Very well."

The thought occurred to Hunter that Jack's affable attitude wasn't being forced, as it would have been had he felt guilt over being discovered in a compromising situation. He obviously perceived their walk as just that — a walk — and nothing else. This realization did nothing to improve Hunter's somber mood, though.

In the fading light, Reena's eyes were glowing sapphires, wide and searching. "What's the matter?"

Stone reached inside his breast pocket and pulled out the telegram. Without saying a word, he handed it to her and waited.

She gasped and looked at it but didn't take it. "The last time someone handed me one of those, my mother had died. Tell me this isn't like that, Hunter."

His jealousy melted away as he saw the vulnerability in her face. He'd intended to tell her the news instead of showing her the telegram, but his surprise at finding them together — so *happy* together — had clouded his thinking, and now guilt filled him. To read a telegram was coldly impersonal. It only passed along the briefest of information, devoid of the emotions behind it, filled with annoying STOP STOP STOPs that cluttered the message.

Besides, it was only a walk, he told himself. *It wasn't like you caught them in a passionate kiss.* He glanced at Sheffield, who misinterpreted his hesitation.

"Would you like me to leave?" he asked.

"No, that's not necessary. Reena, the news isn't as bad as you think, but it's not good. Your uncle Faron wired us from Dakota Territory. Somehow he fell in with General Custer's troops and got himself wounded pretty bad."

Reena gasped and put a hand to her mouth.

"He wants you to come down and take care of him."

"Uncle Faron . . . with Custer . . . but how . . . ?"

"That's what it said."

Sheffield asked, "Doesn't Custer have surgeons with him? Why does he need Reena?"

Stone shrugged and repeated, "That's just what it says, sent by Custer's own hand." He and Sheffield watched Reena as she absorbed the news. Her eyes were fixed on a spot over Hunter's shoulder, and she stood perfectly still. "Reena?"

"I've got to go to him," she whispered.

"I know," Stone replied.

"What?" Sheffield said, aghast. "You can't go down there, Reena. There's about to be a *war!* Talk some sense into her, Hunter."

"To her it makes sense, Jack."

"Why, that's . . . we can't —"

"*You* try if you like. I'm not wasting my breath."

Sheffield stared at him in disbelief, then turned to Reena. "You can't do this, Reena. Do you remember that Sioux brave that rode in here the other day? Remember the way he glared at us with hatred? If we'd been out on the prairie, alone, he wouldn't have thought twice about scalping us. The Sioux and the Cheyenne have declared war on the white man, Reena. I really don't believe they take prisoners, either."

"I'm going, Jack."

"Wait a minute. What I just said was wrong. They *do* take prisoners — women. You're just a commodity to them. Don't you understand that?"

Sheffield's words seemed to roll over Reena as harmlessly as a light breeze. "Are you going with me, Hunter?"

"Yes." That she'd known he would agree was obvious by her nodding acceptance. Her confidence and trust in him washed away his earlier doubts.

"I'll go get ready. When can we leave?"

"We can't leave until dawn. Del's behind me with a wagon loaded down with supplies."

"All right." Reena spoke as if she were far away, either still in a bit of shock, or already planning what she would need for the journey.

"I'll gather some things together, too," Jack said.

"What for?" Stone asked. Sheffield had already turned his back and taken a few paces toward his tepee. Stone reached out and grabbed his arm and stopped him, more roughly than he'd intended. "I said, what for?"

Sheffield looked down at the arm gripping him, and Stone reluctantly let go. "Because I'm going with you."

"Uh-uh — forget it."

"And why not?"

"This isn't going to be an easy trip, Jack."

"I'm well aware of that, I just —"

"You're not going," Stone stated flatly.

Sheffield faced him fully. He was half a foot shorter than Hunter, yet he met Stone's gaze directly. "You don't have any say in it, Hunter. This isn't a vacation outing, I know — but neither is it a commission of the North-West Mounted Police. You have no authority here. I'm sorry to be so blunt, but that's the way it is."

Reena had been listening in a distracted way but suddenly asked, "*Why* do you want to go, Jack? You don't even know my uncle Faron."

"I've never told you, but I met Crazy Horse once. It was a few years before either of you came to the Territories. For some reason one summer — I think it was '71 or '72 — the buffalo didn't return to the Sioux hunting lands. They stayed up here. So the Sioux came up here, and they made a visit to the Sarcee camp where I

170

was at the time." He paused and shook his head, his eyes gazing far off. "I'd never met anyone like Crazy Horse. I was so young and intimidated I just stayed in the background, watching him. He just ignored me. But he has this presence. . . ."

"What does that have to do with this?" Hunter asked impatiently.

Sheffield focused back to the present. "We had a visitor the other day, Hunter. He was a Sioux warrior, and he was trying to recruit the Blackfoot to go fight with them."

"Why didn't anyone report this?" Stone asked accusingly.

"He went away — no harm done. But I want to see Crazy Horse and try to convince him not to make war."

Stone almost snorted in derision. "What makes you think — ? Your ideals are a mite high, aren't they, Jack?"

Sheffield again turned and headed toward his tepee. Over his shoulder he asked, "Did you ever hear of anyone accomplishing anything with low ideals?"

Dear Megan,
I'm sure you've heard the news about Uncle Faron from Vic by now, and I just wanted to write you a quick note before I

171

leave. It's late, and it's quiet in the village right now. In many ways it's my favorite time of the day — time to reflect and read God's Word and think about things. To listen to the sounds of the night and the forest.

Tonight it isn't the same, though. I'm packed and ready, but I'm scared, dear sister. It's such a long way, and the trip will be filled with danger at every turn — not just from Indians, but we all know there are evil men on the prowl everywhere on the plains. I'm just so glad Hunter is going with me, though I haven't told him.

When he got here, I was walking with Jack, and we almost bumped into him. When he saw us I was so embarrassed. We were laughing and talking, arm in arm, not paying attention to where we were going. Oh, Megan, the pain in Hunter's eyes was so apparent and real! I wanted to apologize right then and there, but there was no easy way to say it without hurting Jack's feelings. Then I thought how ridiculous that was — why should I apologize for going for a walk in the evening with a friend? It was completely innocent. The only reason I was holding on to Jack was because I was barefoot and had just stepped on a particularly sharp stone and stumbled —

Reena put down her pen, dimmed the oil lamp beside her, and rubbed her tired eyes. "You're rambling, Reena," she whispered, then laughed at her own choice of words. The smile quickly faded from her lips, and she continued writing.

Forget all that . . . it's not important, and it will all work itself out.

I pray, as I'm sure you do, that Uncle Faron is all right. I don't understand why he's asking me to come down there, but I'll do it. It seems one of my duties in life is to bring wounded men back to life, as strange as that may seem. First Hunter, then Vic, and now our own kin. Why is it that I find myself in the position of rescuer so much?

"Reena?"

She looked over at the closed tepee entrance in irritation, then back down at the paper in front of her. Suddenly she had the urgent need to answer that question — to write her thoughts down quickly and find the answer inside her.

"Reena, are you awake?"

"Come in, Hunter." She laid down the pen reluctantly.

He had to duck his head low to enter. He wore the same outfit he'd had on earlier — dark blue denim shirt and thick, fawn-colored cotton trousers tucked into calf-length leather boots. Try as she might, Reena couldn't get accustomed to seeing him in civilian clothing. In a moment of comprehension, she realized she would certainly have the chance with the long trip ahead of them.

He stopped just inside the entrance and gazed around the tepee.

"I'll just be a moment," Reena said, then gathered up the letter and extra paper and placed them in the small desk drawer. Her vulnerable thoughts exposed in the letter made her uncomfortable, though she knew Hunter would never attempt to read something without her permission. After capping the inkwell, she found him staring at the large trunk beside him, smiling slightly. "What is it?"

He turned his grin on her. "I was just trying to picture the young girl who packed this trunk four years ago and headed for the Canadian wilderness."

"I was twenty, thank you very much."

"Twenty, then. What did she pack?"

Reena sighed and sat back in her chair. "You wouldn't believe what that girl packed. Every sort of cosmetic that she owned, all sorts of bathing perfumes and combs — she even crammed her favorite spices from the kitchen in there, somewhere among all the bloomers and bonnets." He laughed, and she was glad that she could make him laugh because he did so rarely. Her annoyance at his interruption was fading.

"I wish I could have seen her," he said.

"My dear sir, are you saying that I've aged that much?"

"On the contrary," he returned, moving to the chair opposite her on the other side of the desk and suavely seating himself, "my conviction is that the woman before me is ten times more fair than the youngster of that day."

"You're too kind," Reena said, a demure smile turning her lips upward.

"Thank you." He sprawled his long legs out and folded his hands over his belly.

Reena had never seen a man transform himself so quickly as Hunter Stone could. His natural movement appeared slow, methodical, and deliberate, yet at times she'd seen his reflexes explode from him with a catlike swiftness hard for the eye to believe. His awareness of his surroundings seemed total and complete to Reena, yet Vic had told her once that on long patrols Hunter could fall asleep in the strangest of circumstances — while riding Buck, on short water stops, catnaps after eating — as if he was able to turn his mind on and off at will.

Now she looked across the desk at a playful boy, who earlier had been grim and sober. The twinkle in his gray eyes wasn't just the lamplight — it was the excitement of sportive banter.

"Why are you looking at me like that?" Hunter asked.

"Like what?"

"Like that."

"I don't know what you mean," Reena said.

"Gauging. Assessing. Contemplative."

"I was just —"

"Like I was some sort of peculiar species, unknown to man —"

Now Reena started to laugh, and it felt good. "You've cured me."

"What do you mean?"

"I was trying to work up a good bout of self-pity before you came in — and doing a pretty good job of it, I might add — and now you've spoiled it."

"Sorry."

They talked easily for half an hour about inconsequential things — anything but the long trip that lay ahead of them. His voice was calm and soothing to her. She watched as he became animated at certain subjects, pensive and speculative on others. He was as interested in her opinions as much as his own.

Finally Hunter caught her stifling a yawn, and he rose to his feet. "I'd better go tuck Del in."

"That must be an interesting job."

"Mmmm. But someone has to do it." He leaned down and kissed her lightly on the forehead. "Get some sleep."

"I will — now." Just before he disappeared through the flap, she called, "Hunter?"

"Yes?"

"Thank you for . . . not being angry about Jack."

In the dim light a shadow passed over his face, then quickly disappeared. "All right."

"And for cheering me up."

"You're welcome."

"And for being you."

He smiled and murmured, "Go to sleep." Throwing her a kiss, he ducked through the flap and stepped into the night.

"Wonderful you," Reena whispered and made ready for bed.

"Now this here," Del Dekko announced to his audience of three braves, "is a flush."

One of the Blackfoot braves tasted the word on his tongue, even as he stared at the five cards Del had fanned in front of them. "Flu — flusssssshhh."

"No, not flussshhh . . . flush. Real quick and easy."

"Flush," the boy said, struggling with the strange word.

"There you go. And this" — he quickly sorted through the deck of cards in front of him and rearranged his hand — "is a straight flush. See all them numbers in a row?"

The young braves stared at the displayed cards blankly.

"Don't you fellas know your numbers?" Del asked in irritation.

Stone stepped up to the gathering around the fire, shaking his head. "Del, you can't teach these people poker!"

"Why not? They're catching on pretty fast — faster than many a white man I've played with."

"That's not what I mean." Hunter nodded to the braves, recognizing only one of them by name. "Red Elk, this game is not right."

"Not right?" Red Elk's brow wrinkled in confusion. He was a handsome young man, with many colorful beads decorating his ebony hair.

"Gambling. Especially with an old horse trader like Del."

As one, the three braves looked across the fire at Del.

"I resent that remark," Del grumbled. "It's just a friendly game, Hunter. I wasn't gonna take anything from them."

"Then what's that you're trying to hide under your leg?"

Del looked surprised to find the hand-made quirt under him. The handle was made from cottonwood, polished carefully, with an engraving of a bear on one side. "Now, how did that get there? Red Elk, here's your quirt."

Red Elk took his possession back with a wary eye. "But you say you win that fair —"

"Never mind what I said! It was only a *learnin'* experience, you understand."

The braves headed toward their tepees for the night, casting suspicious looks over their shoulders at Del, which he ignored.

Stone unrolled his bedding a few yards from the fire and unceremoniously plopped himself down with his saddle for a pillow. The thoughts of the long journey ahead made his bones feel more tired than they were.

Del, after settling in his blankets, asked, "How's Miss Reena?"

"She's fine."

"Scared?"

"Probably."

Del gauged him with one eye, while the other seemed to be peering into the fire. "What about you?"

"What about me?" Stone said matter-of-factly.

"You know."

"Del, I have no idea what you're asking me."

"Are you scared?"

Stone thought about the question for a moment. *Now that he mentioned it. . . .* "Any man who goes into hostile Sioux territory is either scared, or he's lying if he says he's not."

Del grunted and was silent for a long time. Hunter was half dreaming about Reena's eyes, almost asleep, when Del said softly, "They say the Sioux do things to a man when they capture him that are pretty awful. Not to mention what's done after the poor sod's dead."

"I don't plan on getting captured and ending up in their camp."

"Hunter, I'm serious!"

Perching himself up on an elbow and facing his friend, Hunter told him, "It doesn't do any good to worry about it, Del. We're in God's hands, and wherever those hands lead, He'll take care of us."

"Well, that's a pretty simple philosophy — if not simple-minded."

Stone held up a finger. "Watch what you say. Faith in God is not something to scoff at. Faith *is* simple, if applied every day. One day you'll learn that, my friend."

"Yeah, I guess you're right."

At that moment, Stone had never seen Del so frightened. "Listen to me . . . those atrocities you're afraid of are the very same things that have been happening to the Indians since the white man came here. Did you know that they learned scalping from the French a long time ago? They never treated their enemies that way before we came. They respected their enemies. Now what's to respect? They've been run off their land, countless promises to them have been broken, and they've seen their villages burned and wives and children massacred. I'd say all that has fueled their fires for revenge, wouldn't you?"

Del nodded slowly, not meeting his eyes.

"Now, stop worrying about it and get some rest, will you?" Stone kicked some dirt on most of the fire and turned his back to it. His words were brave, but deep down he harbored the same fear as Del. His experience with hostile Indians had been limited to one — Red Wolf — and that renegade Crow had proven to be almost more than Hunter could handle. What would happen when they were among a thousand or more?

"Just don't wanna get caught," Del mumbled, and then he began snoring softly.

Chapter Ten

On the Missouri

They left before dawn the next morning for Fort Benton, where Del said they could catch a riverboat to the lower Missouri and thereby cut down on the wear and tear on horses — and travelers.

Reena was very anxious about the distance they had to cover to reach Custer's camp. After Hunter talked to Del about it, they decided to leave the wagon behind and all ride horses. Macleod had lent Stone two extra horses, so they divided the supplies between them and headed out.

The mood was silent and somber at first, despite the excellent weather. Each person seemed to be occupied with his own personal thoughts and satisfied to ride in silence. Stone controlled the pace of their travel, alternately urging the mounts into an easy gallop for a few miles, then slowing to a walk so they could catch their breath.

Del had scowled when he'd discovered

that Sheffield would be going along. "He'll give out."

Stone had shrugged. "That's a possibility, I guess, though I doubt it."

"What would we do if he did?"

"Leave him. I'm more worried about Reena."

"Hmmff. She's got scrap — I ain't worried about her."

Stone had noticed that Del's opinion of Reena seemed to grow with every passing year. Del never failed to defend her to others, and Stone could only guess what the curmudgeonly old scout saw in her that made him hold her in such high regard. If asked to, Stone was sure Del would defend her to the death.

Halfway to Fort Benton and just across the border, they stopped to water the horses at a small clear stream. Stone took Reena aside and asked her about going any farther that day.

"Don't slow down because of me, Hunter," she insisted.

"I saw the way you gingerly got off Buck." He'd let her ride Buck because his canter was the smoothest of the horses, and therefore caused less discomfort on the rider. "We can stop and rest if you want."

"No," Reena countered firmly. "I'm the one in a hurry. I can ride as far as any of you." Then she squatted down beside the stream and began splashing water on her face and neck.

Stone watched her for a moment, then joined her. The water was cool and refreshing, and he took a long drink. When he looked at Reena, she was staring into the sun-brilliant surface of the creek with a faraway gaze. "Is something wrong, Reena?"

"No." She saw his doubt and amended, "Not really. I don't know."

"That's some answer."

"I'm not too sure about leaving Plenty Trees' tribe alone. Jack should have stayed."

"Why didn't you tell him that?"

"Because I thought he should make his own decision. But what if something happens? Such as the crops burning down, or a major —"

"Reena, those people were getting along just fine before any of us got here. They can take care of themselves without us."

"You're right. I know I shouldn't worry, because God will take care of them."

He tucked a finger under her chin and tilted her head up to him. "That's right."

She didn't return his smile.

"I'm sure your uncle is all right."

"I hope so."

"He's an O'Donnell, isn't he?"

His words of comfort brought a small smile to her lips, and it was enough for him at the moment.

Jack Sheffield filled his canteen, glancing over at Hunter and Reena occasionally. Whenever he happened to watch them together as he was now, Jack was amazed at how they were able to block out their surroundings completely. At this moment, their world consisted of a four-foot-square cube in which they talked easily and communicated by subtle gestures and looks. Jack admired that. He admired Hunter Stone.

Jack had never experienced a closeness with a woman as Hunter knew. And, from what he'd heard, Stone had enjoyed the same relationship with his deceased wife, Betsy. Jack had often wondered why God had not given him the gift of a wife, but he knew that it was foolish to question God's will. He longed for a woman as dedicated as he was, to share the mission work with him and be by his side. He knew he had a lot to give to a wife, and sometimes the desire was almost too great to bear.

Jack shook his head at his momentary lapse into self-pity and took a drink of the cool water.

"Something bothering you, preacher?" Del asked.

Sheffield had completely forgotten the scout was standing beside him. Del was adjusting his horse's saddle while it drank deeply from the cool stream. Forcing a grin, Sheffield asked, "Why do you ask that?"

"I never saw your eyebrows draw together like that. You're deep in thought about something — something pretty serious, I'd say." His piercing eyes skittered over to Reena and Stone, then came back to Sheffield, unreadable.

Understanding Del's fierce protective nature, Jack's strained smile turned genuine. "You're to be admired, Del."

"Oh? Why's that?"

Sheffield ignored the question. "How long have you known them?"

" 'Bout three years."

"And what do you think?"

"Well, that's a pretty broad question, so I'll answer it the way I want to. Over there are two of the finest human beings I ever knew. That answer your question?"

Jack grinned. "I suppose so."

Del knelt down beside the water and soaked his bandanna. In a much kinder tone, he said, "I understand your feelings, Reverend. Land sakes, I'm prob'ly in love with Reena myself a little bit. Who wouldn't be?" He placed the wet bandanna on his neck and squeezed. "But there's always been somethin' special between those two, from the moment I laid eyes on 'em back in '73. They maybe didn't know it then, but I sure did."

"Know what?"

Del looked at him, surprised. "Why, that they was meant to be together."

Sheffield considered the simplicity of Del's logic and nodded.

"I ain't sayin' that I'm smart, or that I've got some kind of talent for predictin' the future. All I'm sayin' is what's written plain on the air when they're together."

"Yes. I understand." The truth of Del's words was undeniable, and Jack felt a surge of happiness for Hunter and Reena. "Maybe you do have a talent, Del. What about me? Is there a good woman in my future?" He was washing his hands when he asked, and as the silence grew he looked up.

Del was staring at him in a disturbing

way. The man's strange eyes went from Jack's face, to his hands in the water, and then away to the prairie. Finally, he stood up and mumbled, "Gotta see to the buckboard horses."

"Del?" Not receiving an answer, Jack shook his head and checked his own saddle. Del had been the least accepting of Jack's presence since he'd arrived, and apparently that wouldn't change for a while.

They arrived in Fort Benton just in time to catch the *Rose Maiden*, a riverboat departing for the Musselshell River. On the way would be a convenient stopping-off point for them to make their way to the Yellowstone.

The boat's elegant name was a mystery. At the waterline and below on the hull could be seen the discolorization of rust and the sludge of sediment. The outside walls of the two decks were covered with a permanent, camel-colored grime. She tilted back and forth in the muddy water of the Missouri listlessly, as if aware that she fell short of perfect, or even vaguely presentable.

Sheffield, Stone, and Reena stood on the dock facing the boat, each with their own degrees of doubt shadowing their features.

The horses were being loaded on board by way of a long pier by sunburned, disheveled dock workers. The horses sensed that their world was about to be changed, and they were skittish, giving the workers as much trouble as they could. Stone was just about to go forward and try to calm Buck, but as he watched, the palomino shook his head one last time and led the way onto the deck. The other horses followed his lead.

Tentatively, Reena asked, "Are we sure this is the way to get to where we're going?"

Stone shrugged. "According to Del."

"I hope he's right about this."

"He says it will save us a lot of time."

"Are you sure?"

Stone turned to her, amused. "Has he ever steered us wrong?"

Del emerged from the harbormaster's office beaming. "See? I told you we'd find transportation."

"You call this transportation?" Reena said. "It looks more like a one-way ticket to the bottom of the Missouri." When she saw his hurt look, she said, "I'm sure it'll be all right, Del."

"So convince *me*," Sheffield muttered under his breath and promptly received a discreet stomp on the toe from Reena's boot.

When everything was loaded on the *Rose Maiden*, an energetic little man appeared by their side. He was dressed in faded tan trousers and shirt, with a battered Union artillery cap tilted jauntily on the side of his head. Through a mouth that possessed absolutely no teeth, he lisped, "You folks ready to sail?"

"Absolutely," Stone said, sounding more confident than he felt.

"Then we'll shove off!" His *s*'s *came out in an astonishing whistle.*

Despite the grimy outward appearance of the boat from the dock, they were pleased to find the deck clean and immaculate, with spare ropes, chains, and other equipment stowed neatly against the main housing.

Reena was aware of the looks she received from the sailors and tried her best to appear as if she sailed down the river every day. She smiled at one man, whose expression didn't change as he threw off the mooring ropes.

"Hold on there!" came a shout from the dock.

Three grimy men waved at the toothless captain as they strode down the pier. All wore knee-length light coats that flapped in the breeze. None had shaved in days. The one who spoke wore a bear tooth necklace and a felt hat that had seen much better days.

"I told you boys we were leaving," the captain called out. "You nearly missed out."

"But here we are," the leader returned as all three leaped aboard the crawling vessel. One of them stumbled and fell, then righted himself unsteadily. The other two laughed. "I swear, Dale," the leader gasped through fits of laughter, "you're the clumsiest man I ever saw *sober,* much less drunk!"

As if on cue they all swung around to Reena, and their laughter subsided into looks of surprise and pleasure. Stepping over to her and ignoring the men beside her, the leader removed his hat and half bowed. "Cliff Cutter, at your service, ma'am." His gaze lingered long, and dark thoughts filled his mind.

Reena felt Hunter shift his position beside her and somehow force his presence between her and Cutter in a non-threatening way. Cutter ignored him.

"What would a pretty lady like you be doing on this voyage, if I may ask?" He smelled strongly of dirt, whiskey, and horses.

Sheffield was less subtle than Stone. Taking her arm and moving her away, he said, "Let's have a look at the stern, Reena."

"Hey, I was talkin' to the lady! Hey, you!" Cutter reached for Sheffield but found his forearm encircled in a viselike grip. "Get your hands off me, blondie, before I throw you overboard!"

Stone tightened his grip, keeping a wary eye on the other two men. "We don't want any trouble here."

"Well, you sure got a way of showing it!" Cutter roared, unable to keep a grimace of pain from his face. "Putting your hand on me and all."

Stone let him go.

Cutter jerked his arm away, held it gingerly for a moment, then reached under his coat.

Everyone heard the unmistakable sound of a hammer cocking. "Stand aside there, Hunter," Del said easily from behind him. "I've been feelin' a bit of the palsy in my trigger finger the last couple of days, and there's no tellin' when this gun could go off accidental like."

Stone moved, leaving a clear line of sight

for Del to Cutter and his men, who froze in the same position as their leader — reaching for weapons.

"You fellas didn't make a very favorable entrance, now did you?" Del asked. "Care to try again?"

They looked at the receding dock, fully fifty yards away and growing farther.

"Don't wanna swim?" Del asked, shaking his gun at them.

They shook their heads.

"Then behave yourselves." Del holstered his pistol but kept his hand on the butt. He and Stone followed Sheffield and Reena's path to the stern of the ship, glancing back occasionally.

"You boys are pretty brave when you got a man bushwhacked," Cutter called to their backs. "May not be the same next time."

Over his shoulder Del said, "We'll take our chances with the likes of you."

"Don't provoke them any more than they already are, Del," Hunter warned.

"They's just prairie trash, Hunter. Driftin' buffalo hunters — or skinners, which is worse."

"Prairie trash with guns. I'd just as soon avoid any trouble on the way."

"We're the ones walkin' away, ain't we?

That looks like avoidin' to me."

Stone cast one more look back before they moved out of sight. The drifters were grumbling among themselves, but Cutter was watching them with piercing, restless eyes.

At Tobias Pate's mountain cabin, Vickersham and Becker watched the man nervously go through his belongings, searching to see if anything was missing. He'd balked at the door, stating that it was just too soon to go back there. Vickersham had informed him that if he didn't cooperate, the alternative would be a long stew in the jail at Fort Macleod.

Becker had given Vic a long look but didn't comment.

Pate went through the kitchen, the spare bedroom that was basically a storage room for odds and ends, and finally Becker walked him out to the small shed for a quick inspection.

When they came back inside, Vickersham was sitting on the well-worn couch, legs crossed, staring out the back window into the woods beyond.

Becker stopped beside the couch, with Pate just behind him. "Vic?"

He didn't answer.

195

"Vic?" Becker said again more forcefully.

"What?"

"Pate says some whiskey stores are missing."

"*All* of them are gone," Pate corrected.

Vickersham didn't respond immediately. His eyes still had a strange far-off cast to them. "How much?"

Pate calculated a moment, then said, "Three cases."

"Look in the bedroom."

"For the whiskey?"

Vickersham gave him a withering look. "For anything missing."

"I ain't going in there . . . no way." Pate's glance skittered to the door of his bedroom, clearly imagining horrors inside.

"Get in there, Pate!" Vickersham snapped.

Becker moved around in front of Vic, keeping his voice calm and level. "He doesn't need to go in there, Vic. It hasn't been cleaned, and —"

"Then clean it!" With a heavy, exasperated sigh Vickersham rose to his feet. "Never mind, I'll do it." He strode into the bedroom, found a spare blanket in the small closet, and spread it over the stained bare mattress. Finding a grimy set of sheets tucked away in the corner of the

196

closet, he placed it over the stains on the floor beside the bed. When he turned for the door, he found Becker watching him. "Well? What do you think? Can he come in now, Dirk?"

"Vic, what's wrong with you? You're acting very strange."

"Oh, not you, too!"

Becker's eyebrows raised. "So Megan noticed?"

"Don't give me that self-serving leer, Becker. Bring Pate in here."

"Yes, *sir*. Pate, you can come in now. Just look around for anything missing or out of place."

Vickersham let Becker's sarcasm pass, though he seethed to call him down on it. He brushed past Pate, who was slowly moving toward the room, and again sat down on the couch. His eyes followed Becker as he went into the kitchen, grabbed a chair, and brought it over. "Shouldn't you be in there with him?"

"Why?" Becker asked, placing the chair down with the back toward Vic and straddling it.

"In case he tampers with evidence in there."

"What evidence? The room's nearly bare."

"I don't like your tone, Becker."

"With all due respect, Vic — and yes, I'm well aware that you outrank me — I haven't liked your attitude the past two days. I want to know what's going on."

"I don't know what you mean."

"Yes, you do. What's got you so spooked about this murder? What is it?"

Casually, Vic answered, "It's just another reminder of the brutality of this Territory. After a while, it tends to become tedious."

"*Tedious?* Is that the only word you can come up with for what happened in that room?"

"It suffices."

Becker shook his head in disbelief.

Pate appeared in the doorway to the bedroom, his face pale and drawn. "There's nothing missing, but . . ."

"But what?" Vickersham asked.

"She had a bag packed, like she was leaving me. All her things were in it."

Vic nodded.

"You knew?" Pate asked.

"I suspected."

"And you didn't tell me?" Pate demanded, his voice rising. "You let me walk in there and find out . . . this way?"

"I wasn't sure, Pate. For all I knew she always kept a bag packed for —"

Pate suddenly cursed and sprang across the room at Vickersham. Vickersham rose from the couch in a defensive position, but Becker planted his large bulk between them, restraining Pate, who was furious.

Eyes wild yet uncomprehending, Pate roared, "I didn't have to go in there! Why did you make me go in there?"

"You're still a suspect, Pate," Vic answered calmly.

"Come on, Vic," Becker pleaded. "You know he didn't kill her."

"Never leave a stone unturned, Becker," Vic said, turning to the front door. "Remember that."

"Sure, Vic." Realizing he still held Pate by the arms, Becker released him and wiped sweat from his eyes. When he looked up he found Pate staring after Vickersham, his face filled with confusion. "I'm sorry, Mr. Pate."

"What are you apologizing for? *He's* the crazy one."

"He's not usually like this. I don't know what's gotten into him." Pate shook his head slowly, and Becker saw the hollow look of a man whose world had come apart.

"Why was she leaving me? I was good to her. I never hit her or anything."

Becker didn't know what to say.

"If I'd been here, she wouldn't be dead."

"Don't talk like that. You couldn't have known."

"It's true, though," Pate whispered.

From the yard Vickersham called, "Let's go, Becker!"

Becker cast an irritated glance over his shoulder at the door. "Will you be all right, Mr. Pate?"

His face became hard as he looked around the small room of the simple cabin. Then his pale-colored eyes stared hard at Becker, full of bitterness. "Oh, I'll be better off than you, I suppose."

"What do you mean?"

"I'll be here all alone," Pate said wryly, with a nod to the door, "but you have to go with *him*."

Chapter Eleven

Unheeded Warnings

The cramped dining room of the *Rose Maiden* was filled with the sound of clinking silverware against dishes, grunts of pleasure, and the strong odor of sweat. The occupants — Stone's party, Cutter and his men, and the captain with some off-duty crew — sat elbow to elbow at the long crude table fighting for space.

Reena was crushed between Sheffield and Stone, trying to ignore the obvious leers of some of the men. She was determined not to let it bother her because she knew that the boat trip wouldn't be that long. Besides, Hunter would never let anything happen to her. However, the nagging thought kept running through her mind that four or five determined men might be able to overwhelm him.

"Er . . . um . . . Captain Borland," Cutter said around a mouthful of food, "what's to be the sleeping arrangements on this here barge?" His eyes, bloodshot and darting, landed on Reena for a moment.

The toothless captain was forced to eat squashed food. At the moment he was working mashed potatoes around in his mouth with gusto when he answered, "The sleeping arrangements on this *boat*" — one bushy eyebrow raised in direct reproof — "is to be that my crew gets their regular cabins, Miss O'Donnell one of the others, and the gentlemen with her may divide the other one amongst them as to how they see fit."

"What about us?" one of Cutter's men complained. His name was Lowry, and his lanky figure supported a head that seemed too large in contrast.

"Yeah," joined in another man, who was referred to as Skinny. He was even lankier than Lowry, but his head seemed to fit his frame. "Ain't we good enough to earn a cabin?"

"You were the last on the *boat*," Borland reminded them, with another evil eye cast in Cutter's direction, "and therefore will take what's left over."

"Which is?" Cutter inquired.

"Hammocks on the deck."

"Hammocks! What if it rains?"

"I'm sure you've slept in the rain before, Mr. Cutter."

"Doesn't mean I *liked* it." Cutter's gaze came around to Reena, who quickly looked down at her plate, trying to avoid him. "The lady's got a cabin all to herself," Cutter continued boldly, "and there's *two* bunks in there, one on top of the other."

"Mr. Cutter . . ." Borland growled in warning.

"Seems to me there's room enough for one of us — maybe even two if we . . . um . . . crowd a little bit."

"Shut your mouth," Stone warned, pointing his fork at him.

Cutter grinned wolfishly. "Shut it for me, pretty boy."

"That's enough!" Borland declared. "I'll have no fighting on this boat. Mr. Cutter, if you don't like the arrangements, maybe you'd prefer me to put ashore and let you make your way to your destination as best you can." Borland's unfortunate lisping somehow lessened his authority.

"What *is* your destination anyway?" Stone asked Cutter.

"None of your business."

Borland said, "They're going to the mouth of the Musselshell for a hunting party, isn't that right, Mr. Cutter?"

Cutter's eyes narrowed. "I said it was none of his business, didn't I, Captain?"

"No need to be so standoffish, Mr. Cutter. We're all friends and fellow travelers together."

"Good. Then maybe pretty boy wouldn't mind me asking where *he's* going."

The only sound in the room was the creaking of the swaying ship and the dull thump of the rear paddle wheel working its way down the river. All eyes turned on Stone, who merely kept on eating.

"I'm talking to you, pretty —"

"The name is Stone." His gray eyes came up and fixed on Cutter, who managed to keep the grin fixed on his face.

"And what's the lady's name?"

"She's with me."

"Are you married?" Cutter winked at his men. "Don't see no rings."

Stone didn't answer.

"So that means you'll be sharing the cabin with —"

"That's none of *your* business."

"No need to get huffy, friend."

Del spoke for the first time. "Hunter, why don't you just bash that boy and be done with it?"

"Look, old man, nobody's talking to you."

Stone looked at his companions. "Is everyone through eating?"

Reena had barely touched her food, and Sheffield was still in the middle of his. However, both of them nodded at him.

"Good. Let's go." Stone rose, and the other three got up with him.

"Hey!" Cutter said. "We're just havin' a pleasant dinner conversation. Where you goin'?"

No one answered him.

"Well, at least you could leave the lady here so we have somethin' pretty to look at."

Del muttered, "Prairie trash," under his breath as he turned toward the door.

"What was that?" Cutter asked sharply.

Del didn't turn around or respond.

"Hey, I'm talking to you, you old coot!"

"Mr. Cutter!" Captain Borland roared.

Before Del could fully turn back, Stone grabbed the lapel of his coat and pulled him out the door into the passageway. "Leave it alone, Del. They're not worth it."

As they walked off toward the cabins, they clearly heard Cutter say, "That's a snobbish bunch, Captain. You need to watch who you take aboard."

"That could have gone better, I think," Sheffield commented wryly.

"Don't matter," Del informed him.

"That kind's always gonna make trouble, whether you ignore them or not."

"Is that supposed to make me feel better?"

"What are you afraid of, preacher? We'll protect you."

Sheffield gave him a sour look over his shoulder.

They stopped at one of the vacant cabins and Sheffield let Reena by him to open the door. It swung inside with a faint creak, and the three men craned their heads to see over her shoulder.

After a long silence, Reena asked, "Do you think there are rats in there?"

Del shook his head. "Too small for rats . . . they prefer breathing room, space to stretch their legs."

Reena moved inside to the far bulkhead, which proved to be a scant four paces away. To her right were narrow bunks, one on top of the other, and to her left stood a tiny washstand with a burning oil lamp. The washbasin contained nothing but a fine sheen of green-gray slime. There was nothing else in the room.

"I'll go get your trunk," Stone announced.

"No, there's no room for it. I'd just end up stumbling all over it in these cramped quarters. I'll go with you and get what I need out of it."

Sheffield and Del inspected the other cabin and found the exact same sparse furnishings minus the washbasin. "I don't know if that's good or bad," Del mumbled. "Reena's basin kinda looked like somethin' was growin' in it."

"Let's take Reena's and wash it out with fresh water and find our own."

Their gear was lashed to the starboard bow of the ship. As Reena and Hunter emerged on deck into the purple twilight, Reena filled her lungs with fresh air, wishing she could *absorb* it and cleanse herself of the grime below deck. She closed her eyes for a moment, and when she opened them, the boat seemed to be somehow askew. Disoriented, she half fell against the guardrail.

Hunter took her elbow, steadying her. "Reena? What's the matter?"

"It's nothing. I just got dizzy there for a second."

"You're pale . . . do you feel sick?"

"A little."

"I don't think this boat trip was such a good idea."

"No, I'll be all right. I just need to get my . . . what do they call it? Sea balance?"

He grinned at her. "Sea legs."

"Yes, my sea legs under me."

"Have you ever been on a boat before?"

"Not this big. I went out in a dinghy every once in a while with Liam in a small cove on Lake Michigan."

"It takes some getting used to."

They stood at the guardrail while Reena regained some sense of balance, then she retrieved some essentials from her trunk. As they started below again, Reena took one more longing look at the wild prairie and another deep breath, imagining she could store the precious air inside her until morning.

When they reached her cabin, Stone placed her things on the bottom bunk and turned to her. "You need to get some rest. We still have a long way to go when we get off this boat."

"I know. I'm just afraid lying down will make me sick."

"Don't think about it — and whatever you do, don't try to read. That'll just make it worse."

"Where are you sleeping tonight?"

He pointed to the ceiling. "Up top on the deck."

"Oh no! What about those nasty men?"

"What about them?"

"Shouldn't you . . . ?"

"Sleep with Del and Jack?" Hunter finished with a smile.

Reena realized how ridiculous that proposition was and at the same time saw that there was no way Jack — gentle, sweet Jack — could be thrown to the wolves. "What about Del?"

"Del would just pick a fight, and I'd end up having to go up there anyway to save him from being heaved overboard. Don't worry, Reena, I'll be fine."

He kissed her lightly on the forehead, but before he got away from her, she pulled him down and pressed her lips against his briefly but firmly. "Good night."

" 'Night," Stone said, then turned and left her cabin.

Reena noticed the fresh water in the washbasin and silently thanked Jack and Del for their thoughtfulness. She washed her face and brushed her teeth, glancing over occasionally at the imposing tiny bunk. When she'd changed into her night-gown, she stood in front of the bed and said softly, "Okay, I'm tired and don't feel too good. But you're going to give me a good night's sleep, right?"

She extinguished the lamp, found herself

in cavelike darkness, and promptly barked her shin on the low-lying bed. Biting her lip, she crawled in, adjusted the flat, well-worn pillow, and found that her feet hung off the end of the bed up to her ankles.

"Who's been sleeping here — midgets?" she mumbled in the darkness. Heaving a sigh, she said her prayers and thanked God for what she *did* have. Surprisingly, sleep came over her rather quickly. But just when she was drifting off and starting to dream, her eyes popped open and she remembered her uncle Faron. What kind of night was he having?

The thought worried her all over again, and this time sleep eluded her for almost an hour.

Faron knew someone was talking about him — talking about him very close, in fact — but he was powerless to join in the conversation. He slipped in and out of consciousness, sliding from crazy dreams to the sound of thunder and the sight of a swaying lamp, then back to crimson delusions. Once he saw his wife, Margaret, and he was coherent enough to know *that* wasn't real. He felt chilled from the sheets beneath him that were soaked with sweat from the fever that raged in his body.

He heard the words "fever" and "come off" and "dead," and decided that, by his own Irish whiskers, someone was contemplating some outrage of mutilation against him. He struggled mightily with his own brain's betrayal and managed to open his eyes and find his voice. "Who's there?"

A face loomed over him, stark white and bulbous. "It's Dr. Denton."

"Ye wouldn't still be tryin' to take my arm, now would you, Doctor?"

"It's time, Mr. O'Donnell. If I don't, you'll die from the gangrene."

"Not till I say so."

"Mr. O'Donnell, I'm sure you can't see your arm because you can't even see me, but it's turning."

"Turning? Into what?" Faron had the sudden image of his arm transforming into a wing, or some sort of appendage with an awful claw at the end of it, then knew that it was the fever making him delirious. The life-draining fever.

"It's got to come off," Denton said quietly but firmly. He didn't move when he heard the cock of the pistol.

With gargantuan effort, Faron raised the Colt with his good arm and swung it over to the doctor. At least, he thought he did.

For all he knew he was waving it at the ceiling. He'd had the kid, Norton, put the pistol in his hand the last time he'd been here — whenever that was.

"Now, Mr. O'Donnell," Denton said soothingly, "you wouldn't kill me for trying to save your life, would you?"

"Nope. But I'll sure maim you for it."

"The gun's not loaded."

"That's what you think. The lad wouldn't give me an unloaded gun. He's my friend."

"He gave you a loaded gun. I *un*loaded it hours ago."

"Why, you sneaky —" A coughing fit seized him. Denton's face disappeared from Faron's view and was replaced by a red curtain, then a black one darker than the other side of the moon.

He never knew when the sawing began.

Hunter spent some time talking with Sheffield and Del about the trip before going topside. They tried to talk him into staying, saying one of them could sleep on the floor, but he would have none of it. He didn't think that Cutter or any of his men would have the energy or the will to start any trouble. Hunter had seen his kind many times in the past — they were basically harmless if you didn't mind their brave talk. The only way they would make a move against someone was if the prey was helpless, alone and outnumbered, like a pack of wolves stalking a stray sheep. Stone was anything but helpless.

As Hunter moved toward the door to leave, Del said, "What about that conversation we were going to have?"

"What conversation?"

Del jerked his head and danced his eyes toward Sheffield. "You know."

"Oh, that. Um . . . Jack —"

Sheffield held up a hand. "I know what you're going to say, Hunter, and the answer's no."

"See? I told you, Del. He's determined to go through with his crazy idea."

"You're just gonna let him off — just like that?"

"What do you want me to do, arrest him?"

"That might not be a bad idea!" Del turned one of his eyes on Sheffield, with the other pointed somewhere over Stone's shoulder. "Preacher, in the first place, Crazy Horse has been runnin' circles around the United States Army for years! What makes you think you'll find him?"

"They're gathering somewhere in the mountains. Crazy Horse will be there."

"Yep. Probably waitin' to put your head on a stick."

"He's not a savage, Del! He's a highly intelligent man who probably cares more for his own people than any white man does."

Del leaned toward Sheffield, his voice a harsh, whispered rasp. "He's killed people in cold blood."

Sheffield didn't flinch but instead came almost nose to nose with Del. "He's *survived* — the only way he knows how."

"How you gonna take care of yourself if things turn nasty?"

"I can take care of myself."

"Bah! Preachers are hard to talk to, Hunter. You ever notice that?"

"Not really."

"They're stubborn, too."

Jack Sheffield grinned.

The half-moon in the sky reminded Stone of a tilted porridge bowl. The *Rose Maiden* felt her way through the river with the aid of a powerful lantern at the bow, with a crewman keeping watch for snags and sandbars in the water ahead.

He went to the storage bin where Captain Borland had told him they stored the hammocks and withdrew the one that had the least number of broken knots. Cutter and his men had strung theirs along the starboard side between the main housing and guardrails. Stone could see four lumps in the hammocks and grunted with satisfaction that there would be no trouble tonight. His body was weary from the long ride to Fort Benton, though he would never admit it, and he looked forward to sleeping under the stars to the gentle rocking of the boat and the moist sighing of the passing river.

He made his way to the stern of the ship, checked on the horses, patted Buck a few times, and tied up his hammock between the tiller arm and the high guardrail at the very rear of the boat. Removing his boots, he wondered if Jack and Del knew what they were missing — leg room. Stone had noticed right off the short length of the bunks and figured that even Del might have some trouble sleeping tonight.

He almost chuckled as he settled into the hammock. Then he nearly tipped himself over and this *did* bring on a chuckle. Finally he set himself right and laced his hands behind his head.

Idly he wondered if he would have the courage to do what Jack Sheffield was doing. *If God told me plainly to do something as dangerous, would I do it?* Then he remembered that even Reena had had the courage to step out into a harsh land on faith. He admired them both and hoped that if it came down to the same dilemma for him, he would have the strength to follow it through.

He knew he had so much to learn about trusting God and making his faith real in a world so filled with dangers at every turn. He realized the only way to learn more and advance in knowledge was to read God's Word, and he wished he weren't so tired so he could read by moonlight before falling asleep.

Over the rush of water lapping against the boat he heard a soft scrape behind the buckboard. He didn't have time to look in that direction because the hammock suddenly spun over and he found himself face down on the deck, the breath half knocked out of him.

The tip of a heavy boot planted itself into his back with brutal authority.

"Not sleeping with the *missus* tonight, *partner?*"

The emphasized words were accompanied by vicious kicks, each one more painful than the previous.

"That's too *bad!*"

More feet joined in the cruel beating.

Stone covered himself as best he could, but he couldn't avoid the onslaught of kicks. With one of the kicks the rest of his breath escaped him with a *whoosh* from his gaping mouth.

"Maybe she gets *lonely* all by *herself!*" another voice chimed in with derision.

It was becoming a brutal game. Stone couldn't tell whether it was Skinny or Lowry because of the roaring in his head. He opened his eyes just in time to see one of the six boots in front of him make a beeline for his face. At the last instant he lowered his head but still took it on the edge of his scalp. Sparks danced across his vision.

"Hold it, boys, hold it!" Cutter ordered.

Stone didn't know why Cutter called them off, but he was grateful as he gasped for breath. Well aware that they could very well kill him, he quickly rolled over and raised himself halfway up and sunk his fist into Cutter's belly. Now it was Cutter's turn to *whoosh!*

A flurry of arms tried to grab at him, and he felt another kick to the back that made him cry out. He battled the groping hands and swiftly jerked back an elbow that landed solidly into flesh. He heard a groan as one of his attackers fell to the deck.

Two down.

But he couldn't get to his feet. The rain of kicks had taken their toll, and his muscles wouldn't obey his instinctive commands. The other man easily restrained him while he was on his knees.

Cutter, holding his stomach and sucking in a much needed breath, looked at Stone with a mixture of hatred and wrath. His gritted teeth seemed to glow in the moonlight. He took aim with malicious pleasure and exploded a right hook to the side of Stone's jaw.

Then another.

Then a left to the sternum.

Stone was out cold.

"Heave him over the side," Cutter breathlessly told the others.

Skinny looked up. "How 'bout into the paddle wheel?"

Cutter grinned.

Part Three

THE MASS OF FORCE

Force, if unassisted by judgment, collapses through its own mass.

Horace
Odes

Chapter Twelve

Dark Results

The large paddle wheel of the *Rose Maiden* churned against the strong current as the paddles cut deep into the river and thrust the boat through the murky water.

Stone tried to struggle against the arms that half dragged him to the back of the boat, but he didn't have the strength to break free after the brutal beating. He heard Cutter curse him as they threw him over the side. When he crashed into the wheel, it didn't knock him further into unconsciousness. Instead, the sudden impact snapped his addled brain back to some semblance of life, alert enough to know he was in serious trouble.

His shoulder connected solidly with one flat paddle, and one of his ankles slammed against the wheel support that held the whole mechanism in place on the stern of the boat. The flash of pain in his ankle awakened him even more. He heard the wet splash of water below him and knew he was being carried straight into it. He had just enough time to take a deep breath before he went under.

Stone knew the Missouri was very shallow in certain spots, having seen a few sandbars that day, and prayed they weren't passing over one now. If they were, he would be ground into the mud like a fish that had been stepped on. He kicked and struggled to break free of the wheel but couldn't move. He doubled his efforts, but he was helplessly caught in the big paddle wheel.

Feeling the resistance at his waist, he felt around and discovered that his gun belt was caught in something on the wheel. When he burst clear of the water, he took a deep breath of air and tugged at the gun belt. It wouldn't give. The darkness and blinding water prevented him from seeing what was snagging the belt. Desperately he gave up trying to find the cause and fumbled at the belt buckle. His hands were slick, and the belt was so taut that he couldn't break it loose.

He was going under again.

As he plunged beneath the water again, he felt the brush of solid ground scrape his side, and he clung desperately to the paddle on which he was hanging to keep from being torn in two. He heard a dull creak behind him, and when he cleared the water again, he saw the huge rudder, only a foot away from the paddle wheel, turn to avoid grounding.

The wheel groaned as it dug its way through the sediment that had suddenly come up to meet it. The spotter at the front of the boat must have missed this shallow inlet completely as the pilot tried to correct course. The paddle wheel plowed harder. Stone knew that if he went under one more time, he might drown with a nose and mouth full of mud.

At the very apex of the wheel's cycle, the gun belt tore loose — how, he didn't know. He was so surprised he simply stared down at his waist for a moment, then leaped clear of the wheel, bracing himself for meeting the shallow riverbed just beneath the water. Instead, he sunk down past his head, gave a surprised gurgle, kicked his feet, and surfaced.

The *Rose Maiden* was already fifty feet away and leaving him stranded in her foamy wake.

Reena heard the moisture-tarnished hinges of the door squeal as it opened, even though it wasn't that loud. She'd noticed the rusty sound when she'd first looked in the cabin and hadn't given it a second thought.

Now, in what she could tell was the middle of the night despite her grogginess, she knew that something was wrong. Her mind sorted out the squeaking instantly and she stiffened. If it were Hunter, Jack, or Del, they would have knocked. Her heart lurched in fear.

Dimly she saw the unfamiliar figures against the lighter passageway and opened her mouth to scream. The room was so small that one of the men was on her instantly with a grimy hand over her mouth. The pungent aroma of alcohol burned her nasal passages.

Hunter, where are you? she tried to scream, but the sound only escaped her as a dismal moan. Besides, in the darkness as black as ink, Hunter didn't *feel* near.

No one felt near.

God, please help me! she thought as she tried to struggle.

Jack Sheffield woke thinking he heard a stealthy squeaking, but he couldn't be sure of *any* sound over the deep snoring of Del Dekko. Sheffield had never heard such a racket.

But the noise had been different from the normal groaning timber of the *Rose Maiden*. For some reason it sent off a warning in his sleepy head. Despite the feeling, sleep almost enveloped him again when he definitely heard a muffled groan. Quickly slipping on his trousers, he went to the cabin door and opened it.

Reena's door was open.

Then, as he watched, it shut quietly. Instantly, he knew something was wrong.

Without hesitation he rushed to the door. Though he was by nature a cautious and overly sensible man, Reverend Jack Sheffield lifted his leg and kicked open Reena's door, destroying the jamb as if it were paper. Directly in front of him stood a man with his back to him, leaning over slightly, shoulders rounded. Sheffield saw other shadowy figures in the room also and didn't hesitate. He grabbed the man in front of him and swung him around in a wide circle, using the momentum to send the man crashing through the splintered door and face-first into the bulkhead across the hall with fearsome force. He crumpled to the floor and didn't move.

"What the — ?" a gruff voice cried inside.

Another man suddenly appeared in front

of Jack and sent a roundhouse right directly toward his nose. Jack dodged smoothly and landed his own right hook, sending the intruder sprawling backward against the lower bunk. He hit the lower bunk as loose as a marionette.

Sheffield heard the rustle of movement and a whispered curse. His peripheral vision took in the shape of Reena sitting up on the bunk and a figure dashing toward him. He felt rather than saw the man swinging and ducked beneath it. Pivoting, Sheffield brought his clenched left fist around into the man's chest, stopping him solidly. Pain shot through his hand as it connected with the inflexible ribs that surrounded the heart.

With his eyes adjusting to the darkness, Sheffield saw that he was indeed dealing with Cutter and his men, and instantly he knew what was happening in the dark cabin. Black anger washed over him in waves. "You . . . you . . . *animal!*" he stammered through numbed lips.

Cutter must have seen something in Sheffield's eyes, for he began to back away, still holding his chest.

"Animal!" Sheffield heard himself roar. Without thinking, he took the stance of a boxer — left protecting the chin, right leading in front — and moved against Cutter.

"Now, hold on there. Nothin' happened here!" Cutter pleaded as he stepped away, but his back ran up against the bulkhead with nowhere else to go.

Like a well-oiled machine, Sheffield began striking Cutter with incredibly fast combinations to the face and body. Cutter tried his best to cover up, but wherever he placed his hands, it seemed that Sheffield had already foreseen it and directed his punishing blows elsewhere.

All the while, Sheffield was consciously aware that he was out of control, and it was only with gargantuan effort that he managed to stop himself from inflicting permanent damage on the defenseless man. Someone was calling his name — screaming it, actually. Reena. Male voices joined in, and what seemed to be a thousand hands dragged him away from the pitiful, bloodied form of Cutter.

Reena's face was suddenly in front of him. She was trembling, and the look of concern in her fear-filled eyes was so intense that he felt like taking her in his arms and telling her that everything would be all right. Right then he heard a deep voice order, "Get him out of here *now!*" Then he was practically dragged back to his cabin and thrown inside. The door slammed shut behind him, and he turned to find Del and Reena staring at him, both as breathless as he. For a moment, he was confused over their fearful looks.

"What's . . . what's the matter?" he stammered.

"What's the *matter?*" Del echoed, breathing hard.

"Come over here," Reena told him, stepping to the washstand.

Sheffield dutifully went to her.

"My stars!" Del declared. "He don't even know. . . ."

"Give me your hands," Reena said as she tried to steady her trembling hands.

When he saw his bloody, torn hands in Reena's smooth ones, he snapped out of his dazed state. He heard his own tortured breathing, smelled the aggression leaking from every pore, felt the throbbing pain in his hands.

"I'm gonna go get Hunter," Del announced and left.

Reena gently dipped Sheffield's hands into the washbowl, and they both watched the water turn burgundy. Delicately she ran a finger across his hands, searching for any cuts.

"You have a few scrapes, but none serious. Most of the blood isn't —" She stopped abruptly.

"Isn't mine?" he finished.

Reena didn't answer.

"Reena, are you . . . did they . . . ?"

"You got there just in time, Jack. Thank you."

"You're not hurt?"

"No. Just scared."

The door opened and Sheffield turned, expecting Stone and Del. Instead Captain Borland entered, carefully inspecting Sheffield with inquisitive dark eyes. "You're not hurt." It was a statement rather than a question.

"No."

"Amazing." His eyes ran up and down Sheffield's lithe frame in a strange, speculative assessment. "If you don't mind my asking, where did you learn to take apart three men at once, sir?"

"I . . . I studied pugilism before I became a minister."

"Mmmm." Borland turned to Reena. "Are you hurt, Miss O'Donnell?"

"No . . . just shaken."

"I must tell you that Mr. Cutter has never displayed that sort of aggressiveness before this night. He wouldn't be on this

229

boat if he had. And he will, I assure you, be brought to justice when we stop at the next township. Until then, he and his pals will be tightly locked in a hatch below. My apologies for your trouble, Miss O'Donnell."

"Thank you."

Borland squeezed by Sheffield and out the door.

Jack stared down at his hands. "I can't believe this. When I realized what they were doing, I just lost control."

"You weren't yourself. You just reacted, Jack."

"I wasn't myself?" he said louder than he'd intended. "I should say I wasn't myself! A minister is supposed to . . . to . . . keep control, supposed to —" He stopped and took a deep breath. "I suppose I'm still out of control." He could still feel the effect of the anger coursing through him.

Reena moved closer and placed her hands on his arms. "Listen to me, Jack. Those men were . . . well, you know what they were trying to do in there. They had me cornered, Jack. I don't know what brought you to the rescue, but I thank God you were there. Your actions saved me from certain harm."

"I don't know, I —"

"*I* know, Jack," Reena said softly, fervently. "If you hadn't shown up when you did, they would have —" She stopped, shuddering at the thought of it. "Thank you."

Sheffield moved to his bunk and sat down heavily. He heard men talking and moving outside and wondered if Cutter was really all right. From the way Sheffield's hands hurt, he couldn't imagine the pain Cutter was going through. A dark thought crossed his mind, and he uttered, "But he deserves it."

"What did you say?" Reena brought the washbasin to him and began bathing his hands again.

"Men like Cutter make me ashamed to be a member of the same species." He noticed that her hands were shaking, and he locked eyes with her. "Are you sure you're all right, Reena?"

"Yes . . . thanks to you."

"No, thank God. Something woke me up over the roar of Del's snoring."

At that moment Del burst into the room, startling them both. On his face was a look of utter confusion, and he was out of breath.

"What is it, Del?" Reena asked with alarm.

"Miss Reena . . . Hunter ain't on this boat."

He rode with the swift-flowing current of the river for a while, all the time watching the *Rose Maiden* pull farther away. His socked feet bobbed in the air in front of him. He swallowed water a few times and felt his backside bump against the shallow bottom. Overall it was just a matter of keeping his head afloat, paddling his arms a few times a minute, and steering around obstacles such as tree limbs or rocks. The half-moon shone bright in the cloudless sky and cast its silver light on the river, showing him the way.

He didn't know how far he traveled this way, but when the lights of the *Rose Maiden* disappeared around an unseen bend in the river far ahead, he knew that it was only a matter of time before the current ran out and he would be forced to travel on foot. He only hoped they would discover his absence before too long and stop to come back for him. Any way he looked at it, he would be forced to walk at some point — through darkness in broken country, bootless, wet and cold, with a crippled ankle. The possibility wasn't heartening.

Stone knew, however, that it could have been much worse. He could very well have drowned at the bottom of the river, knocked unconscious by the paddle wheel. He silently thanked God for sparing him and concentrated on his predicament.

The reason for the attack on him was only too clear. He clung to the hope that the spotter in the bow of the *Rose Maiden* or the pilot perched above the main cabins had heard the scuffle and investigated. Yet if that were the case, the boat would have stopped long before now to search for him.

The only other possible hope hinged on the fact that Reena's cabin was close to Jack and Del's. The thought of Reena sleeping helpless in her cabin bothered him so much that he refused to think about it.

When he reached the bend in the river and still couldn't see the light of the boat, he paddled to the north bank. Grabbing at the tall prairie grass, he pulled himself onto the bank, grimacing at the sharp pain in his ankle. The rest of his body also cried out in protest from the severe beating it had taken. For a moment he just lay there, catching his breath. It would be easy to rest for a while in the cool grass — just let the aching in his muscles pass, and . . .

Irritated, Stone got to his feet painfully.

He knew that if he stayed prone any longer, his aching muscles beneath the wet clothes would begin to tighten and cramp. He had to keep exercising them.

He began to limp and hop downriver.

Captain Borland was horrified to discover that he'd lost a passenger some time in the night without any of his crew knowing about it. True, this wasn't a passenger boat in the strictest sense, like ones on the Mississippi, but he took pride in not losing paying customers overboard. That was bad for business.

After he woke up the entire ship and ordered a thorough search, Captain Borland berated the sheepish mates relentlessly as they went about their hunt. Many of them swore afterward that, even if the captain lacked a tooth in his head, his words bit as deep as the tusks of a wild boar.

When no one could turn up the missing Hunter Stone, Captain Borland waved to a huge man named Gunnarson whose bulging muscles looked like steel cords. Together they went down to the tiny hold where Cutter and his men were being held and closed the door.

The nearest crew members below heard voices raised in anger, then a healthy thud or two. What was being knocked around was up for discussion, but they all had a pretty good idea of what it was — someone's head.

Borland and Gunnarson emerged, with the captain unable to hide a look of Viking triumph. He quietly ordered Gunnarson to carry a message, then went straight to Jack Sheffield's cabin.

"They threw him off," Borland informed them without preamble.

Reena, Jack, and Del looked at one another, stunned.

"What . . . what for?" Reena asked, trying to control the fear gripping her on the inside.

Borland shrugged. "Probably were scared of him being around when they" — he cast a look at Reena — "did what they did. The three of them jumped him and tossed him overboard."

"*Tossed* him?" Reena fairly screamed. She couldn't believe the disasters that had occurred in so little time, and all thoughts of her attack faded at once. She was trembling again, afraid to ask the question, but she forced herself. "Was he alive?"

"They claim he was when they threw him over," the captain said.

"How can you be so *calm* about this?"

She felt Jack's hands on her shoulders and a slight squeeze. Now *he* was trying to keep *her* under control. She knew that Borland was the captain of the ship and the only one who *was* calm, as it should have been, but his calm demeanor still irritated her.

Del asked, "You're going back for him, right? 'Cause if you're not, I'll take my leave right now and go overboard myself."

"I have a plan, Mr. Dekko. Never fear," Borland assured them all.

About ten minutes later, the *Rose Maiden* put in at the mouth of the Musselshell. Reena, Sheffield, and Del accompanied Captain Borland to the top deck. By the dim light of the moon Reena could see some sort of construction on the banks they were facing, but it wasn't until some lanterns were lit on shore that she could discern what it was.

A small dock, hastily built from fresh timber, extended some twenty feet out into the river. All around behind the area were stacked dozens of cords of firewood.

"We'll replenish our wood supplies here," Borland informed them. "Mr. Dekko, you may borrow two horses from these woodhawks. If they give you any trouble, mention my name."

"Much obliged." Del moved down closer

to midships in order to be the first one off the boat.

"Woodhawks?" Sheffield asked the captain.

"Woodcutters, if you will. That's all these men do — cut timber for steamboats like the *Rose Maiden*."

"Isn't it sort of dangerous? Being out here in the middle of nowhere?"

Borland gave him a wry look. "Oh my, yes. Hardly a month goes by that one of these fellows isn't killed by Indians or a large bear."

Sheffield couldn't seem to grasp why anyone would risk their lives like that. "Are they paid well?"

"Hardly."

"Then . . . why do it?"

Borland looked at him strangely. The lamplight accented his lower jaw, deformed because of the lack of tooth support. "Because it was a good idea at one time. When the Missouri became a major source of transportation west, the need for fuel stops presented itself. Unfortunately, every mother's son who owned an ax and a strong back thought of it at the same time. Now there are countless woodhawks all along the river, fighting for scraps." He paused, gazing down at the men, and a sad light came into his eyes. "Some of those poor souls are just sodbusters who headed to California and ran out of money. They do what they can to save up enough to complete their journey."

Reena barely heard the conversation. Hunter was out there somewhere, and he could be hurt badly. *Or worse,* she thought morbidly. Quickly she pushed the terrifying thought from her head and continued praying as she'd been ever since they'd found out he was missing.

They watched Del jump down to the dock, nod at two men lugging a small wagon full of wood toward the ship, and stop to talk to a man with a tall felt hat who seemed to be supervising the activity.

"This Del Dekko," Captain Borland explored cautiously, "he . . . um . . ."

Sheffield nodded. "You can count on him finding Hunter and returning the horses, Captain. You won't find a man more honest than Del."

"Good. I sensed that about him, but I've been taken before." Borland glanced over at Reena. "We'll find him, miss. Don't you worry."

Reena wished she were as confident as he sounded. Suddenly she turned to Jack.

"We'll go below and pray for him, Jack."

"Of course."

Borland watched them go with a strange look, then shook his head in wonder.

Stone was admiring the spectacular purple-tinged dawn he was walking toward when he saw the rider across the river. Immediately he knew it was Del. He waved his hands high over his head, but Del had already spotted him. Exhausted, bruised, and sore, Stone sat down on the shallow embankment and waited for Del to come to him.

"Good to see you alive, at least," Del drawled. He stopped the roan he was riding and fumbled in the saddlebags.

"What happened on the boat? How's Reena? Did Cutter try anything that —"

"Hold on!" Del cried, throwing Stone a canteen. He drank greedily as Del spoke. "Reena's fine, and them bushwhackers are locked up."

Stone closed his eyes and said a silent prayer of thanks.

"You wouldn't believe what happened," Del said with a grin.

"Try me."

"The Reverend Jack Sheffield saved her. He was spittin' lightnin' and swingin' thunder."

Stone stood quickly, grimaced at the pains in his body, and threw the canteen back to Del. Mounting the spare horse with a groan, he said, "You can tell me about it on the way."

"How'd they get you, Hunter?"

"Caught me daydreaming . . . or nightdreaming."

"I didn't think anyone got the jump on you."

Stone gave him a wry look. "It can happen to anyone, Del."

Del removed his coat and threw it to him. Stone put it on, noticing the sleeves stopped well above his thick wrists, but he was glad to have something between his damp shirt and the crisp morning air. The eastern horizon was on fire now with the sun's impending arrival. River smells of moss and mud were strong in his nostrils.

"I thought we'd lost you for sure, Hunter," Del said.

Stone nodded. "So did I there for a while."

Chapter Thirteen

Days Gone By

"Vic," Becker nodded.

"Dirk. Hello, Jenny. Come on in." Vickersham stepped aside to let the couple into his home.

Jenny had been in the Vickershams' new household only once, and that was a hurried affair to decorate just before the wedding. Since then, Megan had added a comfortable touch that was pleasing to the eye. In the corner of the parlor stood a quaint corner chair with French cut-wool upholstery. Beside it was a serpentine-front card table with four silver candlesticks at each corner. The New England settee in the middle of the room was gold-colored with dark mahogany legs. Jenny hoped that someday she would have a house of her own with such nice furnishings.

Becker surrendered his hat to Vic and stood just inside the door uncomfortably. He was wearing civilian clothes, black pants with a simple white shirt buttoned to the neck, much the opposite of Vic's impeccable dark blue suit with crimson string tie. They hadn't seen each other since the day before at Pate's cabin. The trip back to the fort had been strained and silent, and Becker expected nothing less on this evening that was intended to be a festive dinner, celebrating the newlyweds.

"Where's the reverend?" Vic asked him.

"You didn't know?"

"Know what?"

"He went with Hunter and Reena. And Del went along as a guide."

Vickersham's eyebrows raised in surprise. "What for?"

"I don't know. I didn't know myself until I heard it from Macleod this morning. The colonel wasn't too happy about it."

Vic considered the implications of this news and frowned.

Megan came into the parlor from the kitchen, wiping her hands on her apron. After greeting the visitors, she too asked about Sheffield. "So it will just be the four of us," she said, trying to sound cheerful. "We've got a lot to eat to make up for the reverend — you know how he likes home-cooked food."

No one said anything to this. They stood staring at one another for an uncomfortable moment until Jenny asked, "Do you need help in the kitchen?"

"Of course," Megan answered, a bit too anxiously. She gave a pointed look to her husband before leading Jenny away.

"Sit down, Dirk," Vic offered. "Can I get you some coffee? Lemonade?"

"No, thanks. I'm fine."

Vickersham seated himself across from Becker on the settee and crossed his legs. As an awkward silence filled the room, he picked lint from the knee of his trousers.

Becker held his hands in his lap and kneaded his thumbs together.

Faintly, the sounds of men shouting came to them from the western corral of the fort, where fresh horses were being broken. The mantel clock over the fireplace softly chimed the half hour of six. Twinkle moved restlessly on the front porch.

"She looks like she's grown in only a week," Becker observed.

Vic looked at him blankly.

"Twinkle."

"Oh yes. Grown outward, if not upward. Megan's been feeding her only the best vegetables."

Becker nodded.

"Her favorite, believe it or not, is squash."

"Interesting."

"Boiled, no less."

"Mmmm."

The setting sun escaped from behind a cloud over the mountains and burst through the western window, falling directly on Becker's face. He squinted and turned his head.

"I'll get that," Vic said. He went to the window and drew the curtain, then sat back down.

Their eyes met, then skittered away.

From the kitchen, just inside the doorway, Megan and Jenny stood with their heads cocked toward the parlor trying to listen. Megan shook her head and whispered, "This is ridiculous."

"I know," Jenny agreed.

"Why are they acting like that?"

Jenny shrugged. She knew that something more must have happened between the two men at the mountain cabin, but Becker hadn't spoken of it. In fact, he'd hardly said a word to her at all on the way over. Jenny could pardon his silence easily since she was much the same way when something was bothering her. Megan, she knew, was much different. Judging from her frustration, Jenny concluded that Megan had been getting the same silent treatment and could barely stand it.

"Look at them!" Megan said crossly. "They're just . . . sitting there like two stubborn little boys."

In the silence of the parlor, a joyous roar carried down the lane from the fort.

"How many horses trained today?" Vickersham asked. From Becker, he'd learned to refuse to use the word "broken."

"About twelve. I think we just heard number thirteen."

Vickersham put on a grin, trying to break the ice. "And of those twelve, how many were yours?"

"Three."

"Good job."

"Thank you."

Vic scowled for a moment at the short answers he was receiving, then said, "Dirk, about yesterday . . ."

Becker waited, not willing to make it easier on him.

"I may have been out of line in my treatment of Mr. Pate. It seems that —"

"Why are you telling me this?"

"What do you mean? I was just trying to —"

"Go tell it to Pate."

"Why are you being so harsh, Becker?"

The use of Becker's last name created an unseen wall in the uncomfortable space between them. Vickersham had, consciously or unconsciously, elevated himself due to their rank. The room now seemed larger, the men physically farther apart, and the fading sunlight dimmer.

From the kitchen, Megan could stand it no longer. She marched into the parlor with ill-concealed irritation and announced, "Dinner's ready."

During the meal, the ladies tried to draw Vic and Becker into light conversation. They talked about the weather, the school, the growing burg of Fort Macleod, cheerful local gossip — all to no avail. The men answered with "Oh, really?" and "You don't say?" but that was about it.

Finally Megan slammed her fork down. "What's the matter with you two?"

They looked at her in startled surprise.

"And don't ask me what I mean. It's written all over your faces, your voices, and your attitudes. What's happened?"

Becker looked over at Vickersham, who suddenly found his plate very interesting. Softly he said, "There's been a murder."

"I know about that!" Megan said. "Everybody in town knows about it. What I don't know — and I think I can speak for everyone else at this table — is what this murder has to do with you crawling into a hole."

"Excuse me." Vic placed his napkin beside his setting and stood.

Megan shook her head and buried her face in her hands. "I give up!"

Becker, angry now, cast a glare at Vic. "Yes, why don't you go sulk somewhere else so we can have a nice dinner?"

"Now, you listen to me, Becker —"

"Stop it!" Jenny cried, slamming down her fork and getting to her feet. Standing, she only came to Vic's shoulder, but the thunderous look on her face and the tightly clenched fists made her stature seem more forbidding. "Just stop it!"

Becker reached for her hand. "Jenny . . ."

She jerked her hand away, eyes blazing, then turned to Vickersham. "I don't know you very well, and it may not be any of my business, but you're being mean."

Vic stared at her, open-mouthed.

Jenny plunged on. "I know that you're a kind man, and everyone thinks the most of you, just like they should. But when you act like you do, closing everyone off, it's so unlike you that the people who care about you are worried out of their minds. Does that make sense?"

Vic and Megan stared at her in surprise. Jenny didn't think they'd heard her speak so many words at one time.

When Vic didn't answer her question and she saw that she'd shocked all three of them, Jenny lost some of her momentum. She looked at Becker, wrung her hands, and sat back down. Seeing Megan's thoughtful look and misinterpreting it, she said sheepishly, "I'm sorry, Megan. It's none of my business."

"Nonsense. You're my friend." She glanced up at Vic. "You're *our* friend."

Vic was staring over Jenny's shoulder, through the small kitchen window and beyond. Then his lithe frame seemed to sink into itself a little, as if he'd come to a conclusion and dreaded facing it. Slowly, he sat back down.

Jenny watched him, and all at once she didn't want to hear what he was going to say. She didn't want Megan to hear it, nor Dirk. Somehow she sensed he was about to say something that wasn't going to be good. Silently she chastised herself for letting her frustrations come out in the open.

"All right," Vic said softly, "you want to hear it, I'll tell you."

No, Jenny thought, *we've changed our minds — we don't want to hear it. Solve it on your own, Vic.*

His gaze swung around to his wife. "The girl who was killed? I knew her."

Becker's first thought was, *Uh-oh.*

From Megan's look, she'd been expecting anything but this, and her face registered nothing but confusion for a moment. Then she swallowed and said in a tiny voice, "Oh?"

Vic's long, slim fingers played at the corner of his cloth napkin, but he kept his eyes locked with Megan's. "Yes."

"Knew her . . . how? From where?"

"From two years before you and I met."

I've got to get out of here, Becker thought. *I've got to grab Jenny's hand and whisk her out of here before this goes any further.*

"Did . . . did you know her well?" Megan asked, still in that small childlike voice.

"Yes."

Vic's eyes cut over to Becker for a split second, and Becker knew somehow. He didn't know if it was a man-to-man matter or some sort of mind reading, but in that instant he knew. He also knew that he *had* to get out of there, and very soon.

"How well?" Megan asked. When she didn't receive an answer immediately, Megan shifted to another question — by the pasty look on her face, one she hoped was more safe. "Where did you meet her?"

Becker said, "Jenny, I think we'd better —"

"You stay right there, Dirk," Megan told him, not taking her eyes from Vickersham. "Where did you meet her, Vic?"

"It was on a lone patrol. I was after a whiskey runner, but he crossed the border. I'd been away from the fort for days and it was very cold. I started to fear for both myself and my horse if we didn't find shelter." He paused, then finished, "So we did."

Becker tried again, this time more determined. "Let's take a walk, Jenny." He took her hand, and this time Megan didn't stop them.

On the porch they were met by Twinkle, who leaned up against Becker's legs. He scratched her head affectionately.

"Vic must have known that woman pretty good to be so broken up about her dying, don't you think, Dirk?" Jenny asked.

Becker realized that Jenny didn't understand the full implications of what Vic had just admitted to Megan. "Yeah, pretty good, I guess."

Megan, buying herself some time to think, put on some water to boil for coffee.

The white curtains on the window to her left burned bright orange with the sun's last rays, making her face glow a cinnamon color. A hundred questions ran through her mind, nagging at the edges, wanting immediate answers from Vic, but she knew there was only one that really needed addressing.

She turned from the stove and said, "What was her name, Vic?"

"Her name was Fran Meyer."

"Fran," Megan repeated, tasting the name on her tongue and finding it momentarily bitter. Then she remembered two men talking outside the dry goods store earlier that day. She hadn't heard about the murder yet and caught the word "butchered." Megan thought they were talking about the cattle business until she heard, "Her husband was pretty broke up . . . must've been pretty messy." Then at school Jenny had told her that a woman had been murdered in the mountains.

Megan felt sorry for Fran, and then guilty about blaming her for giving Vic shelter that cold night. It was *how much* shelter she'd given him that bothered her.

"I'm sorry, Megan. As I said, it was before we'd even met, long before I'd become a Christian, and —"

"How did you feel about her?"

Vic looked at her. "We were both lonely."

"That's not an answer."

"Oh, come now, Megan! Have you ever seen someone that you know cut up and murdered?"

"No," she said, trying to quell the fear rising in her heart.

"It's very traumatic, I can assure you. It doesn't matter how you felt about that person — I don't think I'd even like to see an *enemy* so mistreated!"

"So you . . . didn't love her?"

Vic went to her and put his arms around her. "No. I was . . . we were lonely, and —"

"Just speak for yourself, Vic."

"*I* was lonely. It was before I'd met you and before I became a Christian. I'm not excusing it at all. It was very stupid of me. I just need you to forgive me, Megan. I'm sorry I've been out of sorts since it happened, but it's like a sand burr in my pocket — it bothers me to no end. I can't get the vision of her out of my mind."

The water began boiling, and Megan pulled away from him to make the coffee. It gave her time to think, but she couldn't get past the picture of Vic and her together. They'd never discussed any of his past relationships before they married. She knew it was silly to think that he'd been out of touch with any female his whole life until he'd met her, but that didn't make it any easier.

Pouring the steaming water over the coffee grounds, she asked, "Why didn't you tell me before we married, Vic?"

"For many reasons. It never came up, it was a mistake on my part that I didn't like admitting, and —" He stopped and put his arms around her again. "Megan, I'd never even *thought* of Fran for a long time. She was in my past, before God came into my life. My mind has always been filled with you from the first day I met you."

Megan gently pulled herself from his arms. The confusing emotions that swept over her came in wave after wave. She felt like a drowning swimmer, struggling against a strong current. "I need some time to . . . to understand this, Vic."

"All right." He stood there for a few seconds, then nodded his head once and moved toward the parlor to leave her alone. As if in afterthought, he turned and said, "This is still a murder case that needs to be solved, Megan. I'll be leaving in the morning to question Plenty Trees about some evidence. From there, I don't know where it will take me." He held his eyes on her, watching for a reaction.

Megan carefully kept her face neutral.

"That should give you enough time to think this through, Megan."

"Why does it have to be you, Vic?"

"Because I found her," he answered simply. "And I want to be the first one to look into the face of the man who did this."

Vic wasn't too pleased that Macleod had allowed Becker to be assigned to the troop. Becker was a direct reminder that things weren't well at home — that Megan and his best friends were observing him with a wary and concerned eye — not to mention a palpable suspicion. Guiltily, he knew the suspicion was well-founded, since he hadn't told Megan what he had discovered. The pain of holding something back from her was tearing him up inside. He wanted nothing more than to sit her down and tell her everything, but truthfully he still hadn't come to terms with it himself.

As they rode along, he reached down and patted his saddlebag with the diary in it, as if to reassure himself that it truly existed and said what it did. It existed. He could feel the hard outline of it.

Besides Becker, D'Artigue had insisted on going, along with four other Mounties. The party was being led by Jerry Potts, the sad-faced scout who was the undisputed master of knowing the Territory. Vic glanced over at Potts as he rode beside him, contemplating the man's silent nature. Potts avoided conversation like a plague, and only a few could remember him putting more than two sentences together at a stretch. Usually Vic tried to draw him out into conversation when they were on patrol together — never succeeding, as a matter of fact — but on this day Vickersham was more than happy for the lack of talk.

As usual, many of the Blackfoot people met the troop as they rode into the village. After giving a few greetings to the gathering, Vickersham spotted Plenty Trees. He was smiling at Vic, but it faded quickly.

"What is wrong with my English friend?"

"My heart is heavy this day, Great Chief." From his saddlebag Vic withdrew the Indian armlet that was found beneath Fran Meyer's bed. Holding it up, Vic felt a surge of guilt at the trap he was springing on his friend. He had to be sure of where they stood by seeing Plenty Trees' reaction to the sight of the armlet.

"That is Blackfoot," Plenty Trees confirmed. His face showed only a mild puzzlement.

Vic was relieved that the chief had nothing to hide. "I know. What I don't know, Chief, is why it was found beneath a dead white woman who had been killed in a very bad way."

"Bad way?"

Vickersham looked at Jerry Potts. "What's the Blackfoot word for massacre?"

Potts released two guttural syllables from his throat.

Plenty Trees looked startled. "I know nothing of this." As Vic stared back, offering no answer, the first sign of anger spread over Plenty Trees' strong features. He gestured at the people around him. "The Blackfoot are friends to the white man!"

"Are you certain that all are friends here?"

"Yes! Why do you dishonor me?"

Vickersham held up a hand. "I am sorry, Chief Plenty Trees, but I had to be certain. Do you understand?"

Still offended, Plenty Trees asked, "Now you are certain?"

"Yes. We . . . I thank you and hope you

can forgive my momentary mistrust. But this is a bad man, or men, we are hunting, and we will stop at nothing to find them."

Plenty Trees considered him a moment, then nodded. "I will help you."

Vickersham admired the chief's ability to accept and forgive the wrong that had been done to him. To question a Blackfoot's friendship or word was a serious, and sometimes dangerous, matter. "We know that you will, and we thank you. Now we wonder if —"

"Bad Weasel. You should find this man."

"Who?"

"The Sioux warrior that is going from tribe to tribe, trying to get the Blackfoot and others to join him."

"Join him where?"

"To fight the bluecoats in the Powder Hills."

Vickersham exchanged glances with Potts and Becker. "Plenty Trees, why didn't you report this to Stamixotokon?" Stamixotokon was the name given to Macleod by the Blackfoot, meaning "Bull's Head."

"We ran him away," Plenty Trees shrugged, as if the Sioux warrior had disappeared from the face of the earth when he'd left their camp.

Hiding his frustration, Vic asked, "Have you not heard about him since? Where he has gone?"

Plenty Trees consulted with a few of the braves around him in their tongue.

"What are they saying, Potts?"

Potts shook his head once and held up his hand to silence Vickersham, listening to the conversation among the Indians.

When Plenty Trees was finished talking, he turned to Vickersham triumphantly and pointed east. "They go where the sun rises."

Meaning east, Vic thought. "How far east?" he asked the chief.

"One day's ride. At the village of the Sarcee."

Vickersham turned to Potts with a questioning look.

"Not good."

"Why?"

"The Sarcee don't trust us very much yet."

"And how is your friendship with them?" Vic asked.

Potts' father was Scottish, and his mother was a member of the Blood tribe, related to the Blackfoot. Growing up, Potts had spent most of his early life with the Bloods and was well respected. Vickersham knew that if Jerry Potts was unwelcome with the Sarcee, they could be riding into danger.

With characteristic nonchalance, Potts shrugged lazily. "We'll see, won't we?"

Chapter Fourteen

Departures and Arrivals

When Faron O'Donnell woke from what seemed like a coma-slumber, the first thing he was aware of was moisture. All over. Everywhere except the inside of his mouth, which was cotton dry. His ears, however, felt full of water, and he automatically lifted a hand to explore.

His eyes popped open.

His hand wasn't there.

And neither was his forearm, or elbow.

Faron stared at the stump of his left arm silently while the rain blew into the covered wagon. The appendage was so unreal it might as well have belonged to someone else. It seemed like the head of a sledgehammer was dangling from his shoulder. He wiggled it.

"Oh no," he groaned. "They've gone and done it." He laid his head back and closed his eyes again, hoping that when he opened them the nightmare would be over. But it wasn't.

He felt a strange, chilling sensation as a distant memory filled his thoughts.

Ten years ago he'd met a trapper in the mountains who was missing half of a leg — Faron couldn't remember which one. The old man was open and comfortable with the handicap, so Faron had questioned him about how it had happened. He asked him if he still felt pain. Then, finding himself almost afraid to know, Faron had asked, "Is it true that it still itches?"

The trapper had looked up at him from where he was cleaning a beaver, and his expression had turned painful. "Yeah. Sometimes so bad I can't stand it. How did you know about that?"

Faron couldn't remember where he'd heard about mysterious itching limbs that weren't there anymore, so he'd ignored the man's answer and quickly changed the subject.

Now, contemplating the empty sleeve at the end of his arm, he knew the old trapper was correct. It *did* itch. Very badly. The incredible itching was bad enough, but he was also soaked to the skin. Fierce anger washed over him at the injustice of taking his arm without his permission and the added insult of poor care afterward. Whoever had left him in the back of a wagon, in a driving thunderstorm, with the back flap open was going to suffer his Irish temper.

Faron truly believed that if that drunk doctor showed his head at that moment, he would put a bullet through the man's eye. Faron raised his head to look for his pistol, but an excruciating pain shot through his shoulder and what was left of his arm that sent him back to the pillow gasping.

Someone was going to pay for this.

Despite the pain and wet clothing, he fell back asleep. When he woke again he found Norton beside him in the wagon. Faron looked over Norton's shoulder through the back of the wagon and saw that the rain had stopped, though the steel-gray clouds seemed heavily laden with more to come.

Norton wore a dark blue caped slicker and restlessly spun his hat in his hands. He was staring at something outside the wagon, unaware that Faron was awake. Faron wished he could remember the boy's first name, but it escaped him.

"Who do I blame for this, lad?" he asked in a croak.

Norton spun around quickly, dropped his hat, then picked it up and gazed at Faron with large blue eyes. "You're awake!"

"Aye. That surprise you, does it? That

I'm still alive?"

"Well . . . um . . . nossir. You just . . . I wasn't prepared, that's all. Scared me."

"Then what will ye do, lad, when ye come across Crazy Horse and his bunch if you're afraid of an old one-armed Irishman?"

"I . . . uh . . . didn't mean it like that —"

"I know, I know. But you still haven't answered me question."

"Question . . . ?"

"What devil took me arm off?" Faron saw the boy glance at the stump, then quickly look away. With a sinking heart, Faron realized he would see that reaction many times for the rest of his life — if he lived.

"It was pretty bad, Mr. O'Donnell. I mean, it was turning black and beginning to smell, and your fever was so high that we were wondering why you were still alive."

"We?"

"Me, Dr. Denton, General Custer —"

"Custer! What was he doing here?"

"We were on a delay like we are now — waiting for a bridge to be built so we can cross with the wagons — and he stopped in to check on you."

"Mmmm. Ain't I the lucky one," Faron grumbled.

"It was the general who ordered Dr. Denton to go ahead and ampu— do the procedure."

Faron knew something was different from when he'd last been awake. Then he realized what it was. "Who put the dry clothes on me? And the blankets?"

"I did. Dr. Denton is real busy with a few accidents we had today. The flap of the wagon must have blown open during the storm. Sorry you got soaked to the bone."

"It's not your fault, laddie." The boy's concern touched Faron, but he was very tired of having to be taken care of. And this was only the beginning. "What about my niece? Any answer to that telegram?"

Norton didn't meet his eyes. "No, sir. No answer."

Faron tried to put a cheerful tone in his voice, though he was very disappointed. "Ah, well. My darlin' Reena's probably gone back to Chicago by now. Never could picture her spending the rest of her life in the wilderness."

He turned his head away from the stump and closed his eyes. In spite of the boiling anger he felt because of what had been done to him, he again fell into a deep sleep.

Reena stared at Jack Sheffield in shock.

"You're not serious?"

"Completely."

They stood on the shore of a natural inlet where Captain Borland had anchored to let them off. Behind them rose a gentle incline to the floor of the prairie. A grove of cottonwoods to their right shaded them from the sun.

"That's ridiculous, Jack," Hunter said shortly. "Get on your horse."

"I'm going on, Hunter. I told all of you what I was planning to do when we began this journey, and I haven't changed my mind. In fact, I'm more determined than ever to find Crazy Horse and talk to him."

Hunter, who was gently trying to calm the excited Buck, faced Sheffield fully. Hunter's left cheek was bruised purple and pale green from his attack, and his eye was severely bloodshot, making his appearance more threatening than it was. "They'll kill you, Jack, before you get a chance."

"I know you don't understand," Sheffield shrugged, "but I've got to try."

Sheffield had been very quiet and subdued since the night of the attacks, choosing to spend most of his time in his small cabin. When Reena had asked Del what he did in there with all his time, Del replied, "Reads his Bible mostly — you know, the one that has the pretty embroidery on the outside?"

"It was made for him by a chief's wife," Reena said. "It's an eagle in flight."

"Yeah, it's pretty. He just don't have much to say right now, I don't guess, Miss Reena."

Reena had worried about Jack, but she supposed that he'd been in deep prayer over his journey ahead.

Now she looked up at his clear cornflower blue eyes. "When will you be back?"

"I don't know. Whenever I feel the Lord calling me, I suppose."

Del, who'd remained silent and watchful, stepped up to him and held out his hand. "We'll miss you, preacher."

"Even you, Del?"

"Yup."

Sheffield took the offered hand and said, "Somehow I think you're the only one here who understands what I'm doing."

"Take care, Reverend," Del said with a wink.

When Sheffield turned back to Reena, Stone was right in his face.

"This is foolish and unnecessary, Jack. There's nothing you can say to the Sioux that will change their minds."

"You don't know that, Hunter. Maybe

God is waiting to use a man just like me."

Stone looked at him for a moment, pondering the possible truth in what he'd just said, but reluctant to agree. Finally he reached out and shook Sheffield's hand. "If you feel God's leading in this, then go with Him, Jack. We'll pray for you."

"Thanks, Hunter." He leaned forward and whispered, "Take care of her."

"I will."

Sheffield grinned and turned to Reena, who was shaking her head and staring at him defiantly.

"What's the matter?"

"This isn't right, Jack. It doesn't feel right at all."

"It does to me."

"What if . . . ?" Reena couldn't finish her thought and was surprised to see him smile.

"I can feel it, Reena," Sheffield said with conviction. "Don't you see? I know in my heart that God is leading me to go this way. Something's waiting for me. I know it."

Reena crossed her arms and wouldn't meet his eyes.

"Do you remember Him speaking to you? Telling you to come west and work with the Indians?"

"Yes."

"Very clearly?"

"Of course. It was . . . as you say, very clear."

"Did people doubt you?"

Reena hesitated, knowing she'd been trapped. People *did* question her decision and probably looked at her as she looked at Jack right now. "I just don't want you to go, Jack. You're all alone, and from what we've heard, the Indians are in no mood to listen to reason right now."

"I'm going to try," he said simply.

Reena shook her head in frustration, but she knew he had to go. Biting back tears and not caring if it made Hunter jealous or not, she went into his arms and hugged him tight. "Take care of yourself."

"I will."

"Our Blackfoot tribe needs you. Don't stay gone long."

"I won't."

Reena watched him walk up the gangplank. As he mounted his horse and rode up the bank toward the prairie, she wondered if she'd ever see him again.

"How much farther, Del?" Reena asked.

" 'Bout twenty miles. Should be there by tomorrow sometime." He removed his battered hat and scratched his head. "You know, Miss Reena, I hate to bring it up, but it'll be mighty chancy meeting a big army like that. What if they've already arrived there and moved on?"

"Then we'll ride on till we find him," Reena said immediately. Then her face softened, and she asked, "You *will* find him for me, won't you, Del?"

"Oh yes, ma'am. I will do just that," Del assured her.

The country was badly broken up by plenty of gullies and ditches. It was necessary to carefully weave the horses around the obstructions for most of the first day, a feat made more troublesome because of the animals' eagerness to run. They were very glad to be off the steamer, and therefore difficult to control at first. Nostrils flaring, ears twitching, hooves dancing, they pulled against the reins with the want — the *need* — to break all out into a dead run. Reena's horse, a bay gelding, succeeded in defying her wishes by running headlong for almost a half-mile before she could rein him in. In the process, the horse narrowly missed disaster by stepping in a gopher hole. Luckily it was a well-worn hole, widened by an earlier rain.

When she finally had the bay under control, she saw Hunter grinning at her and made a face at him. She still thanked God that he hadn't drowned in the muddy Missouri after the fight with Cutter and his men. When she'd seen him galloping up to the *Rose Maiden* with Del, she'd felt an indescribable sense of relief and ran into his arms when he'd dismounted. She also noticed him wince, but he hadn't gone into detail about his injuries to her. He only told her shortly, "They caught me when I wasn't looking and threw me overboard like a trash fish." Reena found she didn't want to know the details, since enough had already happened that she *did* know about. He hadn't questioned her either, and she guessed that he'd gotten the story from Del. They were both content that the other was alive and unhurt.

All three of them were silent most of the day, just enjoying the open air and being away from the cramped boat. They saw a group of pronghorn bounding away in the distance, and Reena couldn't count the number of prairie dogs she saw running busily here and there. The thought of Jack's departure still disturbed her at times, but she knew she would have to accept his leaving as something between him and God and pray for him.

That night Reena couldn't help but consider the long miles they had traveled already, not even knowing if Faron was still alive. If he wasn't, how foolish would she feel to have brought Hunter and Del all this way? Then again, if he *had* died, she wouldn't really care about that — she would be too heartbroken. She hated to admit it — had even cried about the feeling when younger — but Reena felt closer to her uncle than to her own father. She knew it wasn't a measure of love. It was simply the fact that Uncle Faron had always been more easily approachable than her father.

Jack O'Donnell was a driven man when it came to establishing himself in the cutthroat business world of Chicago banking. Even after making it to one of the top rungs of the ladder, his obsession didn't stop. He loved his family, of that there was no doubt, but he constantly seemed to be preoccupied even when at home. After feeling neglected when growing up, Reena finally accepted the fact that her father measured his worth as a family man by how much he could give them materially instead of emotionally.

Faron, on the other hand, cared not one whit about money or possessions. Fun-loving, adventurous, and unassuming, he was the very antithesis of his brother. Whenever he came to visit, even Reena's friends would follow him around. They would all laugh at his jokes and gasp at his irreverence concerning ideas that were basic tenets for high-society children to believe in. They sensed the child in him, ill-concealed beneath a gruff nature and scraggly appearance, and took him into their hearts and loved him.

"Oh, please, Lord," Reena whispered that night, "let him be alive."

She fell asleep with tears drying on her cheeks.

For the first time, Faron began to doubt his own ability to overcome his wounds. The fever that gripped him raged like a furnace throughout his body. He couldn't seem to stay awake for more than an hour at a time, and that time was spent being jostled in a wagon over rough country. His whole body was sore and weak. Unable to hold any food down besides some broth lightly sprinkled with prairie chicken and mashed corn, he longed for a huge, juicy buffalo steak and regretted all the times he'd taken it for granted.

Another thing that irritated him was that he couldn't keep track of time. Living in the mountains, alone, he'd carefully kept track of what day and month it was every evening. Other mountain men he'd known had scoffed at him, saying there was no room for such nonsense in their rugged way of living. It defeated the very purpose of leaving the world of cities and men and time behind. But Faron *wanted* to know those things — he didn't know why, it was just important to him. Now he awoke at all times of the day or night, disoriented, and it galled him.

Whenever he awoke from a fitful sleep, he never failed to look down at the ugly stump, harboring a faint hope that he'd been dreaming all along about the whole ordeal. But he was continually disappointed. The half arm rested beside him, a painful reminder that he was no longer whole. Often when he felt consciousness returning, he didn't want to wake up and found it disturbingly easy to sink back into that slumber where landscape blurred with a sky as black as the smoothest onyx.

He was dying. He became sure that the first sign of death was the willing release of life, and he was well on that road. Strangely, he didn't really care. He was vaguely aware that the fever made him feel that way. It was like an ocean wave to be ridden out until it crashed against un-known shores.

Faron thought back to his voyage across the Atlantic to America, and the wondrous time it had been. He remembered looking out across the blue expanse and thinking the ocean was limitless. Someone had made a mistake — those Spanish explorers with their fancy outfits, he thought — there *was* no land called America so far from Ireland. Just water, water, and more water.

But he'd made it, along with the other people from his homeland, and he would never forget the grand celebration. He saw Reena first, her almond-shaped eyes shin-ing a bright aquamarine, just like the sea he'd just crossed. She seemed so happy, so full of joy that those beautiful eyes were wet with tears.

No, that wasn't right. He hadn't seen Reena. He'd seen fishing boats, what seemed like hundreds of them, outside of New York harbor.

"Uncle Faron?" Reena said softly.

He tried to answer but couldn't, and that only made his beloved niece cry more. He didn't want to disappoint her. *I'm here, lass,* he tried to say. *I made it across.*

Faron heard a man's voice and knew that

someone else had intruded upon his wonderful vision. He jealously wanted the man to go away. This was no place for talk of blood and fever and dying.

Faron drifted away again. If the despicable man wouldn't go away, then by the leprechauns *he* would. He would rather watch the sporadic, brilliant lights against that timeless sable sky rather than listen to any more depressing talk.

"Uncle Faron . . . please look at me."

A cool hand against his forehead reluctantly brought him back from his dream world. If that man was still there . . .

"That's it. Look at me," the soft voice pleaded.

Her voice was like he imagined an angel's to be — soft, musical, soothing. How could he help not looking at her?

Reena leaned closer now, and his whole field of vision filled with her. "You hold on, Uncle. You take my hand and hold on and don't let go. Stay here with me." She tried to smile, but it was one of those that turned down instead of up. A single tear fell from her jawline, and he felt it — actually felt it — strike his bare collarbone on the side where the useless stump lay.

Faron swallowed, though there was no saliva around his thick tongue. "Only one, lass," he croaked.

"What did you say?" The cool hand stroked more urgently.

He swallowed again and concentrated on making himself heard, though his throat was on fire. "Only one . . . hand . . . to hold yours."

Reena smiled, and this time the corners of her mouth went up, not down. It was a real smile that moved her cheeks up and squeezed more tears from her eyes. "I know. But that's plenty enough for me."

He tried to say more, but the effort was too great. Besides, he wanted to hear her talk in that clear, calm voice again. Just before he reluctantly drifted off to sleep once more, he heard her say, "I'll hold your hand in both of mine, Uncle Faron, and I'll be here whenever you wake. I won't leave you."

His dream no longer held a forbidding sky that clashed tendrils of lightning and streaking meteorites.

It was deep blue and serene now.

When Reena first saw him, she thought there was some mistake. This man couldn't be her uncle — not this husk of a man with sunken cheeks, bone-white skin, and a bandaged but bloody amputated arm.

She turned to the lieutenant who'd brought her, Hunter, and Del to the tent to tell him that he was wrong, that her uncle was somewhere else. His sympathetic look had stopped her.

Instead, in a tiny voice that surprised even her, she asked, "He's alive?"

"Barely, ma'am. I'm sorry."

Reena knew it wasn't the young lieutenant's fault, but she turned on him anyway. "What do you mean, barely? If he's still breathing, he's still alive, isn't he?"

"Yes, ma'am, he is." He touched the tip of his hat and left after a knowing look at Hunter.

Reena wanted to call him back and apologize, but she couldn't take her eyes from Faron's still form. He'd been so *vibrant* all her life! What she was staring at was an old man who was knocking on death's door, if not already opening it and peeking inside.

"He's a tough old coot."

Reena turned and found a slumped, disheveled man with a bulbous nose and an exhausted smile standing just inside the tent.

"I'm Dr. Denton. I'll answer any questions you might have."

Why did you take his arm? was what first popped into Reena's mind, but she knew it wasn't this man's fault. She asked about medication, just to be asking something, because she couldn't get her mind off the pitiful figure lying on the bed.

When Denton was through describing a list of medical treatments that meant nothing to Reena, he waited patiently for her to ask another question. When she didn't, he glanced at Hunter with raised eyebrows.

"What's the prognosis, Doctor?" Hunter asked quietly.

"Rest, obviously. As many fluids as you can possibly pump into him. Food, also."

"That's not a prognosis, that's directions."

Denton looked at him sharply. "And who might you be?"

"Sub-Inspector Hunter Stone, North-West Mounted Police. This is my scout, Del Dekko. We are . . . friends of Miss O'Donnell."

Denton glanced at Reena pointedly, but she was staring at Faron.

"You may speak freely," Hunter assured him.

Shrugging his rounded shoulders, Denton said, "Two of the bullet wounds are healing nicely, but the other one shattered his forearm and became infected, forcing me to amputate to save his life.

The trauma, however, has caused unforeseen problems." He stopped and looked at the men knowingly. "Had quite a time taking his arm, I can tell you that. He threatened to shoot me if I did."

Del commented dryly, "Then you're prob'ly in a hurry to get out of here, I'd expect." One of his eyes fixed on the prone Faron O'Donnell admiringly, and he murmured, "I'da done the same thing."

Denton noticed that Del's other eye seemed to be gazing at him, and he stood transfixed for a brief time. Ignoring the threats of being shot, he continued. "The only thing that has me worried is the fever he's had since before the amputation. It won't break, and I don't know why. I'm almost sure the infection is gone."

Reena had moved to the bed and laid her hand gently on Faron's laboring chest. She was only half listening to the conversation behind her.

"Fever is very bad, Sub-Inspector. I don't think I have to tell you what damage it can do over a long period of time."

"No, you don't."

"That's why you *must* force fluids down him — clean fluids, preferably boiled water that has cooled to lukewarm. Hold him down if you have to."

"Thank you, Doctor."

After he left, Faron woke and Reena spoke to him. She thought it very significant that the only words that had come from his mouth had been bitterness over his amputation. Reena had known as soon as she'd seen it that the handicap would be foremost in his mind, and the hardest to deal with. She'd heard the doctor's puzzlement about the fever, but after talking with Faron, it was clear that he really didn't care if he lived or died. Maybe, just maybe, seeing her would give him some hope of living.

When he'd lost consciousness again, Reena turned and buried herself in Hunter's arms.

Chapter Fifteen

Crescent Moon

Stone was afraid to leave Reena alone. Even when she stopped crying, he could see the tears still pooled in her eyes, ready to spill out again at any time.

Now that they had found Reena's uncle, Stone had no idea what she planned to do with him. Furthermore, he doubted she'd even considered it. Should they stay right where they were until Faron could travel, or should they go with the army? Custer had reluctantly been forced to call a temporary halt of the command to wait for fresh food being shipped upriver, but Stone knew they would be marching on either the next day or the day after.

He glanced over at Reena. She stared blankly in the direction of her uncle, eyes far away. Now was not the time to discuss what would happen tomorrow.

Stone turned to Del, who was sitting on an overturned crate and whittling. "Del, why don't you go see if you can find out what Custer's plan is tomorrow?"

"Okay. Why?"

"We need to know. I have no idea if this area is safe for us to make camp, or if we should follow the army."

"What makes you think Custer will tell me what his plan is?"

Stone grimaced. "I didn't mean ask *him*. Ask around. Maybe one of his scouts knows." Then he saw Del grin and knew he was only joking.

"I'll see what I can do." Del sheathed the knife and stepped outside, then stopped. "On second thought, Hunter," he said without turning around, "why don't you ask the general himself?"

"What do you mean?"

"I mean here he comes right now."

Stone looked out and saw Custer striding toward them. At his side were two men, one of whom went running off after Custer murmured an order to him. The other man bore a striking resemblance to the general, and Stone knew that he was Tom, Custer's brother. Unlike Custer's buckskin, Tom wore the cavalry uniform of dark blue blouse and tan trousers with a yellow stripe down the sides. He wore his blouse open at the top and carelessly buttoned. A smile seemed to be constantly playing at his mouth. Stone remembered hearing that Tom had won the prestigious Medal of Honor in the war, a glory that even Custer couldn't claim. Stone wondered if Custer was jealous of his brother because of that.

They came right up to Del and Stone. During the introductions Custer didn't shake hands, but Tom did. His grip was strong and sure.

"So," Custer said, placing his hands on his hips, "you're our new visitors. I was beginning to wonder if O'Donnell had dreamed up his niece."

"It was a long journey," Stone nodded.

"You're a Mountie, eh?"

"Yes, sir."

"I hear it's a fine outfit."

"We think so, sir."

"Ever do any Indian fighting?"

Stone remembered the renegade Red Wolf and nodded. "A little."

"Nothing like this, though."

It was a statement, not a question, and Stone didn't bother to answer. He was taller than Custer by about six inches. If it bothered the general to look up at him, he showed no sign of it. The man exuded a confidence that was almost surreal.

"Who *have* you been fighting?" Custer

asked suddenly.

Stone touched the bruise on his face gingerly. "We had some trouble on the river."

Custer nodded, watching him a moment, then he spun on Del. "How about you?"

"Sir?"

"Have you ever fought the red man?"

Del seemed surprised and pleased that Custer was interested in him. His chest swelled a bit as he answered, "A few. I'd prefer to be friendly with them, though. Easier on the scalp."

"Mmm. Sometimes that way is impossible," Custer said grimly, sweeping an arm around the area filled with troops. "Witness the result when the Sioux are unreasonable about staying in their assigned posts."

Stone wanted to tell him that the Sioux weren't in the army, and their "assigned posts" — to them — meant free movement on the prairie.

Custer swung his piercing gaze back to him, and his face changed. "You don't agree, Stone?"

"Well, now that you ask — no, sir."

Tom looked quickly at his brother, and Stone braced himself for some sort of outburst. Custer said nothing but again gave him a calculating once-over.

Finally he asked, "Where is O'Donnell's niece?"

"In the tent with him. He's not . . . doing well."

"I know. I've checked on him from time to time. Felt as if it were a bit my fault, him getting himself wounded."

"How's that, sir? How did it happen?"

Custer told Hunter of the hunting party at the beginning of the trek west. "The man claims it was Crazy Horse himself in that grove."

Stone was shocked. "Really?"

"I have my doubts about that, to tell you the truth." He took off his hat and scratched his head, revealing the famous auburn hair.

Stone had heard the stories about his hair being long and flowing, most of the time carrying a cinnamon scent. He was surprised to see it cut short.

Tom spoke for the first time. "Why would he lie about that, Autie? Maybe it *was* Crazy Horse."

Stone wondered why he'd called Custer "Autie," and reminded himself to ask Del about it later.

A captain rode up to them, dismounted, and saluted. "Scouting report, General."

"What is it?"

"Still the same news, sir. Plenty of travois and pony tracks, but they're old."

"Mmm. I expected as much."

"General, I must say that these tracks are the most we've ever seen. There must be . . ." the captain paused, calculating, ". . . over a thousand lodges."

For the first time Custer showed real emotion. "A thousand? You must be mistaken, Captain."

"I don't think so, sir. Even Bloody Knife agrees. The scouts are getting a bit antsy, I believe."

Custer waved a hand. "Leave the scouts to me, Captain. Dismissed."

The captain saluted and led his horse away.

Stone and Del exchanged identical glances, each thinking, *A thousand lodges? And he's not worried?*

"What plans do you gents have?" Tom Custer asked. He seemed as unconcerned as Custer about the news of over a thousand Indians passing through a couple of miles from where they were standing.

"I don't really know," Stone told him. "We were just wondering when the army would be moving on."

"As soon as possible," Custer assured him. "And I would strongly recommend that your party come along with us."

"That depends on Mr. O'Donnell's ability to travel."

Custer swiped at his flowing mustache with an index finger and smiled. "I wouldn't bet against that man in anything, Stone. Do you know him?"

"I haven't had the pleasure."

"Oh, it's a pleasure, all right. Take my word." Abruptly he swung on his brother. "Come, Tom. We have a lot to do. Gentlemen."

Stone watched them walk away arm in arm. Tom said something to Custer, who threw back his head and laughed heartily.

"Thick as thieves, those two," Del drawled.

"Oh?"

"Yep. Custer's got his nephew with him, too, count on it. And his brother-in-law."

"Nepotism, eh?"

"What?"

"Never mind."

"There you go, throwin' them fancy words around like they was gold. If it ain't you, it's Vic." His bushy eyebrows came together in sudden concentration. "I wonder how that limey's doin'?"

Dirk Becker was trying his best to keep

the whole Mountie troop from being massacred. Vickersham's fiery words to the Sarcee chief, falling just short of calling him a liar, had thrown a pall of distrust over the area like a blanket.

Trying to ignore the spear that was pointed at his throat from only a foot away, Becker told Jerry Potts to translate. "Tell Chief Tall Bear that the white chief's words are spoken in anger. He does not mean to insult Tall Bear."

Potts, who was the only man without a Sarcee weapon trained on him, spoke in his usual lazy, calm voice.

Tall Bear barely acknowledged the words and kept his fierce gaze on Vic. Despite his name, Tall Bear was only of average height. Around his neck hung a necklace made from tufts of black hair. Becker hoped it was bear or buffalo hair and not human.

Vickersham sat calmly on his horse and returned Tall Bear's black gaze without blinking.

"Vic!" Becker whispered. "Back down. Now!"

"He's hiding something, Becker. I know it."

"Then let him go on hiding it! It's better than having your scalp grace the front of his lodge."

"They won't attack," Vic said with calm assurance.

"How do you know that?"

Vic ignored the question and asked the chief, "Does Tall Bear forget the man who saved his son from the bad white men?"

Potts translated, and everyone saw Tall Bear's stunned reaction.

"Yes," Vic nodded. "It was me. Last summer. He was about to be taken by them and put in prison, and I saved him. Does Tall Bear remember this?"

Tall Bear replied, "That man was you?"

"Yes."

Potts looked at Vickersham strangely before interpreting.

The result of this news was instantaneous. Tall Bear ordered his warriors to back down, then told Vic that "the fierce Sioux" had gone south from the Sarcee village. To Vic's embarrassment, the chief offered gifts of furs, stone jewelry, and food. Vic refused politely, saying they had to be on their way.

When they were back on the prairie and headed south, Vickersham ordered a full gallop. Becker knew they were at least fifty miles from the border, with no hope of reaching it this day. It was nearing twilight, a dangerous time to be traveling so fast because of the shadowy prairie dog holes that could break a horse's leg. Becker knew Vic was aware of that.

Something else occurred to Becker, and he eased his mount beside Vickersham. "That was a brave thing, rescuing that Indian kid from those men. Strange I haven't heard about it before."

Vic said nothing.

"I seem to remember the story some time last year, but I sure didn't know it was you."

"It wasn't."

"Then you lied to him."

Vickersham turned a cool gaze on him. "I did what was necessary to get information on the men we're tracking."

"We don't even know if that Bad Weasel had anything to do with that woman's death."

"We don't know that he didn't, either."

Becker looked around to be sure they were still out of hearing distance from the other men. "Listen to me, Vic. When we start lying to the Indians in this country, we'll end up no better off than the Americans. For that matter, these tribes will be just like the Sioux and Cheyenne and every other one down there. They'll be defending their land against treachery. Is that the way you want it?"

"We'll use any means at our disposal to arrest criminals, Becker. I didn't make the rules."

"That's strange. I didn't see anything about lying to the natives in a manual."

"I don't like that word."

"All right . . . how about manipulation? Is that better?"

Vic's jaw clenched. "You're on dangerous ground, Dirk. I'm still your superior officer, and this is an official patrol. What did I tell you about crossing the line?"

"I'm a junior non-commissioned officer, that's true, but I can still question your methods."

"Officially, yes, but not out in the field. File a report on me when we get back to the fort if you like."

Becker was shocked at Vic's cold and uncaring tone. "Use any means available, eh?"

"That's right. If you don't use your initiative, you'll never rise above a constable, Becker."

"That's how you got your commission? Initiative?" It was the wrong thing to say, and Becker knew it as soon as the words left his mouth. Vic's arrogant tone had caused him to react without thinking.

When the Mounties first formed, they lacked enough experienced officers to fill the ranks. It was no secret that some men received their commissions purely by way of their wealth, political status, or title. Vic fell into the latter category, since his father held the prestigious title of earl in Britain.

Vickersham's reaction wasn't what he expected. He raised a hand and stopped the galloping troop, then faced them with a stony look. "Mr. Potts and Constable Becker will be riding ahead to scout the Sioux we are following. Nelson and Steers will accompany them."

The two sub-constables came to the front and reined in beside Potts. Becker stared at Vickersham, wondering what this new order meant.

"Did you hear the order, Constable?" Vickersham asked flatly.

"Yes, sir." Becker decided that he'd done all he could for his friend and moved behind Vic's horse toward Potts. With a curt nod to the scout, Becker led them ahead.

Megan sat on the front porch of her house and tried to concentrate on the Bible she was reading but wasn't having much success. She shifted uncomfortably in the caped yellow dress she was wearing made of wool, which was much too heavy for the warm day. Twinkle, asleep at her feet, felt her movement, looked up at her with mud-colored eyes, and stretched her legs.

"You have such a hard life, Twinkle, I don't know how you can stand it." Megan smiled at her own words, but it quickly faded. *I've been married for just over a week. If I'm still a newlywed, why am I so sad?*

The answer, when she dared to think about it, was simple. Why was Vic so upset over a woman he'd been intimate with so long ago? Was it guilt? Fear? Hidden feelings?

Megan tried to shake off her sullen mood by checking on the roses she'd planted in front of the porch fence. Twinkle lazily followed her down the steps, tagging along as she always did when Megan was outside. The rose bushes, given to her by Mrs. Howe from the boardinghouse, were showing signs of life. An ant mound was starting to develop at the end of the row, and Megan made a mental note to shovel it out. Absently she fingered the leaves of the bushes, her mind elsewhere.

Vic was out there on the prairie, rolling around like a loose cannon on a ship's deck. Megan had never known him to be so subdued and disturbed as he'd been the last few days, so she couldn't venture a guess as to his mood when he was away from her. She had a feeling that he was being hard on his men, by the evidence of Dirk's reactions. She was glad Dirk was with him wherever they were.

He doesn't love you.

"Stop it," she said aloud, plucking a dead leaf from one of the bushes.

He loved her.

"That's not true. He *married* me."

Maybe she wouldn't have him. Maybe he asked her.

A small growl of frustration escaped from Megan's throat.

Twinkle's huge ears raised, zeroing in on Megan's confusing sounds.

"I'm not angry at you. I'm angry at me." She reached out and scratched behind one of Twinkle's ears.

The nagging voice in Megan's head had tried the tactic over and over. She couldn't, however, prepare herself for the things it said, no matter how many times she heard it.

Vic had seemed so happy with her, and they'd both been overjoyed now that their newfound faith had brought such peace and harmony into their lives. Was it not enough for him? Was he disappointed with his new life? The foolish voice had tried to whisper to her that maybe Vic had been interested in her father's money, but that was beyond all reason. Vic cared nothing for money, and even if he did, he knew that Megan would never ask her father for help unless it was a dire emergency.

Then what was it? Was *she* displeasing to him in some way? She tried to envision in what manner she'd changed since the ceremony, but she could think of nothing. The only thing she could imagine was that she'd pretty much decorated the house on her own without any input from Vic at all.

Megan shook her head. That was too trivial.

Twinkle dutifully followed her around to the small shed at the back of the house. The shovel handle still shone a new ivory color from the virgin ash it had been cut from, but the iron was grimy from when Megan had buried the roses.

In the rosebed, she dug deep beneath the anthill and carried the mound to the far backside of the house at the edge of a small creek. For a moment she contemplated throwing the whole hill into the water. Could ants swim, or would they drown?

She didn't know, but she *did* know she was being childish.

Megan dumped the dirt a few feet from the creek. She didn't watch to see in which direction the ants scurried away.

That night, Megan prayed for Vic and the men he led — for safety, for wisdom, a safe return — just as she did every time Vic was away leading a patrol. But this night was more earnest and pleading, more *concentrated* than ever before. She sensed that Vic had reached an important crossroads in life that he'd never experienced before and was having trouble coming to grips with it. He was standing on the brink of some discovery — about himself, his job, life in general, she didn't know — but she was determined to help him through it in any way possible.

While she was on her knees praying, the thought occurred to her that Vic's troubles had started, and had some connection, with the discovery of the dead woman's body. Fran. The woman he knew and hadn't told her about. But Megan knew that interruption was Satan attempting to intrude on her prayer time, and she banished him as quickly as she had the ants in the garden. The only thought she gave to the idea was to acknowledge that Fran's death had triggered something inside her husband that had been dormant for a long time. It had nothing to do with their relationship itself.

After almost an hour, Megan got up and began making preparations for bed. She felt infinitely better and silently asked the Lord to forgive her for not coming to Him earlier. The whole matter was in His hands now, not hers.

Just before extinguishing the parlor lamp, Megan paused to admire a thin moon outside the window, low on the purple horizon. It was hanging heavy side down, grinning at her. She grinned back. Then she sensed rather than heard soft footsteps on the porch, and it wasn't the thud of Twinkle's small hooves.

The door rapped with three knocks.

"Who is it?"

"It's Jenny."

Megan opened the door, surprised. Jenny's short light brown hair was slightly disheveled, as if she'd been in bed and had just gotten up. "What is it? Is something wrong?"

"There's been another murder."

He felt the strength and the power surge

through him like the humming and vibrating of railroad tracks in the path of a locomotive. Even *that* didn't really describe it. It didn't convey the sweaty palms, the knees knocking together, every nerve standing on end and tingling with sensation.

He didn't know why it had come to him so late in life, though he wasn't an old man by any means. Young, in fact, to his way of thinking. But now he knew. Fulfillment wasn't something that you worked toward, planned for, sweated for — it was a thing you reached out and grabbed. Until recently, he just hadn't known how.

Now he did.

And it was so simple. Too bad it was against their law. He had his own laws to follow now.

No longer would he be forced to admire others who were more confident than him, who looked down on others just as they gazed down their noses at him, who walked through life as if they were untouchable. Now *they* could admire *him*.

He would only tell certain ones about the strength — the ones who saw its glory through fear-clouded eyes. They would stand in awe that one solitary man could be so powerful, just like the other two.

It was the fear he liked the most. In all his life no human beings had displayed pure fear toward him as the woman and man who'd witnessed the strength. Animals had, of course, because he'd always shown *them* who was in control. But the cowering of animals meant nothing to him now that he'd seen the fear in the eyes of humans who'd wronged him.

Riding his horse through the dark on the way to his cabin, he looked up at the orange tinted moon split in two by a single strip of black cloud. His father had told him that he'd been born one night when the moon started out full, but later had turned to a thin silver crescent, then full again. He hadn't understood that — how could that happen? — and he'd shrugged it off as some sort of mistake. That night had been bad enough — his mother had died giving him life. But ever since his father related to him the events of his birth, he'd often stare at the moon for an hour or two when it was swollen to its limit, hoping he could see the same thing. He wondered if his mother saw it before she died, but he'd never thought to ask his father about it.

Tonight there was no chance of the phenomenon, so he paid the moon no attention. Then, when he was almost home, he began to think of it again. A virgin moon, on its way toward fullness yet again for no one knew how many times through history. A renewing, a coming of age, a blossoming. . . .

Just like him.

Maybe he and the moon had more in common than he'd originally thought.

Chapter Sixteen

A Long Night for Reena

Faron woke in the middle of the night, calling out her name.

Asleep on a chair with two army issue blankets covering her, Reena sat up instantly. The glow from a few low-burning fires outside the tent tossed strange dancing reflections on the side. For a moment she had no idea where she was.

"Reena, are you there, darlin'?"

"Yes, I'm here." Her surroundings came back to her, and she rose, rubbing her face to clear it from sleep. Shivering, she turned back to the chair and draped one of the blankets around her shoulders before going to the side of the bed. "What's the matter, Uncle Faron? Do you need something?"

"Ah, you *are* here. Thought I'd dreamt ye."

Reena lit the small lamp by the bed to a low setting and looked at him. His face was pale but no longer coated with a sheen of sweat. The bandages on his arm had seeped a bit and would need changing before long. His eyes glittered like diamonds in the dim light as he focused on her.

"I'm not, am I?"

"Not what, Uncle?"

"Dreamin'?"

Reena smiled. "No, I'm here and you're alive."

The stump moved and he gave a pained look, then he brought the hand up on his other arm and scratched his nose. He noticed her look and said, "Got to get used to doin' everything with this one hand, even scratchin' me nose. It's a sad state, lass."

"I'm sorry."

"Don't ye be sorry fer me, Reena. I've enough self-pity in meself to cover all o' ye. Blasted sawbones . . ."

Reena didn't know what to say, so she made her hands busy by pouring water in a cup and letting him take a few sips. His lips were red and cracked. She gave him time to swallow, then made him drink some more.

"Pour some on me lips, lass. I don't care if it runs down me neck. That's the girl." He pressed his lips together appreciatively. "Ah, that feels wonderful. What's the date?" he asked abruptly.

"The date?"

"Aye."

"It's the sixteenth, I believe."

"Of what?"

"June."

He thought a moment, then said, "I take it it's still the year of '76, eh?"

Reena laughed. "Yes, it's still 1876."

"A hundred years," he muttered, shaking his head.

Reena didn't know what he meant and was beginning to wonder if he was still in the grip of a hallucinating fever. She felt his forehead and found it hot, but not the furnace it had been when she'd checked last.

"This country of yours is only a hundred years old, girl. Don't ye find that amazin'? It's unthinkable to someone from the old land. Are ye doin' anything special for the Fourth o' July, Reena?"

"I don't know, really." Reena retrieved her chair and carried it to the other side of the bed so his amputated arm wouldn't be between them. It seemed to have a presence all its own, and he kept glancing down at it as he talked. It distracted her also because she was trying to be careful not to look at it.

Faron watched her strangely. "It's your country's independence day, and you've no plans to celebrate it? That's unnatural."

"Uncle Faron, I live in Canada now, remember?"

"So? Do they have laws against you celebratin'?"

"No, I don't think so."

"There ye are, then. Hmpf . . . I wish Ireland had an independence day. I guarantee there'd be some fireworks. Enough to put the Chinese to shame, I'd wager. As it is, the limeys make us celebrate kings' and queens' birthdays and the like."

Reena was glad to see him awake and talking, but his voice was still very weak. She wondered if she should make him rest, then thought of how silly that was — *make* Uncle Faron do something? She knew he would be the worst patient she'd ever encounter, including the extremely stubborn Hunter Stone.

Faron yawned hugely, but he refused to drop the subject. "A hundred measly years old, and already had, what, two wars? Three if you count fightin' the lobsterbacks 'til '81 or '83. Then this last business" — he stopped and his face lost some of its animation — "mercy, that was a bad one. All those lads killed — all

Americans, mind you — pitiful." He closed his eyes slowly.

Reena waited to see if he would go on, but his breathing slowed and became deeper. She pulled the blanket up over him and tucked it around him tighter. He hadn't been awake long enough for her to warm some broth, so she made a mental note to make that the first thing to do when he woke again.

"Prussians, that's what ye remind me of," he mumbled, eyes still closed. "Always spoilin' for a war. Don't matter who with, mind you, just wantin' one. Now it's the red man's turn to feel the bite."

His words bothered her as she extinguished the lamp. What he'd said was true, she realized, but she didn't like being included in the bloodthirsty group he'd just described. Was his the common opinion of the courts of Europe, or just that of a cranky old Irishman?

It seemed as if she'd just fallen asleep when Faron woke again. She gave him some more water and watched him to see that he didn't choke. He looked uncomfortable lying on his back so much, and she reminded herself to check for bedsores. Dr. Denton seemed to know what he was talking about, but Reena wasn't sure if he'd had the time to give Faron the proper attention. So much to do, so much to think of. . . .

"Was there someone with ye, Reena? When I saw you first?"

"Yes. Two of my friends brought me down here."

"Friends, eh?"

"Yes." She knew what was coming before the words were out of his mouth.

"Have ye snagged a lad yet?"

"Well, I don't know if 'snag' is the right word —"

"Ye know what I mean."

Reena sat down and took his hand. It felt hotter than before. "I care for someone very much."

"And him? Does he return it?"

"Yes."

"Is he one o' the ones who came with ye?"

"Yes. His name is Hunter Stone."

"Stone, huh? Sounds like a limey name."

"He considers himself a Canadian now."

Faron had barely opened his eyes while talking and seemed much more subdued and weak. "Is he a good man, Reena? A God-fearin' man?"

"Yes he is, Uncle."

"Good. I'm not in much shape to pin a man's ears back who was mistreatin' ye, but I'd give it a go if I had to."

Reena smiled, but he didn't see it. She watched him shift uncomfortably and decided to give him some more laudanum for his pain. He drank some, made a face, then reluctantly downed the rest of it.

"Talk to me, Reena. Tell me about me family. Take me mind off this monstrosity," he said as he held up the bandaged stub with contempt.

Reena wondered how long it took for someone to come to terms with such a traumatic event and decided to let his crude comment pass. Deep down, she was aware that he knew the truth. If it hadn't been amputated, he would be dead. But would he rather be dead? Surely not.

"First you eat something," Reena told him. She prepared some broth and fed him while she began telling about Megan — of her bad marriage ending in Louis' death, her decision to stay at Fort Macleod and teach school, and her recent marriage to Vic.

"She's happy then?" Faron asked hopefully.

"Yes, very."

"Good for her. I had me doubts about

how she would turn out. I'm glad I was wrong."

His forehead furrowed with worry as Reena related her brother Liam's ill-fated journey into Canada. When she finished, Faron grunted. "I always knew that boy was a wild one somewhere inside. But he's doin' well now?"

Reena nodded. "Set to graduate from West Point in two years."

"Glad he sowed his oats, but aren't ye worried he'll be sent out here to fight Indians when he gets out?"

"Yes. But I don't want to worry about that until the time comes, if it does. Right now, I'm just glad he's not in jail."

"This Stone fella arrested him, eh?"

"He was only doing his job, Uncle. I didn't understand that at the time, but I do now."

Faron watched her closely.

"What's the matter?"

"Nothin'."

Reena talked until the sky outside began to turn deep blue with the approaching sunrise, and Faron's eyelids drooped nearly shut. Men began to stir outside, making breakfast and preparations for the day ahead. Hunter and Del were just outside the tent sleeping on cots, and she wondered if they were awake. Her eyes felt gritty and tired from the long night and the release of pent-up worry over her uncle.

When he drifted off to sleep again, Reena debated whether to stay awake and begin her day, or try to catch some more sleep.

Within minutes she was fast asleep again.

Stone and Del drank coffee prepared by Private Norton, who'd stopped by to check on Faron. The army camp was bristling with activity on the foggy morning. The air carried the musky scent of the muddy Yellowstone and wild prairie flowers. As they sipped their coffee, they watched some of the men do some last-minute fishing for trout on the banks of the river. The activity of the camp was different from the day before when they'd arrived, so Stone didn't have to wonder about Custer's plans — they were to move out as soon as possible.

"What do you think, Del? Do we stay or go with them?"

"I don't know. If we stay, there's just you and me against whatever comes along. We're mighty close to Cheyenne country." His hat was balanced jauntily on the back of his head, revealing sleep-strewn hair that stuck out like stray branches.

"Faron would be all right, wouldn't he? He's already come this far bouncing along in a wagon."

"I'd expect so. But I ain't no doctor."

Stone drained the last of his coffee and flung out the dregs. Rolling up the sleeves of his shirt, he said, "I suppose Reena should have a say in it."

"Yep. Though we might not like it."

They went back to Faron's tent. Stone had checked on them earlier and found them both sleeping soundly. A few times during the night he'd heard them talking, so he knew Reena would be exhausted when she awoke. He admired her stamina. The trip had been long and hard, and she'd been under the added strain of worry the whole way.

Inside the tent, he found her in the exact same position as before. She was sitting up in the chair, head turned awkwardly to her left. Her eyelids fluttered slightly as if she were dreaming. Faron, however, was watching them silently. Stone started to say something, but Faron put a finger to his lips and cut his eyes over to Reena.

Stone went to the bed, leaned down, and whispered, "Do you need anything?"

"A little water, if'n ye don't mind."

Stone gave him some, then sat down by

the bed. "Your bandages need changing."

"It'll wait a while longer." His whispered voice was hoarse and strained. "Poor lass. I kept her up half the night with me foolish talk." His eyes came around to Stone and Del, gauging them openly.

"I'm Hunter Stone, and this is Del Dekko."

"I know who ye are. Thank ye for bringing Reena to me."

"We hear Crazy Horse shot you," Del said.

"Nope, you heard wrong. Rumors in an army are like politicians' promises — there's too many of 'em, and the facts are always sideways and turned around."

"So you didn't see Crazy Horse?"

"That ain't true, either."

Del gave him an exasperated look. "You got shot, didn't you?"

"Aye, and right I know it."

"By Indians?"

"Aye."

"So who were they?"

"Didn't catch their names. And keep your voice down, if ye please."

Del turned to Stone and asked, "Did you ever in all your life have more trouble talkin' to someone other than an Irishman?"

"Can't say as I have."

"Me neither. Now, Mr. O'Donnell —"

"Call me Faron. We're about the same age."

Del looked offended. "I doubt that."

"Well, you *do* look older, but I wasn't goin' to say anything —"

"That's not what I meant!"

"Shhhh!" Faron and Stone hissed together.

Del shook his head. "Whatever. Now, Faron, we've established that you might have seen Crazy Horse, that he didn't shoot you, that an Indian *did* shoot you, but you didn't catch his name —"

"Two Indians."

"What?"

"Two Indians shot me. Fine-looking lads, too. I suppose it's best to be shot by a good-looking man rather than an ugly one, don't you think, Stone?"

"Absolutely."

Del was impatient to get the story. "All right, two Indians shot you — does all that sound about right?"

"I suppose."

"Well, does it or doesn't it?"

"Aye, it does," Faron said.

"Crazy Horse didn't have a gun or what?"

"Oh, he had one all right. He just didn't use it."

"Why not?"

Faron yawned deeply. "You'll have to ask him about that. I didn't have the time nor the inclination at the moment."

Reena stirred on the chair and all three men looked over at her. She opened her eyes and squinted against the incoming light, then stretched her arms over her head. "What time is it?"

"About eight," Stone told her. "Why don't you try to get some more sleep while we pack up?" He deliberately asked the question that way to see her reaction.

"No, I've got to get up and . . . what did you say?"

Stone told her about the army moving out and leaving them alone in dangerous country. "So Del and I think we should stay with them. Safety in numbers, you know."

Reena stood and went to Faron's side on the other side of the bed from Hunter and Del. "Uncle Faron, how do you feel about that?"

"Dunno. I've spent the last ten minutes havin' a right silly conversation with Dekko here. Haven't been asked about leavin'."

"Now, wait a minute —" Del began.

Stone broke in. "So what do you think about it now, sir?"

"I'll do whatever me nurse orders, I'll wager."

All eyes turned to Reena. She looked at the three of them in turn and finally stopped when her eyes met Stone's. "I don't know. Would you make the decision please?"

It was not a decision Stone really wanted to be responsible for. What if her uncle died from his poor condition or some unseen hazard? What if they went with Custer and were *still* attacked by Indians? From the evidence he'd heard himself, which Custer had rejected out of hand, the army could be vastly underrating the numbers against them.

"Hunter?"

He knew all the "what ifs" in the world would haunt him if he let them gain a solid foothold. "We go with the army," he told them, nodding firmly.

Two traders' boats had dropped anchor near the army the night before, where the Yellowstone met the Powder River. The soldiers, knowing that they would be in the field for the next couple of weeks, stocked up on tobacco, licorice root, thread, needles, and any other item they could think of. Many bought pen and paper to write a last letter to loved ones.

Reena watched the men writing while sitting in the wagon they'd loaded Faron into. The soldiers sat all around the river-banks, some with their backs against tall lodgepole pines, some sprawled out on the brown grass. Some wrote quickly and without pause, either because they were in a hurry or they wanted to get their thoughts out as fast as they came. Others were more languid, scratching a few lines and then staring off into the gray, overcast sky.

Reena wondered what they could possibly be thinking. As she sat there, she thought about what she would write to her family if she knew that it could very well be the last communication they would ever receive from her. She decided that she would be like the slow writers, painstakingly thinking out every word so that there would be no misunderstanding about how she was feeling in her last days. Then she thought about how much she would have to say in a short amount of time and knew she would write as fast as she could so as not to lose a word. She was glad she wasn't having to write those letters.

Stone and Del had sought out Custer to

see where he wanted them in the line of formation. Too far back would cause immense clouds of dust that would be dangerous to Faron's health. Too far forward would put them in the line of fire should they be attacked. Reena was hoping for somewhere in the middle, where it would seem safer. Her eyes took in the sprawling prairie before them. Once they left the river, there would be little cover in the form of trees or naturally defensive terrain. However, she thought, that could work in their favor also, since the Indians would have none either.

Deep in her heart, she was terribly afraid of the Sioux and Cheyenne. Her only experience with Indians had been with tribes friendly to the white man. She'd heard the tales of butchery and massacre — committed on both sides, of course — and of the high value placed on white female captives by the Indians. Megan had told her a long time ago that she'd heard about white women taking their own lives instead of being resigned to such a harsh fate. Reena knew she couldn't do that because of her faith in God, but the thought still produced a coiled snake of dread in her stomach.

A stiff breeze carried the strangely combined odor of dank river and sharp-scented pine through the humid air. Reena turned and checked on Faron in the bed of the wagon. She'd managed to make him eat some more broth after a few protests and changed his bandages. The sight of the amputated arm had been shocking despite her attempt to prepare herself for it. She'd swallowed hard and tried to keep from making a face, but Faron had been watching and had to have seen her disgust. Reena had seen wounds before, but nothing as graphic as her uncle's surgery.

Soon after she was finished, Dr. Denton stopped by and was surprised that she'd attempted it without him. He'd inspected her work and said, "Couldn't have done better myself."

Reena had found some comfort in that, but the grisly detail had stayed with her all through preparing Faron to travel.

Faron, propped up on two folded blankets and a pillow to relieve congestion in his chest, was peering at her through half-closed lids. "You've a haunted look, darlin'. What's in that pretty head of yours, lass?"

"Oh, nothing."

"A mighty fine thing to be speakin' falsely to a man who may be dyin'."

"Uncle Faron, don't talk like that!"

"It's true and you know it. That old buzzard Denton looked at me this mornin' like he was surprised I was still above ground."

Reena stepped down from the wagon seat and drew some water from a two-gallon pot Del had borrowed from a company cook. Tipping the ladle to his mouth, he accepted it grudgingly. She told him sternly, "If Dr. Denton saw you yesterday, he probably *did* think you were dying." Then she added in a softer tone, "I did too last night."

He watched her over the ladle with calculating blue eyes, then began to sputter. "I swear, Reena, you're tryin' to drown me! Why don't you just throw me in the river and be done with it?"

"I'm sorry," she said, then wiped the spilled water from his bearded chin gently.

Faron suddenly grinned at her. "Can ye see me tryin' to swim with only one wing? I'd be goin' around in circles over and over, then sink like a stone."

"Uncle Faron, why are you being so morbid?"

His good humor vanished instantly. "Why? Why, you ask me?"

A few of the soldiers close to the wagon glanced their way curiously.

"All my life I've asked nothin' from nobody and been content with that. Now I'm bein' tended to like a five-year-old with a runny nose. I can feel the fever burnin' me flesh off me bones as sure as fire, and if that don't kill me, I've got *this* to look forward to," he growled, holding up the stump.

Reena had never seen such a look of pain and despair as she witnessed on her uncle's face at that moment. Stone and Del walked up from behind her, and she was secretly glad for their interruption.

Del said cheerily, "We're up close to the front of the line today, and guess who we're travelin' with? Uh-oh, what's wrong with you two? You look like you've seen a ghost."

The sound of equipment clanging and raised men's voices intensified as the order was passed along the line to prepare to move. The smell of doused campfires permeated the air.

Del gave Hunter a puzzled look.

Hunter interpreted Reena's discomfort correctly and changed the subject. "We need to get moving toward Custer's detail. He wanted us to ride with him, for whatever reason." He and Del moved off to inspect the wagon harness and load a few items that Hunter had purchased from one of the traders.

Reena was grateful for his smooth transition from an uncomfortable silence to busy handwork. She tucked Faron's blanket around him snugly, avoiding his eyes, then placed the cover back on the waterpot. Finally she smiled at him. "It's going to be all right, Uncle Faron. I'll take good care of you."

His eyes softened. "I know. You'll have to forgive me moanin', Reena. It's nothin' short of a shame what happened to me, but it's not your fault nor anyone else's. When I get in a self-pityin' mood, just bash me with that heavy water ladle and I'll come around."

"You've got a right to feel —"

"Now don't go ruinin' me apology, lass. It was so poetic. I despise whinin' in other men, and even more so in meself."

Reena gave him a kiss on the cheek and told him in a heavy Irish accent, "Weel, I think 'yourself' is wonderful."

Chapter Seventeen

Crazy Horse

Captain Borland let Sheffield off the *Rose Maiden* a few miles before reaching Gibbon's troops. The river flowed carelessly by the inlet, carrying along a large tree branch that bumped against the boat's port side. Borland was totally against what Sheffield was doing and said so.

"Preacher, I think you're making a grave mistake. You got some kind of death wish?"

Sheffield was packing his horse's saddlebags with food that Borland had been kind enough to give him. "No, I don't."

"I'm not one to take on another man's business, but this harebrained idea of yours goes beyond all reason." Borland had a rope in his large, strong hands and absently tied knots as he talked. Then he gestured to the vast prairie with it. "Out there's a large contingent of Indians who don't care to be trifled with by a white man right now. And you want to ride up to them and just say, 'Howdy'?"

"That's about it, I suppose," Jack said.

"Well, I doubt you'll get any more words out before they tie you to a post and light a match under you."

Sheffield finished tying down the bags and removed his hat. The constant breeze blew his red hair in all directions. "I'll tell you like I told my friends, Captain — I've got to try."

"You know, believe it or not, there's worse ways to die than burning alive. You could say the Sioux have perfected ways to make a man last a long time before death."

Jack was growing irritated, though he knew the man meant well. "Why all this talk of death? I prefer to concentrate on living, if you don't mind."

"Going out there alone isn't my idea of concentrating on living, but I'll oblige you." His chocolate brown eyes grew wide as he watched Sheffield unbuckle his gun belt. "What are you doing?"

Sheffield handed him the belt. "I won't be needing this."

"Are you *insane*, man?"

"I don't think so."

Borland's mouth worked like a fish out of water, but no sound emerged.

"I won't be shooting any game, thanks to

your kind generosity."

"Look, Reverend, I'm not even going to mention the Indians because that's too obvious, but there happens to be bears, wildcats, and wolves out there, too. You're heading into the Bighorn Mountains where it's wild. Do you understand?"

"I understand," Jack said calmly.

The *Rose Maiden*'s engine came to life with a roar following a quick check by the crew. Across the river, two white herons rose into the air majestically, startled by the noise.

Borland seemed to come to some conclusion that involved giving up his attempt to reason with Sheffield. He held out his hand. "Good luck to you, sir. My prayers may not carry much weight with the Almighty, but I'll say one for you tonight."

"Thank you."

Borland nodded and went back to his beloved boat.

Sheffield led his horse to the top of the embankment and mounted. Looking down, he saw Captain Borland pause at the railing of the boat and lift a hand.

Sheffield waved back. Even from a distance he could see the puzzlement still on Borland's face as he turned and made his way into the wheelhouse.

If Sheffield were to stop and think it through — truly consider the dangers involved with what he was doing — he would find himself mildly puzzled, too. Never in his life had he accepted such perilous circumstances with so little regard for his own safety. The only situation that could be compared to it was when he'd struck out for the North-West Territories to spread God's Word to the Indians. But the Blackfoot and Assiniboine tribes were known to be peaceful and accepting of the white men, while the Sioux were on the warpath.

As he rode along now, with the Bighorn Mountains in sight, he felt peace instead of fear. Calm instead of panic. He took pleasure in the black-eyed susans he saw growing on a bare slope, a prairie falcon making wide loops over the plain, searching for prey, and the scream of an unseen hawk near a grove of cottonwoods.

He felt fine all morning, until he spotted the buzzards.

Ash-gray clouds had taken over the blue sky during his ride, and the air had become stuffy and hot. He'd just spurred his horse out of a dried-out riverbed and started up a large hill when he saw the black scavenger birds. It looked like about ten of them, and whatever the carcass they had their eyes on lay just over the crest of the hill. He stopped the horse and thought a moment. So many buzzards meant a larger-than-average carcass, and therefore bigger predators that could be feeding on it.

Jack patted the horse's neck. "Do you smell anything, boy? Any bears on the other side of this hill?"

The gelding seemed to enjoy the attention but showed no signs of distress.

"No, huh? I sure hope you're right."

He started the horse with a nudge from his boot heels. A large raindrop landed — *splat!* — in his ear, startling him, and it was immediately followed by more. He donned his charcoal-colored slicker while riding just as the heavens let loose a downpour.

From the top of the hill, he saw buzzards on the ground in the valley before him. They completely covered whatever meal they'd found, which was indeed larger than average. With their close proximity to one another, they resembled a huge black anthill on the bare plains.

The rain stopped for a moment, and then just as abruptly began again. Sheets of it swept over the feeding buzzards, but they took no notice. One of them must have sensed his presence because he turned his huge beak in Sheffield's direction, considered him for a moment, then went back to his meal calmly.

A huge crack of thunder rent the air, causing the birds to scatter.

Jack grimaced at what they left on the ground. It was the corpse of a man, or what was left of a man. Red and blue cotton clothing fluttered in the strong breeze. It was barefooted, with both feet turned inward at awkward angles. The bloody hands extended from tattered shirt cuffs as if he were crawling forward when he died. It looked like someone had tipped a scarecrow over on its face.

When the birds realized the noise was from heaven instead of man, they quickly gathered around the body again. Sheffield spurred the horse into a run toward them, scattering them skyward. He was aware that he was screaming at them and waving his hat, but his eyes were on all the arrows around and in the body. When he jumped from the back of the horse, the smell hit him and he gagged.

The wind whipped the slicker around his legs and slapped at his thighs painfully. He barely managed to catch his hat before it was blown away. Jack stood over the figure, hands clenching and unclenching, unsure of what he was doing. It was obvious the man had been dead for some time. Jack felt bad he couldn't bury him because he had absolutely no tools to dig a grave.

He shivered violently, and not just from the cold rain.

Do I want to die this kind of death? Alone, tortured, unable to convince my killers that I'm only here to help? He stood there for a long time, unaware that his knuckles were white from squeezing the reins in his hands unmercifully, and his eyes contained a far-off gaze that saw nothing, yet everything.

Eventually Sheffield said a quick prayer, turned from the sight, and mounted the horse again. The pleasantness of the morning had turned to a hard, charcoal shell that enclosed and swallowed him.

Crazy Horse squatted on the ground in front of Black Buffalo Woman's lodge, gazing upon the young girl with deep affection. She was playing with a quirt and small buffalo hide drum, inventing some sort of game, the rules of which existed only in her head. Her long, ginger brown hair blew around her intent face in the breeze. The bones of her spine formed a neat row down her back as she leaned over the drum, muttering.

Crazy Horse smiled, then quickly sobered and looked around. He was surrounded by women doing odd chores — cleaning tepees, cooking, tending to ponies — and no one seemed to notice he was there. But they were aware of him. He was sure the gossip would be spreading that night like a prairie fire.

Crazy Horse didn't care. He had been the object of idle gossip many times before and would be again until he died. Though he commanded great respect and awe, he knew the People regarded him as they would a pet wolf — good to have around for protection if cornered in an attack, but just wild and unpredictable enough to regard with caution.

If he hadn't felt a burning responsibility for his people, if his natural tendency toward leadership wasn't apparent to others, he would be content to be a nomad, alone and free to do as he chose. But he'd known at a very early age that wasn't to be.

By the time he reached early adolescence, he hadn't had the dream. He'd had the simple nightdreams that everyone experienced, not the warrior's dream that came after fasting and self-denial, the one that defined his future and provided an unshakable sense of self-worth. His friends had all gone through it and received their names, but Crazy Horse was still known as Curly, the name he'd been given at infancy.

For two days he'd fasted and kept himself awake by placing sharp stones under his body when he had to lie down. Nothing came to him — no visions, no dreams — and he was about to give up when the man on the horse appeared, riding out of a lake. The horse kept changing colors as it floated above the ground. The rider wore plain leggings and a simple shirt. His face was unpainted. A single feather decorated his hair, a small brown stone was tied behind his ear.

He told Curly never to wear decorations, and before going into battle, he should throw some dust all over his horse and himself. Then he would never be killed by a bullet or an enemy.

All the while the man and horse floated, brushing aside constant attacks from a shadowy enemy. He rode straight through them, triumphant, but several times the horse and rider were held back by his own people, but he shook them off and rode on.

Finally, after what seemed countless victories, the people closed in around him, grabbing and pulling, dragging him into their embrace.

When he woke, Curly told his dream to his father, whose name was Crazy Horse. His father understood that Curly was destined for great things and gave him his name, taking his childhood name of Worm instead.

Since the dream, Crazy Horse always wore a small pebble tied behind his left ear, always dusted his horse and himself with handfuls of dirt, and never decorated himself or the pony with paint. He often thought of the hands pulling him down in the dream, restraining him from some unknown destination that he would never see — but he knew the shadowy dream rider had had a purpose, an unseen, solitary path that promised untold glory and riches to a man who would travel it alone.

It wasn't to be.

The multitude of hands had pulled him down.

"Crazy Horse?"

He stood abruptly, unaware that he'd been squatting for so long, and felt needles of fire in his legs as he faced Black Buffalo Woman. "Oh . . . hello." He'd thought she was over a mile away at the river fishing, but apparently she'd left early. He looked down and saw a straw basket filled with wriggling fish. "A good day for them?"

"Yes." Her dark eyes glittered as she glanced from him to the girl playing with the quirt and drum. "What are you doing here?"

"Just wandering."

"Right to my tepee?"

"It was an accident."

She smiled. "Since when do you do something by accident?"

Crazy Horse shrugged disinterestedly. His light brown eyes scanned the village, looking everywhere but at her.

"Have you spoken to her?"

He looked at her blankly, but he knew the one she was talking about. "Who?"

"You don't change, do you?" She set the basket of fish down by the entrance to the tepee, near a stump turned upright.

He saw that she'd gained a few pounds since he'd seen her the winter before. The back of her neck, beneath tied-back long black hair, glistened with a light sheen of sweat. He risked a quick look behind him to the little girl and was surprised to find her standing right beside him. Startled, he stepped back from her.

"Do not worry," Black Buffalo Woman told him lightly, "she does not bite."

"What is her name?"

"Blue Sky At Dawn."

Crazy Horse looked the girl up and down, noticing the grimy fingers, a scar on her right knee, and the eyes staring back at him that were the exact same color as his. She watched him silently, sucking on her lower lip.

Black Buffalo Woman said, "Tell him hello, Blue Sky."

"Hello."

Crazy Horse grunted and took the quirt from her hand. "What were you playing?"

"Hunt."

"Hunt? Hunt what?"

"The bluecoat."

"The quirt was you . . . ?"

"And the drum was the mountains. But the bluecoat hid and I could not find him."

Crazy Horse glanced at her mother, who was scowling. He, on the other hand, laughed inwardly. "And when you catch the bluecoat, what would you do?"

Blue Sky made a snapping motion with her hands. "Break his neck."

"Blue Sky!" Black Buffalo Woman cried. "I have told you not to play those games! They are for boys."

Crazy Horse handed her the quirt. She smiled, and something inside him shifted — something that made him want to take her in his arms. "Go play," he said, "but mind your mother."

Blue Sky skittered away to the drum and, it seemed to him, continued the same movements she'd been practicing before.

"She is so stubborn," Black Buffalo Woman said. "Sometimes I cannot make her mind me."

Crazy Horse moved to her to stand close. "Like her father."

She shook her head. This time, it was she who would not make eye contact. "No Water is not stubborn. He is a gentle man."

"Her real father."

"No Water *is* her real father." She squatted down by a stump, removed a fish from the basket, and picked up a heavy cleaver. Her eyes raised to his.

Crazy Horse wanted to reach down and stroke her fine hair that shone in the sun. Her mouth was set in a determined line, the full lips straight and thin. "She is beautiful," he whispered.

"Blue Sky? Yes, she is."

A sadness came over him. "Blue Sky is beautiful, too."

She was surprised and embarrassed by his meaning and turned to the trout on the log. With a sure aim she brought the cleaver down sharply, severing the head neatly. "I saw your white wife by the river. She is getting fat."

Crazy Horse felt himself grow cold inside again. Black Buffalo Woman knew very well that Nellie was of Cheyenne-French heritage, but she insisted on calling her white. His compliment and attempt at intimacy had once again been spurned, just as it had for years since their brief time together. "All women get fat. It is from laziness."

Whack! Another fish head went spinning to the ground, this time with more force. Black Buffalo Woman didn't look up, but he saw her face redden.

"I must go," he said tonelessly. "The Sun Dance is tonight."

This made her look up. "But you do not dance the Sun Dance."

"I must be there, just as your . . . husband, No Water."

"Do not fight, Crazy Horse."

He looked at her. "I have sworn I would not fight him for you, and I have kept my word. When given, it is never taken back."

Black Buffalo Woman said nothing. A

small drop of blood gathered at the edge of the cleaver she held and dropped to the dirt.

Crazy Horse turned to go.

"You may want to go see about the white man they caught over the ridge."

He spun on her. "What white man?"

She shrugged and placed another fish on the stump. "A foolish one. He rode right into some boys who were playing. They were having fun with him. He might not be alive." Black Buffalo Woman stopped abruptly.

When she looked up, Crazy Horse was nowhere to be seen, but Blue Sky At Dawn was. She was running as fast as she could toward the river.

She's chasing after her father, Black Buffalo Woman thought frantically. As she took off after the girl, she thought, *I mean, she's chasing after Crazy Horse, not her father.*

Jack Sheffield hadn't even known he was *close* to a Sioux village, much less Indian boys hunting for antelope less than fifty feet from him. As a matter of fact, he was admiring the white buds on some sort of shrub growing beneath the cottonwoods when an arrow darted from the woods and narrowly missed him. He was so surprised that he couldn't move. The horse heard the arrow whizzing by but didn't react more than pricking up his ears.

From the cottonwoods charged four Indian boys, waving weapons and whooping. As they neared — very quickly, to Jack's dismay — he saw that they were more than boys. They were young men with fully developed bodies and muscles. Their expressions were grim and deadly, not ones of playful chase and capture. His mind registered this in a split second, and he suddenly feared for his life. When he'd played out the scenario in his mind of how he would approach the Sioux, he'd envisioned riding within sight of a few of them, preferably docile women, and waving a hello.

This was completely different, and he was totally unprepared.

His horse pranced away from the screaming boys. Jack could feel the gelding ready to bolt if given the slightest encouragement by his master. Jack decided to wait for them to come to him. Maybe they were just displaying bravado at coming across a white man unarmed in the middle of the prairie.

They weren't.

One of them, burly and muscular, heaved a well-aimed tomahawk that struck flat-side against the front shoulder of the horse. It reared high in the air, tumbling Sheffield from the horse, and bolted. Then the braves were on him.

"Wait!" he called, knowing it was useless. "I mean you no harm! I've come in peace!" When he saw the raised weapons in front of young faces twisted with bloodlust, he covered himself as best he could.

Blows rained down on him, hard blows with vicious weapons that stung and thudded against him solidly. He heard himself still pleading, but his cries fell on deaf ears.

He felt one of his ribs give way with a sickening crunch, snapping him out of his vague disbelief that the whole thing wasn't really happening.

Despite doing his best to cover his head with his arms, something connected that sent his brain whirling, and an ebony curtain closed over his vision.

Part Four

BRAVE HEARTS TO THE FRONT

I could whip all the Indians on the continent with the Seventh Cavalry.
George Armstrong Custer
June 25, 1876

Ho-ka hey! It is a good day to fight! It is a good day to die! Strong hearts, brave hearts to the front!
Crazy Horse
June 25, 1876

Chapter Eighteen

Violation

Reena had been excited at first when Custer told Hunter that he wanted them to ride with him in the column. He was the most famous person she was ever likely to meet. From everything she'd read in the papers before her move to Canada, Custer could do no wrong. Judging from the way he was admired by his men, along with Del's obvious adoration of the boy general, Custer's stature had only grown while she'd been out of the States.

In hindsight, her anticipation at riding with the general proved to be, she thought, a bit silly. He was exceptionally gallant when he met her, sweeping his hat from his head and bowing low on the horse he was astride, but after a few polite questions as to her and Faron's well-being, he returned to his riding companions — his brothers Tom and Boston. To Reena, Boston appeared to be barely advanced beyond adolescence. His face was smooth, as if shaving weren't a serious preoccupation, and he was the butt of many jokes for Custer and Tom. The young man didn't seem to mind, though, as he only laughed at his own expense and tried to return the barbs whenever he was able, which was seldom.

Reena heard her first disparaging words about Custer late that morning from her uncle.

She'd been watching Custer often during the ride when Faron suddenly asked from beside her, "Makes quite a picture, eh, lass?"

"Oh . . . I didn't know you were awake, Uncle."

"Been awake for a while. Watchin' you watch him."

Hunter, who was driving the wagon, turned to her curiously. For no apparent reason, his movement and something in her uncle's eyes made her defensive. "Is something wrong with that?"

"Nope. Kinda hard to keep *from* lookin' at him, I suppose. I was the same way at first."

Reena adjusted the pillows behind his head and reached for the waterpot to give him something to drink. "Was . . . ?"

Faron coughed. "He ain't a god, Reena darlin'."

"I know that."

"Far from it. Was court-martialed back in '67, you know."

Reena looked at him, her mouth open in surprise.

"I'm serious! Among other things, he was accused of shooting deserters in a Kansas campaign against the Indians."

"Shooting . . . ? In cold blood?"

Faron took a drink of the water from the ladle she'd absentmindedly lifted to his mouth. Some of it spilled over into his beard. "Well, he ordered it done, you know. Same thing."

Reena couldn't believe it. She glanced over at Custer, trying to picture the very embodiment of an officer ordering enlisted men killed for something so trivial as trying to get *away* from killing others. "Hunter, did you know about this?"

"Not really."

"What do you mean, not really?"

His back was to her, and after hesitating, he swung his head around halfway. "I've heard of that happening before. I just hadn't heard it about Custer."

"You don't sound surprised," Reena observed with a chill. *How could he be so nonchalant about it?*

"The nature of war, Reena. It's always

been like that."

"That doesn't mean it's right."

Hunter nodded. "I agree."

His calmness about the subject irritated her. She cast a glance over to Custer, who was smiling at something Boston had said. He looked around suddenly, as if sensing he was being watched, and his bright blue eyes looked intently at Reena. When he saw her face, the grin vanished and he promptly rode over to them.

"Is something the matter?"

"Yes, there is —"

"No, sir, not a thing," Hunter interrupted.

She spun on him. "How can you — ?"

"We were just having a friendly little discussion." His eyes bored into hers. "Weren't we, Reena?"

She didn't understand, but she could tell when Hunter was getting angry. She wasn't afraid of his temper, but since she was sure that he must have had a good reason for stepping in, she let it go.

"How are you feeling, O'Donnell?" Custer asked.

"Fit as a fiddle, General," Faron answered.

"Good, good. And, Miss O'Donnell, are you sure there wasn't something you wished to tell me?"

"No, it's nothing."

"For a moment there I could have sworn that you were upset."

Reena didn't answer.

Custer expanded his chest with a deep breath and let it out slowly. "Beautiful day, isn't it?" His worry about Reena completely gone, he galloped away to his brothers.

"Why did you do that?" Reena asked Hunter.

"The general is a vain man, Reena," he explained gently. "If we question him about any of his . . . misdeeds, we may upset him."

"So? He *should* be questioned about something so horrid."

Hunter turned to her fully, and his gray eyes were flat. "He could leave us stranded out here, Reena. He has complete authority over the plains as far as you can see. Would you want that?"

"He wouldn't leave us," Reena said with little conviction.

"Reena, darlin'," Faron said, "would you like to take that chance?"

Later that day, after traveling hours without one stop, they reached the Tongue

River, where they came upon an Indian burial ground. The corpses weren't actually buried. They lay on scaffolds and in trees. Decorative feathers hanging from limbs danced in the breeze. To Reena there appeared to be about fifteen bodies, one of which, to her horror, was an infant no more than a year old. It was wrapped in a buffalo robe, the little body swaying slightly with the scaffold.

Custer ordered a general halt for the troop. "To rest and water the horses," Reena heard him tell a captain, but his eyes didn't sway from the platforms. Tom whispered to him, but he seemed not to hear. Bloody Knife, Mitch Bouyer, and Lonesome Charley Reynolds appeared with Del trailing behind. All of them were unable to hide their uneasiness.

Hunter had stopped the buckboard and was watching Custer.

"Shouldn't we make a wide circle around this place?" Reena asked in a whisper.

"Yes."

"Then why are we stopping here?"

Hunter just shook his head, trying to hear what was being said around the general.

Bloody Knife was gesturing expansively,

and his speech seemed to be peppered with the Ree language as he tried to make some point.

Still Custer gave no evidence that he heard anyone.

Mitch Bouyer spoke, clearly agitated.

Del turned his horse and rode over to them. "This ain't good."

"What's he doing, Del?" Hunter asked.

"Bloody Knife and Mitch are trying to tell him that we need to leave right now, as soon as possible, but Custer's just sittin' there. I don't like it." He leaned over and spat a stream of brown tobacco juice to the side.

More soldiers gathered around Custer, most of them excited. Custer barked something, and everyone became quiet, looking from him to the burial ground. Even though they were about fifty yards from the bodies, Reena felt as if they were too close.

A strange hush fell over the area, as if both man and animal were frozen with indecision and anticipation.

Del spoke, startling Reena. "See that fancy scaffold near the river? The one with painted red and black supports and all the big medicine items on it? That's the mark of a great warrior. You can't get a fancier burial than that."

"What do you think happened to the child?" Reena asked.

Del shrugged. "Disease, pneumonia . . . who knows?"

The small body haunted Reena more than any of the others. It was situated close to the warrior's scaffold, and she wondered if the child had been his. Even in death, the infant seemed vulnerable.

Custer pointed to the warrior's scaffold. Reena didn't know if some trick of the wind carried his voice to her, or if she read his lips. Whichever it was, right before he spoke she felt her heart stop. Somehow she knew what he would say, hoping against it with all her might in that split second, yet helpless to stop it.

"Tear that one down," Custer ordered.

Reena finally found her voice, but it was only a whisper. "No."

Several soldiers shot forward at the order, their eagerness apparent.

Mitch Bouyer and Charley Reynolds paled.

Hunter turned to her suddenly. "What did he say?"

"He said —"

Suddenly Hunter dropped the reins, jumped down from the buckboard, and took off running after the soldiers on foot.

The noise woke Faron. "Wha— ? What's happenin'?"

"It's a burial ground, Uncle Faron. An Indian burial ground, probably Sioux, and Custer ordered his men to tear down one of the scaffolds. It's wrong, it's just —"

"Foolish, is what it is, lass," Faron finished for her. He struggled to raise himself into a sitting position.

"Let me help you." With her eyes still on Hunter, she quickly padded some blankets behind his pillows and sat him up.

"Oh no," Faron groaned, gazing over her shoulder.

The soldiers had knocked two legs from the scaffold. The body and various items tumbled to the ground, one of which was a rawhide bag spilling animal bones and trinkets.

Behind Reena, tethered to the wagon, Buck whinnied and pranced.

Hunter reached the soldiers, breathless, and without hesitation pulled one of them from his saddle. Hunter's face was red with exertion and fury. He reached for another man, but the lieutenant saw him coming and swung down viciously with the butt of a pistol. Hunter dodged the blow and grabbed the arm, deftly using momentum to yank him down, too. The other five soldiers who were still mounted turned their attention on this sudden threat.

Reena turned to Del, who sat frozen on his horse watching the melee. "Del, help him!" she cried out.

Her cry roused him, and he spurred his mount toward the soldiers. Reena willed him to reach Hunter before he was hurt, which would be very shortly. She looked over at Custer, half expecting him to be enjoying the confrontation, but his face was impassive.

Hunter reached for another man, but now he was surrounded not only by those on horses, but the men he'd already rudely dismounted. Then he was lost from Reena's view amidst flailing quirts and angry fists.

"Hunter!" Reena heard herself screaming.

With a word, Custer ordered other men forward.

Del reached the fighting and directed the horse into the middle of the confusion to try to rescue his friend who was receiving a beating. More soldiers joined in, and Reena was reminded of a seething anthill that had been kicked. Another rider was suddenly jerked from his saddle by the unseen Hunter. Del began to whale around him with his rifle butt, clearing some room, but Reena still heard blows connecting with the struggling Hunter.

Mitch Bouyer charged into the fight, apparently without Custer's permission and started whipping soldiers himself. Finally Custer spoke to Tom, who nodded to a burly captain beside him, and both men rode into the fray, barking orders to stand down.

Reena caught a glimpse of Hunter as he went down under three men, still struggling, punching and kicking. Others gained control of Del and his whistling rifle. Bouyer kept them from beating Del senseless.

"Enough!" Tom Custer cried, jumping from his horse and pulling men from Hunter with surprising strength for a man slightly built. The beefy captain joined him, and soon things were under control.

Hunter shook off the hands that held him and sprinted toward Custer, shouting, "This is wrong! You don't have to do this!"

His blond hair was ruffled, his face still cherry red, and Reena saw a new bruise forming on the side of his forehead. She was just thankful he was still alive.

Tom ran behind him to stop an attack on

the general, but Hunter stopped directly in front of Custer, breathing hard and pointing a finger. "Call it off, General. You have no right to dishonor their burial ground!"

"Right!" Custer roared. "Who are you to tell me about my rights? You're not even a citizen of the United States!"

"I'm a member of the human race. That's my right! This place is special to the Sioux, big medicine, and —"

Custer let out a scoffing breath. "You will stand down, Stone, or I'll place you under arrest!"

The hammer of Tom Custer's pistol, held loose at his side, cocked audibly behind Hunter.

"Call the lad off, Reena," Faron warned from behind her. "Now."

"What can *I* do?"

He gave her a knowing look. "Just do it, lass. Before he causes hisself more harm."

Not understanding but willing to go along, Reena stepped down from the wagon and went to Hunter. He didn't watch her approach, though she knew he was aware of it.

Hunter tried once more, this time with iron control of his temper. "This place is sacred to the Sioux. It's like a church is to us. Can't you leave it alone?"

Custer's cool blue eyes stared at the torn scaffold, his attitude dismissive.

Reena put her hands on Hunter's arm, feeling cords of muscle and tendons wound tight. "Come on, Hunter. Come back to the wagon."

He didn't move.

"This is . . . you've done enough." She cast a glaring glance at the general. He was still ignoring them, and one gloved hand slowly reached up and swiped at his mustache. His refusal to look at them made her angry, but she bit back her own words of admonishment.

Hunter turned without a word, placed his hand over hers on his arm, and together they walked back to the wagon. He limped slightly but was trying to hide it.

Reena smiled weakly at Faron, feeling as if they'd lost a major battle, but Faron's eyes were on Hunter.

"Persistence, lad," he said quietly, "is an admirable quality. But it'll get ye nowhere with that man."

Reena wasn't around to see when they finished tearing down the scaffold and a few others. Hunter drove the wagon well away from the activity, and all four of them remained silent.

Some of the soldiers stole the artifacts. The great warrior's body was abused without care, and the wood from the beautifully decorated scaffold was split apart and used for firewood to make coffee.

Two hours later the troop moved on. After the last wagon cleared the burial ground, the scaffold holding the infant, untouched throughout the desecration, swayed back and forth in a strong gust of wind and collapsed.

The Seventh Cavalry moved on toward the Bighorn Valley, the Sioux, and their destiny.

Chapter Nineteen

The Odds of Fate

Jack Sheffield woke to searing pain in his feet, and when he opened his eyes, he found some young children holding a burning stick to them. He cried out and instinctively tried to kick at them, but he was completely tied down.

The children laughed, then pranced away a few feet.

He was staked down outside a tepee painted with red and black buffaloes. His head and cracked ribs throbbed terribly along with his burned feet. Sweat stung his eyes. They'd taken his shirt, and the direct sun was beginning to burn his bare chest.

The children inched closer, mischief etched clearly in their black eyes.

"Get away!" he croaked and realized just how thirsty he was. His tongue was swollen, and he wondered how long he'd been unconscious.

The burning stick was clutched in the hand of a boy, maybe nine or ten, and

Sheffield thought that the playfulness in his face just barely covered a deeper, darker malevolence. He realized he was in serious trouble.

Jack knew that some tribes allowed the women and children time to torture a captive before he was killed. He'd witnessed it once right after he'd joined the Sarcee. They'd caught a Crow who'd been stealing their horses, and the result was more than Jack wanted to think about right now, even though it had been years ago. He'd tried to stop them, but he was still a stranger to them, and they'd regarded him with looks that clearly told him he could be next.

Now, watching the end of the burning stick glow cherry red, Jack understood that he may have made the mistake of his life in coming here.

The boy looked at his companions, two girls and two boys, with a savage grin. He said something, and they giggled. Then he reached out with the stick, and Sheffield felt the coal and fire well before it reached him. "No!" he barked at them. They all flinched except for the one holding the stick. His grin widened.

Sheffield wiggled his foot frantically and tried to keep from crying out when the burn came. Then he growled at them and gave a primal roar, backing them away once again. But he knew they would be back.

He could smell the dank odor of a river or stream nearby and wished desperately for the chance to plunge his foot into the cool water. He decided to try reasoning with his tormentors. "Do you understand me? English?"

Five identical blank looks of incomprehension stared back at him. They also seemed amazed that he was even *trying* to speak to them.

He tried the Blackfoot language. "I'm a man of God. A missionary. I mean you no harm, or anyone else in your tribe." They still didn't understand. Sheffield let his head fall back to the ground. The strain of looking up at the children was causing his neck to tremble with pain and effort. The clouds above him were light and cotton white against the canopy of blue. A flock of geese flew high above him in a perfect V.

He heard movement at his feet and glanced up quickly. The children were moving away, wide-eyed at someone he could hear approaching him from behind. Sheffield hoped it was someone who could understand him.

The sun was blocked out, and he looked

up to see two men standing over him. He couldn't tell anything about them because of the glare. They talked together quietly.

"Hello?" Sheffield said. "Can you understand me?"

They looked down at him silently.

"Does anyone speak English?"

One of them said in English, "I am Swift Bear, and this is Chief Crazy Horse. Why are you — ?"

"Crazy Horse? You're Crazy Horse?" Sheffield tried shifting his head in order to see the famous man, but the blaring sun blocked his vision. The silence became ominous, and he realized that he'd interrupted. "I'm sorry. Please go on." He felt ridiculous lying there on the ground at their feet, bound tightly. It was also the most humiliating experience he'd ever known.

Swift Bear continued. "Chief Crazy Horse would like to know what you are doing here." His speech was impeccable and exact.

Sheffield was overjoyed to finally be able to communicate. "I came here —" He stopped, frustrated at his sudden loss for words. His head ached fiercely from earlier blows and the blinding sun, making it hard to think. If he didn't choose his words correctly at this moment, he didn't think he would last long. The children would be back to torture him, and maybe they'd bring the women with them. He licked his lips with a dry tongue and tried again. "My name is Jack Sheffield, and I'm a minister. I came here to speak with Crazy Horse and the great Sitting Bull."

Crazy Horse squatted down, giving Sheffield his first look at him. Since seeing him four or five years before, his handsome face had become hard and stoic. He watched Sheffield with eyes that had seen too much and endured too many sorrows. He was dressed only in leggings with a knife belt, the very same as before, with no shirt. Corded muscles rippled in his shoulders and torso.

"We've met before, you and I," Sheffield told him. "In the north country, where the buffalo are still plentiful, a few summers ago."

Crazy Horse gave no sign that Sheffield was even speaking to him. His eyes roamed impassively up and down Jack's staked-out frame.

"Crazy Horse was a great man then. I've heard that he has become even more respected by his people and the white man." Sheffield could hear the thickness of his tongue in his speech and wished desperately for a drink of water. A painful twinge in his neck muscles caused him to lay his head down again, though it seemed a sign of weakness in front of Crazy Horse. He didn't want sympathy from the chief, only respect.

Swift Bear said, "You may not speak to Sitting Bull. He hates all white men and would kill you himself if he knew you were here."

Sheffield saw a glimmer of hope. If they were keeping his presence from Sitting Bull, maybe they were willing to listen.

Crazy Horse locked eyes with him, tilting his head to the side a bit, since Sheffield's head was flat on the ground. Then he spoke in Sioux to Swift Bear.

"Chief Crazy Horse says that he remembers you. You were with the Sarcee in the Canadas a few winters ago."

"That's right," Sheffield agreed, speaking directly to Crazy Horse. "Your people were hungry, and you stayed with us awhile. I was very frightened of you."

Interest sparked in the chief's face, and he spoke again.

"Chief Crazy Horse asks if you are still frightened of him."

Sheffield hesitated. This could be the

most important question asked of him — could mean the difference between living and dying. "I fear no man. I only fear the almighty God in heaven, who graciously returns our respect with love and forgiveness." He took a deep breath. "I respect Crazy Horse, but I do not fear him."

Swift Bear cast an uneasy glance at Crazy Horse, then began to translate. Crazy Horse cut him off with a slashing gesture, then withdrew the knife from his belt and said in English, "Every man should know fear. He is not a man if he doesn't."

Sheffield tensed his whole body when he saw the knife come toward him. The sun gleamed brightly along the razor-sharp edge. He knew fear at that moment, sharp and biting, until he prayed, *Father, take me into your kingdom.* . . .

Crazy Horse cut his bonds.

Faron looked at Del accusingly in the failing daylight. "Ye don't have to keep avoidin' me arm that's not there, Dekko."

"I ain't avoidin' it!"

"Oh, yes ye are."

Del shifted in his chair, feeling guilty. "Can't help it," he mumbled under his breath.

"Ye make me more nervous *not* lookin' at it than lookin' at it."

"Sorry." Normally Del would argue about it, but he was feeling very disturbed. They all were, after seeing the Indian cemetery desecrated earlier that day.

Reena had left Del with her uncle while she and Hunter went for a walk. They were both still upset over Custer's insensitivity to the sacredness of the burial ground and wanted some time to enjoy each other's company.

"I need some water," Faron announced.

Del got it for him from the huge pot they'd been carrying all day. While he was at it, Del helped himself to a long drink.

"Don't ye be drinkin' out o' my ladle!" Faron scolded.

"Why not?"

"Ye might have some sorta sickness that I might catch."

"I ain't sick. You're just lookin' for excuses to complain."

"And it ain't hard to find them with you as a caretaker."

"I could leave," Del said casually as he handed Faron the water ladle — freshly cleaned by his shirtsleeve after having his mouth on the edge of it. "Is that what you want? You want me to leave?"

Faron sipped from the ladle and ignored him.

"I asked you a question."

Faron mumbled something.

"What was that?"

"I said no! You hear that?"

"What I thought you said," Del remarked smugly.

The night was cool, with gathering storm clouds to the southwest. Through the tent opening they watched heat lightning pulse and sizzle in the ominous-looking formation. Somewhere a group of soldiers was singing "Buffalo Gals."

"Bad business today at that burial ground," Del commented grimly. He couldn't get the image out of his mind of the warrior's body tumbling to the earth.

"Aye. You a superstitious man, Dekko?"

Del eyed him cautiously. "I've been called that before."

"So ye think the ghosts of thousands of Sioux are goin' to rise up out o' the ground and tear Custer to pieces, eh?"

"Who said anything about ghosts? What are you laughing at?"

"Ah, you're a card, old son. Right now ye look like you've seen 'em yourself."

"I do not." Though he *was* feeling sort of apprehensive about the incident, along with the lightning and storm approaching. "Why do you think Custer did that anyway?"

"You haven't figured it out yet?"

"What?"

"Custer thinks he's invincible," Faron said, adjusting his position on the cot painfully. Then he chuckled. "Come to think of it, maybe he is."

"No, he ain't. Nobody is. Not even Napoleon was invincible."

"Now, what in blazes do you know about Napoleon?" Faron asked.

"Plenty."

"And why are we even talking about him? He wasn't a great general. He was a fool. He went blunderin' into a country that was too big and he was outnumbered."

Del grinned slyly and sat forward, resting his elbows on his knees. "Does that remind you of anybody?"

Reena walked with Hunter far away from the encampment. Her arm was threaded through his comfortably, and they walked mostly in silence. The event of the day seemed to have had a numbing effect on them both, and they were content to sort it out in their own minds before discussing it together.

In the west, a storm announced its presence with growling thunder. The late evening was growing cooler, and Reena wished she'd worn the only wool wrap she'd brought with her.

They were moving down a narrow lane, surrounded by groves of trees. The strong scent of wildflowers hung in the air. The sounds of the camp were mercifully far away, until they suddenly heard the barking of dogs and a gunshot. Hunter tensed with his hand on the holstered sidearm he was carrying.

Reena said, "Do you think — ?"

Right then Custer himself appeared out of the woods ahead of them with four huge dogs bounding around him. He didn't see them at first, and the look on his face consisted of pure joy at his activities with the pets. He carried a pistol loosely at his side, and when he saw them his eyes narrowed momentarily, then registered mild surprise. Without a word, he took something from a satchel he carried and threw it in the air, then raised the pistol and shot it. Pieces of whatever it had been scattered to the ground, and the excited dogs fought over them.

"What's he doing, Hunter?" Reena whispered over the growling.

"I have no idea. Do you want to turn back?"

"Do you?"

"No."

Custer watched the dogs for a moment, then waved Hunter and Reena toward him.

"I suppose we should return to camp," Hunter said, though it was the last thing he wanted to do.

Custer watched them approach in the dying light, standing with his weight on one leg and a hand on his hip. *He always looks like he's posing for a photograph,* Reena thought.

Without a greeting, Custer motioned to the dogs and said, "Magnificent, aren't they?"

The dogs seemed to know that he was speaking of them, for they came to him and sat at his feet expectantly. Custer performed his trick again, and this time it was large biscuits he tossed into the air. Reena covered her ears before he discharged the weapon. She watched the dogs scurry for the bread greedily again.

Custer held up the pistol. "Do you recognize the weapon, Stone?"

"No, sir. The only pistol I know is the Adams."

"This is one of two revolvers, actually.

They're both Webley Bulldogs." He looked over at Hunter as if waiting for praise or scorn, but Hunter remained silent. "Fine pistols, given to me by a dear friend."

Still Hunter made no comment. Reena knew that he was very uncomfortable in the man's presence after the incident earlier that day.

"You own a Henry rifle, don't you, Stone?" Custer asked.

"Yes, sir."

"Ever kill a man with it?"

Hunter hesitated, then answered quietly, "Yes."

Custer nodded slowly and holstered the Webley. "I knew it. You have that look. Not that you look like a killer, mind you, quite the contrary. It's just something in the eyes that I recognize." He patted each dog lovingly as they came to him, speaking low praises. Then he looked up abruptly. "Your friend, Dekko . . . he's never killed, I can assure you of that. And your uncle, Miss O'Donnell — he has."

"No, he hasn't." Reena received a mild, condescending look from him and it made her angry. "I know he hasn't."

"Think what you will," Custer shrugged.

"How can you dare to — ?"

Hunter sensed her wrath because he interrupted. "General, I would think that peculiar talent of recognizing death on men would be a burden. I would rather judge them by their character, not whether they'd killed others."

Custer's cool blue eyes cut around to him. "You surprise me. Judging from *your* character, I'd thought you were a soldier at heart, like me."

"I'm a policeman. There's a difference."

"Which is?"

"We don't get paid to kill. We get paid to protect."

Custer smiled lightly beneath the bristly mustache. "I find it interesting your first inclination is to speak of pay. I don't do what I do for pay. I do it because I was born for it."

The quiet ire that had arisen in Reena because of Custer's comment about her uncle wouldn't keep still. "Born to kill?"

"Born to *lead*, Miss O'Donnell. I sense your hostility toward me and it disturbs me. Is it because of what happened today at the burial ground?"

"Of course."

"Look over there please, Miss O'Donnell." He pointed to the west where the cloud formation hovered over a large hill in the distance. "Somewhere in that direction, less than fifty miles I'd say, are some fierce men. Men named Sitting Bull, Rain In The Face, Crazy Horse, Kicking Bear, Gall . . . incredible names, names that strike fear into the hearts of their enemies. They have many warriors under them to lead against me, and General Crook from the south, and General Gibbon from the northeast. Now, I have no doubt of our success, no doubt whatsoever, but I'll do anything to compound our chances. Because, you see, in the War of Secession I saw chance — or luck or fate, if you will — swing battles from pole to pole in a disturbing manner. Not very often, but enough to where I try to put chance on my side instead of vice versa."

"What does violating a cemetery have to do with your so-called chance?" Reena asked.

"For the very reason you and many others are upset. It's big medicine to the Sioux and Cheyenne. If they see that Long Hair holds no fear of their medicine, then maybe *they* will fear *me*."

"They already fear you," Hunter said quietly.

"Oh? You've spoken to them, I suppose." Custer smiled, not unkindly. "I see you haven't, and none of us can know for sure whether they fear me or not. That's part of the chance, Stone. Don't you see? If I do nothing, I'll never know. If I deliberately try to place fear where it needs to be, even by an act such as today, then I'm attempting to cancel out that chance. Simple."

Reena saw his logic, but it did nothing to cool her outrage at what had been done. "And what about the relatives of those abused? Don't you care?"

"I could sit here and debate with you all night, Miss O'Donnell. But the fact of the matter is that I've been assigned to get those people back to their reservations by any means available, and George Custer is not one to do a job half-heartedly. They broke the treaty, and now they must be punished for it."

"Broke the treaty! And how many —"

"Reena," Hunter said cautiously.

"— treaties have you broken to *them?*"

"None," Custer stated firmly.

"Your . . . your . . ." she searched for words, "bosses then! Washington."

The irritating, condescending tone crept back into Custer's attitude and speech. "I'm a soldier, not a politician. I made no promises of any kind." He watched their reaction, then announced, "I've got a meeting with my staff. If you'll excuse me."

Reena watched him walk away, fuming. "The *nerve* of that man! Hunter, I want out of here. I want to go back home."

"Reena, did you hear what he said? The Sioux could be fifty miles or closer. We can't just ride out of here right now."

Reena sighed and rushed into his arms. "I want to get as far away from here as I can. Please take me home."

"I will." He kissed the top of her head. "Soon."

"We don't belong here." Her eyes locked on the receding back of the boy general, George Armstrong Custer. "None of us do."

They walked back to the camp through the now familiar noises of soldiers on bivouac — the clatter of cookware being washed, low talk and laughter, the metal clang of weapons being cleaned and dry-fired. As usual, wherever Reena went the noises mostly ceased as the men watched her walk by. This close inspection had been disconcerting at first every time she ventured out, but now she merely accepted it as part of the camp.

The thunder was closer now, past the point of being mere background noise, a force of nature that would have to be dealt with soon. She wondered if Sitting Bull and Crazy Horse heard the same thunder. She wondered if the booming reminded them of cannon fire, as it did her.

Chapter Twenty

Enlightenment

Vickersham and Becker didn't catch Bad Weasel. It wasn't for want of trying, because Vic pushed the troop unmercifully, only to find the tracks disappearing across the border hours ahead of them. Vickersham seriously considered venturing over into the United States, since it seemed they were gaining on the Sioux, but this was one thing that Becker, along with input from Jerry Potts, was able to talk him out of.

Becker did his best to keep his distance from Vic, which proved to be no problem at all. Vickersham, normally outgoing and the first to sit around the enlisted men's campfires for stories and companionship, stayed to himself. His silence caused whispering among the men, and Becker brushed aside all inquiries that came his way. He knew that would only start the gossip mill churning even more. In his opinion, Vic's problems were his own, just like any other man, and if he wanted to talk them out, fine. If not, that was fine, too. Becker had learned a long time ago that if a man didn't want to talk about something, it was a waste of time to try to make him talk.

By the time the weary and dejected Mountie troop pulled into Fort Macleod four days after leaving it, Becker had caught a few of the men speculating about Vic's sanity. The exact word "insanity" wasn't used, and no one spoke directly to Becker about it, but he had always demonstrated an eerie sixth sense about the temper of the men around him. There were two reasons Becker hadn't put a stop to the talk. One, he knew it was out of concern instead of malice, and two, Becker wasn't sure he could make a solid argument *against* it. The thought disturbed him.

They left their horses at the stable, and by wordless consent Becker knew he should follow Vickersham to Colonel Macleod's office for a report. When they arrived, with not a word having been spoken between them, they found Macleod holding court. An adjutant, a slim, haggard-looking man by the name of Bristow, told them, "You can wait if you like. The colonel shouldn't be much longer."

"Thanks," Becker returned.

"Have a nice ride through the country?" Bristow asked.

Becker thought it a strange question and said so.

"Haven't you heard? That Sioux you were after didn't kill that woman any more than I did."

"Bristow," Vic sighed, "what on earth are you talking about?"

The adjutant smiled, revealing horsey teeth. "The killer's still here. There's been another murder."

"Another *murder?*"

"Yes."

"Who was she?"

Bristow gave Vickersham a strange look. "Who said it was a woman? It was a man. But you don't have to worry anymore, Vic. We've got the man who did it."

A hundred questions ran through Becker's head, not the least of which was, *Is this man out of his mind?*

Bristow clearly enjoyed the reaction he was receiving from his shocking news and seemed to puff up with importance when he added, "The killer confessed."

Vickersham could tell as soon as they walked in the jailhouse that he wasn't the man.

Hiram Piffer was a sorry sight. First of all, he wore an eyepatch, but it was no ordinary eyepatch — it was a small slab of rawhide held in place by a leather thong wrapped around his narrow head. Hiram's gray hair was falling out; not in a neat withdrawal, but in patches here and there, leaving a tanned skull shining through. His salt-and-pepper beard fell almost to his tattered pants, and the shirt he wore was stained yellow from sweat and lack of washing. One of his boots was missing a heel.

When Vickersham and Becker walked into the building that was capable of housing six prisoners, but rarely was full, Hiram was snoring so loud the guard had stuffed cotton in his ears. "He's been doing that for an hour now," he called to them in a loud voice, though they stood right in front of him.

"Open the door," Vic ordered.

"Hah?"

"Open the door!"

"Oh, right." The guard sailed past them, his finger still tucked between the pages of *Moby Dick* by Herman Melville. Vic briefly wondered how he stayed awake despite the loud snoring.

The key made a racket in the cell door,

but it didn't bother Hiram. The guard managed a look of revulsion and apology at the same time. "Don't want to touch him, you know," he shouted, then kicked the cot firmly.

Hiram came awake and sat bold upright, one eye blinking at the light, then he bent over, clutching his belly in pain. After a moment he saw them and seemed to remember where he was and the reason. "I killed her, yep," he nodded. "Killed him, too. Couldn't help myself."

Vickersham and Becker stared at him for a moment. That was when Vic concluded that Hiram was lying. Vic had seen men like Hiram before as they washed into Fort Macleod from the wastes of the prairie. They'd lived lives in the rough and tumble West so ordinary and trouble free that they themselves were shocked. No one would remember them. It was as if they hadn't even existed. They'd been spit upon, laughed at, and considered just part of the background all their lives. Now they were dying, and in pain, and looking for a reason to be remembered, even if it meant claiming a pair of sordid murders as their own.

Vic nodded at the guard to leave.

Hiram stared back at them, daring them

to contradict him. Then he rubbed his nose and sneezed, which caused him to bend over again in pain. A fine sheen of sweat already covered his face, though the room was cool.

"Mr. Piffer," Becker asked, "have you seen a doctor?"

Hiram squinted at him through his pain. "You're mighty young to be a Mountie, aren't you?"

"Have you seen one?"

"What for?"

"You're obviously very sick."

"Says who?"

Becker looked at Vic helplessly.

Vic said, "Mr. Piffer, you say you committed these murders. I was wondering —"

"I *did* commit those murders. Don't you believe me?"

Vickersham smiled, his first one in days, though it was a sad one. "Just a few questions, if you don't mind, sir."

"Fire away," Hiram said easily with a wave of his hand.

Vic noticed that he was still grimacing and wondered if it was now a constant fixture on his face. He asked Hiram about Fran's murder, easy questions that anyone would know about simply from the local gossip, which was usually disturbingly correct. Hiram, of course, got them all right.

Vic glanced at Becker, then asked, "Mr. Piffer . . . why did you leave the necklace under the bed?"

Hiram had been scratching his knee, bored with the questions, but now he looked up and fixed Vickersham with a knowing smirk. "Nice try, son. It was an armband. An Indian armband."

Vic was stunned. Recovering quickly, he asked, "So why were you trying to blame it on the Sioux?"

"Blackfoot." Hiram's gaze didn't waver. "You need to get your facts straight before you start questioning, boy."

"How many times did you stab her?"

"I didn't count. Did you?"

Vic and Becker again exchanged glances. Becker asked, "*Why* did you stab her? Why her?"

Hiram winked. "That's something I'll take to the hangman with me. It was between me and her, nobody else's business."

"And the man — Sinclair — why did you stab him so many times?"

Becker and Vic had gotten the story on Sinclair's murder from Bristow, who'd been happy to oblige them with all the details.

"I didn't stab him but *three* times,"

Hiram returned. "Are you fellows about through with your tricks?" A coughing fit seized him, deep coughs that brought blood to his lips.

"He's lying," Vic declared on their way to Tony La Chappelle's Tobacco and Candy Store. Tony also had billiards, and where there were billiards, there was illegal whiskey, and where there was illegal whiskey, there was usually trouble. Amos Sinclair had been killed outside Tony's business, in the back by a separate storeroom.

"How do you know he's lying?"

"Come on, Dirk. Do you really think that emaciated, sick old man could have overpowered Amos Sinclair? Sinclair was a big man."

"So how did he know about the evidence? No one knew all those things."

"Think about it, and it'll come to you."

Short, stocky, and hairy, Tony La Chappelle was a Frenchman who'd worked very hard on his accent since coming to the Territories and now spoke with almost no trace of it. He was friendly with the Mounted Police, always had been, but the line was drawn when they requested he refrain from bringing billiards to Fort

Macleod. He told them at the time — and he was absolutely right, they admitted — that if he didn't bring the game to town, someone would. The Mounties had gotten plenty of tips from Tony concerning outlaws and turned a blind eye to the trouble he sometimes had at his place.

He was dressed in trousers and an apron, no shirt, and greeted Vic and Becker warmly. He offered them tea and looked offended when they declined. "Always in a hurry, you Mounties," he chided good-naturedly. "Don't you know it's barbaric to turn down tea? In China, I hear, you could be hamstrung for it."

"We're not in China, Tony," Becker grinned.

"And you, Constable, with your impeccable Southern manners." He clucked his tongue in mock sadness. "What is the world coming to?"

"We're here about the murder, Tony," Vic told him.

"Ah . . . a bad business that. Bad *for* business, too."

Vic asked him about Hiram Piffer, and Tony told them that Piffer just showed up that night, half-starved and weak. Even though he had no money, Tony had given him a hot meal. "He was very sick."

"And still is. Do you think he did it?"

Tony shrugged his hairy shoulders. "I wasn't there." He told them that Sinclair rarely showed up at his place, but when he did, the big man always had liquor and was generally abusive to everyone around him. "I don't like to speak ill of the dead, but he was very mean. No one liked him." Tony told them he had closed up that night and gone home to bed, and that was all he knew.

"Who else was here?" Becker asked.

"Lewis Crane, Billy Blankenship, Skinny Pate, Oscar Williams —"

"Whoa, whoa . . . Skinny Pate? Pate, did you say?"

Tony's eyes lit up. "That's right — he's the one whose woman was killed! I'd forgotten about that."

"How did he act?" Vic asked.

"I don't know . . . normal, I guess. He wasn't mourning, if that's what you're wondering."

Vickersham and Becker looked at each other.

"We go," Vic said firmly as they left Tony's place.

"Vic, we just got into town," Becker countered. "Don't you want to see your wife first?" They were walking back to the fort, and though Becker's legs were longer than his friend's, he was having trouble keeping up.

Vic stopped abruptly. "Why are you so concerned about Megan?"

"You haven't seen each other in four days. Aren't you worried about her?"

"Of course!" he snapped.

"She's been very understanding with your . . . with you, and I'm sure she would want to see her husband before he goes off into the wilderness again."

"Becker, why do you feel you must give me marital advice when you're not even married?"

The two men stood almost nose to nose in the middle of the street, mindless of a few shopkeepers and passersby who stared at them curiously. One of the spectators was a woman with a small boy who asked, "Mama, are those men going to fight?" His tinny voice rang clear in the twilight air, and his expression was mixed fright and hope.

Becker shook his head in frustration, then seemed to come to a decision. "Listen to me, Vic. I'm going to speak my mind for the last time. You're a Christian now. You have *rules* to follow concerning your marriage and your wife, and you'd better read up on what they are."

Vic stood staring at him in stunned silence.

In a gentler tone, Becker said, "Megan's the best thing that ever happened to you, and you're *blind*, Vic, if you can't see that. Whatever's bothering you is something you need to share with her. Do you understand? She's your *wife*."

Vic found himself looking beyond Dirk at some cloudy remembrance of the past week and didn't like what he saw. He'd been a fool — a complete and utter fool. Becker was right. Why hadn't he seen that?

Becker stepped back from him and glanced around at their audience. Then he took Vic's arm and gently guided him toward the fort in the distance. When they were well away from the people watching them, Becker said, "I'm sorry about that."

Vic still felt numb as if he'd been slapped, but he responded, "No, no — don't say it."

"I have to say it. You're my brother in Christ, and I shouldn't be so harsh. But I did have to say something, do you understand?"

"Of course. I'm . . . believe it or not, I'm glad you did."

"Do you still want to ride out to Pate's cabin? I suppose it'll be the best time to find him at home, since it would be midnight by the time we got there."

"After that speech?" Vic asked with the hint of a smile. "No, I'm going home to see my wife and tell her I love her." Becker grinned, and the relief in his young face only reminded Vic of just how good a friend he was.

"Good. I'll see you in the morning, then?"

"Yes. Good night, Dirk."

On his walk home, Vic enjoyed the smell of wildflowers and freshly cut grass that lingered in the air like perfume. His senses were stirred and alive for the first time in days. What had he been thinking all this time? It seemed as if he'd been stumbling around in a dream, feeling his way through a blurry landscape of biting reality that had finally set in on him after years on the prairie.

As he walked, he asked God for that all-encompassing forgiveness. He shed the load of shame and worry he'd been carrying like a boulder on his back. He asked for guidance in dealing with his wife, whom he'd grievously hurt.

Vic's step increased with excitement as

he neared his home. Strangely, no lights showed through the windows, though it was almost dark. She had to be home. He had so much to say, she *had* to be home. He wanted to clear the air between them this minute.

He wasn't sure what Megan's reaction would be, but Twinkle was overjoyed to see him. He stopped and scratched her head, noticing that she really *was* growing. *What do we do with a full-grown antelope anyway?* he reflected good-naturedly.

The front door was open a crack, which he thought strange. Megan wasn't one to be absent-minded about things like that. He stepped inside and paused to let his eyes adjust.

Megan was sitting on the sofa, facing him. Through the dim light he saw that her eyes were wide and staring. "Hello, darling," he said softly. He noticed a dull glint at her throat like a thick necklace. He saw the muscles in her neck constrict as she swallowed hard. "What's the matter?"

From behind the sofa rose Tobias "Skinny" Pate. The silver arc winking at Vic from his wife's neck was a large hunting knife he held in his bony hand.

In utter shock and horror, Vic could only stare with his feet seemingly nailed to the floor. This couldn't be happening — impossible! He had so much to tell Megan, so many things to share with her and apologize for. At that moment he understood, totally and without any selfish interference from his own petty problems, just how much he loved her. He *couldn't* lose her, and certainly not in this way.

The knife flashed at him in the fading light with a mocking, evil brilliance.

Chapter Twenty-One

From the Mouth of Madness

Megan watched her husband tense, the shoulder muscles standing to attention, his fingers jutting out straight from his hands. Her feelings were hopelessly confused, however. She was overjoyed at the sight of him — not just because he might get them out of this madman's hands safely, but his warm greeting to her had been the same Vic she knew and loved, and not the brooding man who'd left the house days ago. At the same time, she was afraid for him. The knife-wielding man behind her hated Vic for some reason.

"Get away from my wife, Pate," Vic said in a low, threatening tone.

"Surprised to see me, aren't you?" Pate returned with a wicked glee in his voice. "Bet you don't feel so smart now, huh? Bet you're *sorry* for the way you treated me."

"Just get away from her."

"Say it."

"Say what?"

"Say you're sorry."

"I'm sorry. Now would you just —"

"That's not good enough. You've got to mean it."

When Megan had stepped inside after coming home from school, Pate had grabbed her immediately. She hadn't even had time to scream. He'd tied her hands and feet and made her sit on the sofa to listen to him. He'd asked about Vic's return, but of course she'd told him nothing. His eyes were dark and empty of everything except his madness, which shone with an evil threat. He'd said he wanted to show Vic something, and afterward he would show her, too. She'd thought it was the knife, but after listening to his crazed ramblings, she knew it was something more, something unspeakable and horrid. She's heard him mention Fran, and she was about to lose all hope until Vic had walked in.

"Say it like you mean it," Pate repeated. "Say you're sorry."

Vic actually smiled and took a step toward them.

Megan felt the knife tighten against her throat.

"Hold it right there, Mr. Mountie. I didn't invite you over here."

Vic took another step.

"I said hold it!" Pate screamed, grabbing Megan's hair painfully and tilting her head back.

Megan worked at the rope on her wrists, but she knew they were too tight. Her hands were numb from the loss of blood circulation. She worked her fingers to bring back feeling in case she found an opening in Pate's defense.

Vic said sincerely, "I'm very sorry for anything I've done to you, Mr. Pate." He moved his eyes to Megan when he added, "I'm not perfect. My actions and the things I sometimes say are wrong, and they cut deeply at times." Looking back to Pate, he said, "Now would you please release my wife and take me instead? This has nothing to do with her."

Pate was silent behind Megan, and she wished she could see his reaction. She heard a low giggle. Soon he was laughing. "Oh, that's where you're wrong, Mr. Mountie. Everyone in this room is involved now. Don't you understand?"

"Why did you kill Fran, Pate?"

"She was going to leave me. Then she laughed at me on her way out the door."

"She *laughed* at you? And you killed her?"

Pate's face glowed pale and sweaty in the murky light. "Nobody laughs at me. Nobody insults me . . . not anymore. That Sinclair fella got what was coming to him, too. Called me worthless trash, and then to top it off he laughed, too. Would've given him the business as bad as Frannie, but somebody came along and interrupted."

Megan felt the tension of the knife ease as Pate talked and briefly considered twisting out from under it. As if sensing her thought, the fingers in her hair tightened their grip.

"So," Vic said conversationally, "you're going to kill anyone who's ever insulted you."

"That's right."

"And my wife? Why are you threatening her?"

"I don't have to give you a reason for everything. Get down on your face on the floor."

"I'll do nothing of the kind."

"Do it!" he yelled.

Once again Megan felt her head pulled back and the cold blade biting deeper. She looked at Vic, trying to keep the fear from her eyes, but knowing she failed. He looked sick, then nodded in defeat. "No, Vic!" she managed to say before her head was jerked cruelly to the side.

Vic got to his knees and leaned forward, still too far away to make a move against Pate. Megan couldn't believe he was giving up. Didn't he know that Pate would only kill her after him?

"Any last words?" Pate asked, gloating.

"Yes." Vic looked at Megan tenderly with a sad smile. "I love you and always remember our trip to Wellington." Then he lay facedown on the floor.

Megan had to bite her tongue to keep from screaming "What?" in frustration. She remembered no such trip — had never even heard of the place. What was he talking about? Wellington, Wellington . . .

"That's a good boy," Pate crooned. "This was easier than I thought. All you Mounties act so tough, but when the chips are down, you're just a bunch of cowards."

Where was Wellington? Megan's mind roared. *What does he mean?* He was giving a hint about something, but what could it be. She was careful not to move her head as her eyes searched the room frantically. Nothing.

Suddenly Pate's face was right beside hers, his breath rank with onion. "Don't you move, missy, while I deal with your husband. Your turn's coming."

At that precise moment she understood. Of course! Vic had always admired the Duke of Wellington, "the Iron Duke," the defeater of Napoleon at Waterloo. He'd brought into their marriage a solid bronze statue that he'd owned for years, ever since England. It was Wellington sitting astride Copenhagen, his favorite horse, and it was almost twenty inches tall. Heavy. Probably almost ten pounds. And it was sitting on a table beside the sofa to her right, out of sight, but not out of quick reach.

In his arrogance and anticipation of dealing with Vic, Pate probably thought Megan was sufficiently cowed enough to only sit and tremble in fear. She *was* trembling, but what he didn't understand was that it was from anger — anger at her house being violated, anger at being tied up for so long and humiliated, anger at what he planned to do to her husband. She wouldn't allow it. This was her *home,* and she would do anything to protect it and the one she loved.

The second he foolishly released her, she lunged to her feet and took one hopping jump to the statue.

"Hey!" Pate shouted in surprise.

Vic was on his feet and on Pate incredibly fast. He brought his fist down hard on

Pate's wrist to dislodge the knife, but Pate cried out and stepped back, switching hands. The knife came around in a vicious, whistling arc that barely missed Vic's midsection.

Because of the tight constriction of the rope, Megan was barely able to grip the statue. She grabbed Copenhagen's legs, right hand on the front two, left on the back two, and lifted. It was heavy — oh, so heavy — but she gritted her teeth and spun around with it.

Pate was swinging the knife back and forth at Vic for all he was worth, taking small steps backward. His eyes were panicked, shifting constantly, looking for a way out. Megan hopped around the back of the sofa to get behind him. Pate moved his body sideways to keep an eye on her, and Vic landed a blow to the side of his neck that made his knees buckle slightly. It was all Vic needed.

He grasped Pate's wrist with both hands, and instead of trying to overpower him as Pate expected, Vic pulled as hard as he could. Their legs tangled together, and they fell to the floor in a heap of flailing limbs.

Megan's forearms trembled with the effort of hanging on to the statue with such

an awkward grip. She was more determined than she'd ever been in her life,
however, and with a few more hops she
made it over to them, raising the statue
above her head. With a grunt of effort, she
brought it down on the back of Pate's
head. At the last moment she was very
aware of the weight of the object and the
momentum with which it was going to
strike Pate. It didn't land squarely, but
most of it connected with the crown of
Pate's head. He fell on Vic at once, limp.

"Oh, Vic!" she moaned. "I think I killed
him!"

Vic rolled Pate off and to the side. "No,
he's still breathing. His breath stinks." He
took the knife and smoothly cut her bonds.

Then Megan reached for him and pulled
him into a sitting position, covering his
head with kisses.

"I'm so sorry, darling," he said, his voice
breathless and muffled against her collarbone. "About putting you in danger, about
acting so rudely toward you —"

"Stop it. Just stop it."

"But I need to —"

Megan clamped her mouth on his firmly,
effectively halting his apologies. There was
plenty of time for talk later. For the
moment, she just wanted to feel him close

and know that they were safe.

Pate stirred and moaned, startling them both. Vic tied him hand and foot none too gently with his own rope.

Megan looked down at Pate, still not quite believing that a double murderer was lying on the floor of her sitting room. "What happened to him, Vic? How did he get so . . . insane?"

"I don't know. Something just snapped inside him, I suppose. I think . . ."

"What?"

"It's hard to imagine, but I think we're lucky that we captured him after only two murders. It sounded like he was well on his way to a real killing spree. Soon he probably would have been imagining slights against him, arbitrarily killing whoever he wanted."

"That's frightening."

"Quite." He turned to her and softly ran his hand down the side of her face. "You were very brave."

"I was very scared."

Vic took her face in his hands and said, "I was too. More than you'll ever know. In the flash of an instant I saw my life without you, and I could hardly bear it." His rich brown eyes bore into hers with a startling passion. "I was so wrong, my darling. I behaved ungentlemanly, and without a thought for your feelings. Can you forgive me?"

Megan's eyes were wet from his impassioned plea, but she smiled. "Of course I forgive you."

He smiled, but then it faltered. "I have something to tell you. About Fran. About why I've behaved so . . . strangely. Please open your heart, Megan, and hear what I have to say with all the understanding you can muster."

Megan waited for him to go on, but he merely watched her. "All right, Vic. You know I will."

"I found something at Fran's cabin. A diary. In it . . ."

"What?"

"At first I was stunned, then sad, then I didn't know what I was for days —"

Megan took his hands in hers and noticed they were trembling. She was afraid of what his words might be, but she knew they could overcome anything if they faced it together with God's guidance. "Tell me, my love."

"Megan, I have a son."

"A . . . a . . . son?" It was the last thing in the world she'd expected to hear. "You mean . . . ?"

"Yes. It's all very clear in the diary, and Fran was certain that he's mine. I know what you must be feeling, and I'm sorry for distressing you so, but I've had more time to think about this than you, and —"

"Vic, where is he?"

"I don't know, that's the thing. She says she left him with her mother, but she doesn't mention her name. He could be anywhere, actually." He bent down and looked at her closely. "I'd give anything to know what you're feeling right this moment."

Megan put a hand to her forehead and shook her head. "So would I. It's all so . . . it's —"

"He's out there somewhere. From the way Fran talked in the diary, she resented him more than loved him. How do we know her mother isn't the same way? He could be in trouble, or —"

"How old is he, Vic? Do you know?" Megan didn't really care at the moment, but it would give her more time to absorb the news.

"I don't know, two maybe?"

"A little boy," Megan breathed. She'd thought about having children with Vic, but not like *this*. The boy's mother had been a wanderer, a lonely woman who took strange men into her home looking for comfort. For all they knew, the mother could be even worse — where else could Fran have learned her behavior?

Then Megan looked at her husband and saw his shining eyes and expectant look. He was so kind and gentle and yet strong — maybe the boy was like his father instead. Maybe he was living in squalor, not knowing that he had a father somewhere who would love him and spend time with him. Teach him to be an honorable man.

"All things work together for good for those who love God." I just read that today before that hateful man came into my home. Do I believe that verse?

"Megan?"

Selfish feelings almost overwhelmed her, but Megan shook them off. This was her husband's son, a part of his very being, and she could see that after days of brooding over it, he'd come to accept the fact that he was a father and had a son who needed him. The very fact that he'd been so reluctant to tell her about what he'd discovered showed that he wasn't sure that she would understand. And she didn't, not right now. But with God's help . . .

"I believe the Word of God, Vic."

He smiled uncertainly. "So do I."

"Then we have to find your son."

The look on his face banished any doubts about God's promise to bring good out of all this.

Chapter Twenty-Two

The Sky Father

Jack Sheffield couldn't believe his good fortune. If Crazy Horse hadn't been close by when Jack had been captured, if he'd been off hunting or fighting . . . But he hadn't been, and Jack could only believe that God had had a hand in it. Crazy Horse not only saved Jack from a sure death, he actually seemed to *like* him. Jack found this remarkable.

Many warriors gave Jack open, hateful glances. There was no doubt how they felt, but they wouldn't go against their greatest chief. Over the two days he spent with Crazy Horse, Jack wondered if anyone had informed the powerful medicine man, Sitting Bull, of his presence. It was told that one word from him decided *anyone's* fate, white man or red, even over Crazy Horse's wishes. Jack figured that Sitting Bull was aware of everything in the huge gathering and could only thank God that his death hadn't been ordered at once.

Crazy Horse was nothing like Jack had expected. The famed chief was a very solitary and quiet man, but his gentleness with children was genuine and sincere. Jack noticed that one in particular, Blue Sky At Dawn, was his favorite for obvious reasons — no one else possessed the same hair, fair skin, and eye color as those two in the whole village. When Jack had tentatively asked Crazy Horse if she was his daughter, the chief gave no sign he'd even heard him.

After Crazy Horse's acceptance, the children who had burned Jack inspected him closely. They fingered his dark trousers and coat, his tie, and especially his saddle. They obviously didn't understand why someone needed a saddle, and Jack had grinned and rubbed his own hindquarters, making a horribly pained face. The children had laughed and laughed. Their earlier cruelty was gone and forgotten, though Jack still limped from the soreness of blisters on the bottom of his feet. To their thinking, they had only performed a ritual that had been in their nation for probably hundreds of years, and Jack was happy to laugh with them instead of being their object of torture.

It was at twilight on the second day that Jack discovered why Crazy Horse had allowed him to live.

Crazy Horse had a passion for fishing. He took Jack, alone, to an offshoot of the Little Bighorn River that proved to be full of trout. They used cottonwood tree limbs and deer gut for fishing gear, and sat by the water mostly in silence. Blossoms from the huge tree behind them stirred in the air, swirling like translucent pink cotton through the sunlight. The smell of fresh dirt and moss surrounded them.

At last Crazy Horse spoke. "I dreamed about you the night before you came."

Jack was surprised but only nodded. Crazy Horse hated unneeded words.

"In it, my brother Little Hawk was leading a sheep. Its coat was as white as the sun and thick like in wintertime. Little Hawk was killed by our enemy, the Shoshone, about ten summers ago. I thought it strange that he was in my dream, because I had never dreamed about him before, and usually the dead have more important things to do than lead sheep."

Jack thought this funny, but he knew that the telling of a dream was very sacred for the Sioux. Besides, he didn't know whether Crazy Horse was joking or not.

"Little Hawk told me that the sheep had gotten lost and strayed onto his burial ground. He had wanted to kill it and eat it, but the sheep told him it wasn't lost, that it was right where it wanted to be. He told me that some intruders are not what they seem, though they look good to eat."

A fish flopped upstream, and the wind sighed through the cottonwood behind them. Green leaves floated by on the sluggish current.

Jack didn't know how to respond to Crazy Horse's words, so he just kept fishing.

"I tried and tried to understand what my brother was trying to tell me, and when I heard that a white man had been captured — only one — I knew what it was."

"You are a wise man, Crazy Horse. Your people are fortunate to have you fighting for them."

Slowly Crazy Horse turned his head to look at him. "Not all will feel the way you say. I know my destiny."

"What do you mean?"

But Crazy Horse didn't answer, and Jack didn't push him. They fished in silence for a long while, then Crazy Horse asked, "That Book you carry — that is the reason you are here?"

"Yes. I had hoped that the Sioux would listen to its words and understand the one true God. Also, I wanted to try to speak the truth to Crazy Horse about the horse soldiers."

A slight smile touched his lips. "And what is that?"

"I know it's hard for you to understand," Jack told him. "But I must tell you, there are many soldiers coming, even after these here now, and many people will die if you don't report to your reservations."

"Many *soldiers* will die," Crazy Horse stated.

"Soldiers *and* Sioux. You know your people will die, too."

Crazy Horse leaned back against the embankment on his elbows, the fishing pole at his side unheeded now. His ebony eyebrows were divided by two sharp lines of concentration. "My men are warriors. It is a great honor to die in battle."

"What if the soldiers break through to your families? What then?"

"It will not happen. There are too many of us."

Jack caught his eye. "I said, 'What if?' "

Suddenly, Crazy Horse flung the fishing pole into the water and got to his feet. As he stomped away, he growled, "I should have let the women and children have you."

★ ★ ★

Late that night Jack was lying by a small fire in the open. It was cool, and he shivered as he read his Bible by the feeble light. Many Sioux warriors walked by him, openly staring. He just smiled at them.

The boy who'd burned Jack's feet came by with herbs wrapped in large thin leaves. He shyly offered it to Jack, who thanked him profusely. Jack asked his name, but the boy just giggled and hid behind a tepee to watch him. The poultice was cool from being soaked in river water. It had a strong odor to it of alkaline, but it felt wonderful. Jack groaned with pleasure and heard the boy giggle harder. Soon Jack saw a half-dozen pairs of eyes peeking around at him. He motioned them over to his fire.

The boy, who was obviously going to be a chief someday with his take-charge attitude, stepped out and waved for the others to follow him. He was strutting now, as if he and the white barbarian were the best of friends.

Jack had nothing to offer them except some fish, but they politely took some. One of them was Blue Sky At Dawn. Jack was delighted.

Their clothes were well-made and cared for. Various ornaments decorated their young bodies, and they'd all been swimming and bathing in the river that day. They collectively smelled of harsh soap and wood fires.

Jack showed them his Bible and the tiny markings on every page. They felt the thin leaves of the sheets tenderly, afraid they would tear, then looked up at him with liquid brown eyes.

"It writes about you in here," he told them. "All of you." He made sign language to try to make them understand, then he turned to the Gospel of Matthew. " 'And at the same time came the disciples unto Jesus, saying, Who is the greatest in the kingdom of heaven?

" 'And Jesus called a little child unto him, and set him in the midst of them,

" 'And said, Verily I say unto you, Except ye be converted, and become as little children,' " — Jack stopped and pointed to each child — " 'ye shall not enter the kingdom of heaven.

" 'Whosoever therefore shall humble himself as this little child, the same is greatest in the kingdom of heaven.

" 'And whoso shall receive one such little child in my name receiveth me.' "

They gazed at him with the incredible intensity of interest that only a child could summon. They knew almost no sign at all, so Jack finally gave up trying to make them understand. Instead, he got the point across that God — "Sky Father" was the best he could translate to them — cared for them so much because they had hearts that were humble and sincere and trusting.

They beamed. Blue Sky flashed white, even teeth at him and wanted to look at the funny scratchings on the page.

"Now, what you did to me the other day," Jack continued, showing them his scarred feet, "was wrong. But you didn't know it was, because no one has ever told you it was wrong. We are to love, not hurt. The Sky Father wants us to love Him and each other above all else."

Suddenly, the children scattered like leaves blown in a strong wind.

Crazy Horse and Swift Bear appeared from behind him, and they didn't look happy. Swift Bear reached for the Bible, but Jack pulled it away and tucked it under his arm tightly.

"You will not talk to our children out of that book!" he growled, eyes wide and furious.

"They *wanted* to hear. They *need* to hear!"

Swift Bear's face twisted horribly, and

before Jack could move, a knife was at his throat.

Crazy Horse grabbed Swift Bear's arm and pulled it away. Swift Bear gave him a seething look, then stalked away.

Jack opened his mouth to thank Crazy Horse, but he squatted down and reached for the Bible. "No, Crazy Horse. I cannot give it away. I don't have another one."

The chief made an insistent motion with his hand.

"Will you give it back?"

"Yes."

Reluctantly, Jack handed it over to him.

Crazy Horse opened it and placed one hand on the pages, fingers spread out, feeling the texture. Cords of tendon and muscle stood out on his forearm like rope. He looked closely at the writing, turned a few pages, and found the daguerreotype of Agnes, Jack's little sister. She was only eight in the picture. Her long red curls spilled around her shoulders, and on her face was a look of interest, much the same as Jack had seen on the Indian children only minutes before.

"Your daughter?" Crazy Horse asked.

"My sister. Her name was Agnes."

"I will not let men put me in the light box. It steals from the spirit."

Jack nodded. He was talking about cameras, and he wasn't alone in his thinking. Many Indians refused to have their picture taken.

"You say her name *was* Agnes. Is she called something else now?"

"No. She's dead."

Crazy Horse grunted in surprise. "This little girl is dead?"

"She was two years — summers — older than that picture when she died." Jack paused, then added, "About the age of Blue Sky At Dawn."

Crazy Horse glanced at him quickly to find meaning behind the words, but Jack only stared at the daguerreotype. He remembered the day it was taken. He'd been fourteen and had to assure her time and again that the light wouldn't blind her forever. After the flash she'd pretended that it *had* blinded her, and she walked around with her eyes closed, hands held out far in front of herself, giggling. Jack had laughed with her, and he'd adored her.

"How did she die?" Crazy Horse asked.

"Consumption. It's a sickness that —"

"I know what it is," he said.

"Of course." Consumption wasn't confined to only white men, nor was smallpox, which had decimated parts of every tribe of Indian at some point since the white man's arrival.

Crazy Horse handed the Bible and picture back. "It is not right for children to die so young."

"Call off the attack, Chief."

He turned to Jack with a look of genuine puzzlement. "It is not I who attacks."

The night turned even colder. Jack had to find some dead tree limbs to add to his fire after everyone else had gone to sleep. Due to the size of the Indian gathering, fuel proved to be hard to find. He ended up resorting to damp limbs he found by the creek. He knew they would only be good to make more smoke and less heat, so he cast them aside on his way back. He was too tired to go searching further, and he doubted he would find any if he did.

Situating himself so close to the dying flames that he was almost lying in it, he closed his eyes and tried to sleep. Despite his exhaustion from his ordeal, his aching muscles and hurting ribs made sleep impossible.

He finally turned on his back and gazed up at the stars. Somewhere to the east he knew a huge army was approaching, a blue snake writhing its way toward the Sioux and Cheyenne camp. The soldiers were out-numbered, but they had guns and cannon to more than make up for it. As always, Jack hated the thought of their intrusion on the innocent Indians. He couldn't understand the action of taking another nation's land and killing and incarcerating its inhabitants. Even though it had happened many times throughout the centuries and in the Bible, it still seemed a barbarous act to Jack.

"Oh, Father," Jack murmured to the sky, "when Adam fell, he really fell, didn't he?"

Jack continued praying until he fell asleep.

The songs of birds woke him, along with the echoing sounds of people moving about at his peripheral hearing. He'd slept so well that his eyes didn't want to open. He wanted to stay there and cover his ears from the noise and sleep all day long. When he did look around, he found that clouds had moved in during the night, dimming the sun's rising and making it feel earlier than it really was.

He saw a group of children — his children, he grinned to himself — running off into a small forest and spreading out as if playing a game. He marveled again at the innocence and inherent happiness in children. They met each day's sun with clear eyes and contentment, the one true lesson they had to teach adults, if only they would listen.

Since he had no coffee to prepare, Jack decided to follow the children and see what they were doing. He still received untrustworthy stares from the adults as he walked along, but he understood why they viewed him with distrust. He showed them his grin and greeted them warmly. Jack didn't know what the day would bring, but he knew that the "Sky Father" was in control. He liked the phrase and would continue to use it with both the children and adults.

He heard the children calling to one another in the woods good-naturedly. Their voices rang sharply through the cold morning air like the clang of thin metal, sending a family of catbirds from the trees wailing their mewing call for which they were named. When they were well away with their distinct rusty undersides flashing against the iron-colored sky, Jack could still hear their strange call. Then he realized that they were *too* far away and that the mewing was coming from the woods.

A boy burst from the underbrush with

eyes wide from shock and fear. He stopped in front of Jack and pulled at his coat, stuttering something and pointing back the way he'd come. Other children burst from the cover in a terror-stricken flock.

"What is it? Is someone hurt?" he asked but received only frantic gestures and excited voices running together in a cacophony of babbling. He dashed off into the forest, ignoring his one tender foot, even when he stepped on rocks, dirt clods, and sticks. Once he tripped, but it barely slowed his stride.

A black bear had Blue Sky At Dawn cornered between three trees that had grown just a few feet from each other. Her wide eyes stared out from between the trunks in utter, frozen horror. The bear stood between Jack and Blue Sky, a little to Jack's right, with his broad back to him. Standing on his hind legs, the large bear sniffed the air, as if he couldn't quite see Blue Sky At Dawn twenty feet in front of him.

Blue Sky's feet were planted in total panic, as incapable of moving as the tree trunk she gripped. Her mouth hung open with a thin pendulum of saliva clinging to her lower lip. Even from Jack's position at forty feet away, he could see her trembling.

The bear picked up her scent and

grunted as he went to all-fours and moved toward her.

Jack was without a weapon of any kind. His breathing was ragged and fierce in his ears, and he thought for a brief moment that he could smell his own fear, rank in his nostrils.

A movement to his left surprised him. Thinking it was one of the other children, perhaps the brave little leader of the children, Jack opened his mouth to warn him back. It was Crazy Horse, looking at the bear with a mixture of anger and grave concern. He was naked except for a breechcloth and held only a knife in his hand. His eyes met Jack's, and Jack saw the same helpless look that he was sure covered his own face.

The bear moved closer to the terrified little girl.

Jack knew there was no choice but distraction. He picked up a four-inch thick limb, stepped out, and screamed, "Run, Blue Sky!" at the top of his lungs while heaving the limb at the bear. Either Jack's movement or his shouting broke the little girl's hypnotic state, and she broke from her spot between the trees and sailed through the woods like an antelope.

The limb struck the bear on its broad

back and did no damage whatsoever, but the bear's reaction was instantaneous and startling. Instead of glancing around at this intrusion curiously, it spun with disarming quickness and charged at him without hesitation.

To Jack, the coming juggernaut was an astonishing display of nature's power, an irresistible force that would not be denied. Jack tried to gauge the bear's speed so that he could jump to the side and run away, but the lack of distance and the creature's pure size caused him to misjudge.

The bear swatted at him with a thunderous paw, and even though it was a glancing blow, it sent Jack tumbling fifteen feet away. Stunned, Jack could only watch as the bear again closed the distance. "Oh, Father, oh, Father!" Jack thought over and over again, his paralyzing fear locking out all thought but the ones for his Savior.

Just before the bear reached him he saw a half-dozen arrows sprout from the bear's side. Help had come, but too late. The bear was on him. Jack tried to protect his head as best he could and heard himself growling along with the bear. Then all was sharp pain and he felt himself being tossed around like a doll. The world was brown fur, razor claws, and yellow teeth, and then it was as black as the inside of a cave.

The voices were babbling in a strange tongue and Jack felt no compulsion to go to them. He was in a warm place, a secret place that he'd never known existed. He didn't want to leave. So peaceful, yet so strange. He could stay there forever.

But he felt himself going toward the voices. His struggles against it were in vain. The world was harsh and cruel and loud that he returned to, and he felt sad that he'd returned. Many faces stared down at him, some young, some older, all with concern. The central face in his vision was an important man — an Indian — but Jack couldn't remember his name. He had deep, wise eyes that looked surprised for a moment.

"You are strong," he said. "Stronger than the bear."

Jack didn't know what he meant at first, then he remembered something important. "Crazy Horse," he whispered.

The man reached out and touched his face tenderly. "I am here."

"That is your name."

"Yes. That is my name."

"But you aren't crazy. I know that."

"Sometimes names are passed down from our fathers, as was mine. No, I am not crazy."

Beside him appeared a little girl who looked much like the great chief. She was crying openly, and in her small hands were handfuls of damp leaves that he gently began placing on Jack's body, though he couldn't feel it. He wished he could feel her touch, wished it mightily, but he contented himself with the fact that she was unharmed. "Why are you crying?" he asked her but was surprised when Crazy Horse answered.

"I cry for a brave man who gave his life for another."

Jack was stunned to see that he really *was* crying. Large tears fell unashamedly from his chocolate brown eyes. Then Jack's mind registered the words he'd spoken. "It is in my Book. If what you say is true, I have been blessed." It was becoming hard to talk, and even harder to think.

"You are a true warrior," Crazy Horse told him, still touching his face with soft caresses. "A warrior of the Sioux, and of the Sky Father."

Jack felt a smile come to his lips. "You know of the Sky Father?"

"The children told me of Him."

"Good," Jack whispered. "Learn more, my friend."

Crazy Horse smiled through his tears. "Songs will be written of this day. From this day forward you will be called Bear Killer in our legends."

Jack felt the warm place beckoning, and he closed his eyes to welcome it. Somehow, he knew it held a promise that could not be found on this earth, and he felt a surge of supreme happiness. He spoke, or thought he spoke, to Crazy Horse. "In your song . . . write of my Book."

An ocean of warmth enveloped him fully, and he rode the waves with pure joy.

Crazy Horse carried the girl back to the village in his arms. Neither of them was weeping now, and they were silent all the way until Blue Sky asked, "Who was that man?"

"His Sky Father sent him so that you could go on living."

Blue Sky thought about his words. "But he told us that the Sky Father was for all of us, not just him."

"Yes, he told us that," Crazy Horse whispered.

Many people were gathered outside the village to see what the commotion was about. Those returning from the woods would tell the story, then it would be told again hundreds of times that day, until by nightfall the whole gathering would know of the brave deed performed by the white man who'd come into their midst for so short a time.

"Tonight, Blue Sky, we will feast on bear meat and begin to make a robe for you out of his warm fur. You will have a necklace of his claws that I will make for you."

She looked up at him from where she'd had her head buried against his shoulder. "Really?"

"Yes."

"And where are we going now?"

Crazy Horse smiled. "To write a song about a man and his Book."

Chapter Twenty-Three
Taking Leave

A hailstorm had peppered Custer's command during late afternoon of June 21. They had stopped by the Yellowstone River, where the senior officers of General Terry's command met on the riverboat *Far West* to devise a plan of attack on the Sioux.

As Reena sat in her uncle Faron's tent, she listened to the sound of ice crunching beneath the cleated boots of the soldiers who passed by outside. Del sat by the tent flap sewing a rip in his shirt caused by a nail protruding from the side of their wagon. Reena had offered to do it for him, but he'd declined. As he worked, his tongue traced his upper lip back and forth.

Faron was finally able to sit up for long periods without growing dizzy and doing so now, practicing loading a pistol. He jammed the barrel of it under the stump of his arm and manipulated the cylinder and bullets with his good hand. He, too, must have been listening to the crunching sounds outside because he said, "Ice in the middle of summer. If the wind isn't blowin' sand in your eyes or the sun not bakin' you in an oven, it's raining ice on you. Ah, 'tis a harsh land we're negotiatin'."

Del grunted and mimicked Faron's accent. "Yeah, and 'tis a lot of complainin' you do. I never saw nobody whine so much when all they do is ride around in the back of a wagon and have folks wait on them hand and foot. *I* wouldn't complain."

"You'd complain if you fell into a mine shaft filled with gold."

"Both of you, stop it," Reena snapped.

They looked at her.

In a softer tone she amended, "Not today, all right?"

The activity around their tent was more intense than it had ever been. Mule hawkers were arranging their wagons, and couriers were running here and there with orders to be carried out at once. A tenseness in the air conveyed a sense of urgency that was palpable. The Seventh Cavalry was preparing to embark on its final leg of a month-long journey.

Reena was overjoyed that her uncle and Del sparred good-naturedly. Usually it eased the tension of being around Faron's amputation and created a sense of home that was badly needed. But on this day Reena sensed a marked danger in the air — something tangible yet just on the horizon that made her jumpy.

She glanced over at Faron, then to Del. Both men were intently occupied with their tasks — perhaps more engaged than was required. "You two don't have to stop talking altogether. I just wasn't in the mood for your bickering today."

They gave her identical blank looks, then considered each other, as if to say, "How do we talk without bickering?"

"Tell each other your life stories or something," Reena suggested.

"Tell . . . ?"

"Life stories . . . ?"

"Never mind," Reena sighed. *Men.*

Del suddenly looked up at someone outside. "Come on in, boys."

Private Josh Norton and another young man entered shyly, removing their campaign hats and twisting the brims in their hands. Norton said, "We . . . uh . . . just came by to tell Mr. O'Donnell good-bye."

"You're leaving?" Faron asked. "Now?"

"Well, we're going to be pretty busy until we do leave, so . . . you know . . ."

Faron hesitated, then said in a surprisingly gentle voice, "What's on your brain, Josh?"

He gestured to the other young man. "This is my friend Denny Simms. He's from Texas, not Ohio like me. We're best friends." He paused painfully, then glanced at Reena.

"I could leave . . . ?" Reena offered.

"Oh no, ma'am, no cause for that." Josh blushed.

Denny Simms spoke for the first time in a rich baritone. "We don't mean to stare, ma'am. We just haven't seen anyone so pretty in so long. A *woman* so pretty, I mean. Not meanin' that we seen *men* so pretty . . ." He closed his mouth with a snap when he realized he was rambling.

Reena smiled at them, but inside she was horrified at how young they were. She recalled some of the fierce Blackfoot warriors she'd seen, and the thought of them galloping through a regiment of boys like these brought an image of wolves among lambs.

"We just came by to give you these," Josh told Faron, reaching into his blouse pocket and handing him something. "You *are* going back to Canada, aren't you, Mr. O'Donnell? Away from here?"

Faron held up two identically wrapped

wads of paper and unfolded one. "You're givin' me a button from your blouse? Both of you?"

Josh nodded. "They're wrapped in our folks' addresses on those papers." The long silence that followed was stunning, and Josh couldn't stand it. "Well, we have to get going —"

"Hold on there, Josh," Faron told him. He swallowed hard, his Adam's apple moving up and down his throat like an acorn. "Have ye written your folks?"

"Oh yes, sir, both of us."

Faron didn't ask where the letters were. Reena knew they'd done one of two things. Either they'd been mailed, or they were keeping them with them in case they were needed for identification purposes later. The thought made her shiver.

"What's the attitude among your comrades, Josh?" Faron asked.

The boys shifted their feet, glanced at each other, and then Josh answered with false bravado, "We're going to whip Crazy Horse, Mr. O'Donnell. Everybody knows that."

With a nod, they ducked through the tent and were gone.

Outside, where they'd vanished, Reena could see sunset clouds on the horizon that glowed crimson and were laced with gold. She heard Faron carefully fold the paper in his hand around the brass button. Del cleared his throat with a grunt, stood, and slammed down his sewing on the chair.

"I'm goin' for a walk."

After a few minutes Faron asked, "What are ye cryin' for, lass?"

Reena didn't answer.

"They're soldiers. They knew the day would come when they had to fight."

"They're *boys*, Uncle Faron. Just boys, playing at soldier like they were in the woods behind their house."

"They'll conduct themselves well," Faron remarked with a touch of pride.

Reena wiped her eyes with the sleeve of her blouse. "I wish they'd conduct themselves well and desert."

"Reena! Ye don't mean that."

"I *do* mean it!"

Hunter ducked into the tent a few moments later and gave Faron a nod, then turned to Reena. The look on his face told her that he was apprehensive about something. "Is something wrong?" she asked.

"We're leaving."

Reena and Faron exchanged looks.

"Macleod has ordered me . . . us . . . back to the fort."

"But," Reena said, "I thought it was too dangerous for us to leave the soldiers?"

Hunter's face seemed to tighten. "I'm beginning to think that it's too dangerous to stay *with* the soldiers."

It did not take them long to get ready since they had very few things to pack into the wagon. Hunter was uneasy during the preparations. Nothing had been resolved with the massed Indians to their west, and he felt that his little band was extremely exposed to attack. He knew everyone wanted away from this place — him included — and he tried to put on a confident face for the others.

When Custer had given him Macleod's telegram that morning, he'd said, "I suppose you'll be leaving us now?"

"It looks that way."

"Godspeed, then." They were in Custer's tent, and he went back to writing a letter to his wife, dismissing Stone without another word.

"General?"

"Yes?" Custer said as he continued to write.

"About the other day, at the burial ground . . ."

Custer waved a hand in the air. "No

need to apologize, Stone. Done and for-gotten."

"I wasn't going to apologize."

Custer looked up sharply.

"I had thought that compassion was a basic trait in every human soul. God made us in His image, the Bible says. Now I wonder."

Staring up at Hunter, Custer's face began to redden.

Hunter went on, unperturbed. "I would be remiss in my duty as an officer of the law if I didn't tell you that had you exhib-ited that sort of behavior in my country, I would have arrested you on the spot. There are some boundaries men don't cross, regardless of the situation or circum-stance. That is one of them."

Through tight lips Custer answered, "Your observation is noted, sir. You may leave now."

Without another word, Hunter left.

Now, as he watched Reena tuck blankets around her uncle in the back of the wagon, he realized that his blunt words probably did no good at all. Custer was a vain, stub-born man whose personal agenda was the law. Hunter didn't doubt that if he'd been a member of Custer's troop, he would have been court-martialed on the spot for speaking against his commanding officer. *But I had to say it,* he thought. *It was too important to let go.*

Del and Reena climbed up in the wagon seat and looked at him expectantly. Around them, the activity of an army preparing to move was like a beehive that had been swatted with a stick, and no one even glanced at them.

"Hunter?" Reena said with a crease of worry on her forehead. "We're ready."

"I feel like we should have a word of prayer."

She smiled. "That's a good idea."

Hunter noticed how tired she was. They had traveled hundreds of miles to get here, and now they had to make the same journey through dangerous country. Through it all he hadn't heard her complain once. She was a special woman, and despite their bleak situation, he felt a surge of love for her.

Astride Buck, Hunter moved to the wagon, took her hand, and they bowed their heads — even Del. "Dear Father, we come to You first with a thankful heart that You've taken care of us this far. Now we face another long journey back, and we trust You to continue to look out for us. Keep us healthy and safe from harm. In the name of Jesus, amen."

When his eyes met Reena's, there was a peace glowing in her that hadn't been there before. With shining eyes she said, "Let's go home."

They traveled through the heat of the day to stop by a small stream amidst a grove of cottonwood trees. Reena could tell that Hunter was anxious to put many miles between themselves and the unrest southwest of them, but Faron was in extreme pain by late afternoon from the jostling of the wagon. They made camp silently and efficiently. As Reena got Faron settled on some blankets beneath a tree, Del gathered wood for a fire. Hunter rode around their position to make sure they weren't camped a stone's throw away from Indians.

Faron, sweating and weak, went to sleep at once. Reena bathed his face with a cloth soaked in the creek, then saw to his dressing. She knew she would have to wake him up to make him eat something in a while. He'd lost a lot of weight since the amputation, and the late afternoon sun revealed his pale, drawn face in a harsh light.

As she and Del started dinner, Hunter rode over a small rise to their west at a dead run. Alarmed, Reena and Del dropped what they were doing and stood. Del reached for his rifle. Hunter reined in Buck savagely and jumped down, sliding his Henry rifle out of its pocket on the saddle.

"Indians, coming this way."

"How many?" Del asked.

"Looks like a small party, maybe ten." He tied Buck to the wagon and said, "Douse that fire. Del, get behind the tree. Reena, get in the wagon and cover yourself with blankets."

Reena went to the wagon, but instead of getting in the back, she reached under the seat and withdrew Faron's rifle.

"What do you think you're doing?" Hunter asked.

After checking to see that it was loaded, she looked for obstructions in the barrel but found none.

"Reena, get in the wagon! This is no time for —"

"If they're here to kill us, Hunter, then they would find me wherever I hid. At least this way I could maybe get one of them."

Hunter didn't argue because the Indians topped the same rise he'd just ridden over. Reena did a quick count — nine of them. They wore only breechcloths, and she had the impression that they were a hunting party, traveling light and quick. They gazed down at them before calmly coming forward.

"Don't shoot unless they attack," Hunter told them. "But make sure they see the rifles. Del?"

Del stepped out from behind the tree and leaned against it almost casually. "Yep, they're Sioux."

Reena whispered a quick prayer and saw that Hunter was doing the same. The sun glittered off the rifles the Sioux carried. They held them pointed to the sky, which Reena hoped was a good sign. They seemed to be in no hurry to kill them, if that was their intention. She thought they would be charging quickly if that were the case. "So what do they want?" she muttered.

Hunter heard her and said, "We'll give them anything — the wagon, the horses, the supplies — we just need to live through this. That's the important thing."

The Sioux leader — obvious because of his center position and headdress — had black eyes that seemed to never blink. He stopped the group ten yards away. Reena had to squint to see them, and she knew that to have the sun in their eyes was planned by the leader. The hot breeze blowing toward her brought their sweaty smell to her nostrils.

The leader looked down at Faron for a long time, and something passed behind his inscrutable features. Then he looked at each one of them in turn, his dark eyes finally coming to rest on Reena. Disturbingly, he was looking at her midsection. She chanced a look down and saw what it was — her cross, carved out of ash by her brother before she came west. It was large and noticeable, and on it were the words *Deo gratias* — Latin for "thanks be to God."

The leader spoke to Hunter.

Del interpreted. "He says his name is Big Tree. He wants to know what we're doing out here."

"Tell him we're going home, to the Canadas."

Del spoke haltingly, then said, "There's no word for 'Canadas' in Sioux."

"Tell him the country of the Great White Mother, the Queen."

Del translated, and Big Tree spoke again.

"He says it's very dangerous out here — like we don't know that — and that we have very fine-looking horses. I don't like this, Hunter."

"Tell him if he tries to take our horses, we will fight, and he will die."

"I can't tell him that! Besides, you said —"

"Tell him, Del." All the while, Hunter's eyes never left Big Tree's. Reena felt her own legs trembling and wondered how he could look so calm in the face of such danger.

Del translated, and Big Tree looked at his companions. Then he smiled slightly and spoke again.

"He says you would die, too. I gotta tell you, Hunter, I ain't crazy about all this dyin' talk. Can't we offer him the horses real nice like?"

Big Tree spoke again, nodding at Faron, and Del looked down at him in surprise. "He says he knows Faron." Then he looked back up at Big Tree. "He says he shot him."

Reena forgot her fear momentarily and felt a surge of anger at the Indian's small smile as he looked down at her uncle. "What are you smiling at?" she asked, taking a step forward.

Big Tree's horse spooked at her movement, and suddenly guns were pointed everywhere. Reena's fear returned instantly, and she stepped backward. She almost dropped the rifle from her slick palms.

Suddenly she *wanted* to drop it and run away as fast as she could.

Hunter, with his rifle now pointed in Big Tree's direction, told her, "Don't do that again, Reena."

"Don't worry, I won't."

Big Tree continued to study her, staring at the cross she wore, then with a head movement and a grunt he ordered his men to raise their rifles. They did so, but slowly and reluctantly. Many of them were watching Reena, the intent of their ebony eyes obvious to all.

Big Tree said something else, then reached down and withdrew a pouch from his saddlehorn and tossed it to Hunter.

Del said, "He claims this belonged to a white man who came to their camp. Says his chief told him to deliver this to the first white people he came across."

"Reena," Hunter said, "see what's in it, would you?"

Glad for an excuse to put the rifle down, any excuse to *do* something besides stand there and be frightened, Reena moved to the pouch at Hunter's feet and opened it. What she found took her breath away, and she murmured, "Oh no!"

"What is it?"

She brought her eyes up to him and

whispered, "It's Jack's Bible."

"Sheffield's?" Hunter asked, looking away from Big Tree for the first time. "Del, ask him what this means."

After another exchange, Del shook his head sadly. "It's bad. He says Jack's dead — he died saving a little girl's life."

Reena ran her fingers lightly over the embroidered eagle on the cover of the Bible. Del's words didn't cut her, because the moment she'd seen the Bible, she'd known that Jack was dead. Tears filled her eyes as she thought of the man who'd shown nothing but kindness to her and a giving spirit that had touched so many lives, both white and red.

Big Tree added to his story.

"He says that Jack was Crazy Horse's friend. Crazy Horse wanted to keep the Bible, but he wrote a song about Jack instead. He wanted white folks to have the Bible, so that they would know he was dead. He also says that Jack was a great warrior, worthy of the Sioux."

While Big Tree told them the whole story of Jack's courageous death, Reena clutched the Bible to herself, tears flowing freely down her cheeks. *So brave. So typical of Jack, to lay down his life for a friend.*

Big Tree finished, proud of his prowess

at relating a good tale of bravery. After telling them it would be wise to leave the area, he and his braves rode away.

Hunter knelt down beside Reena, who was still on her knees by the pouch, and gently stroked her back. "I'm sorry, Reena."

Wiping away tears, she gave him a hesitant smile. "I was, too, for a moment there. But, Hunter, if we've ever heard of God's working in someone's life, this is it. He knew the Lord told him to go to Crazy Horse, and look what happened! Jack gained his respect in just a few days and was able to witness to Crazy Horse at the same time. Isn't that wonderful?"

"Yes, it is."

Hearing her own words made Reena feel even more sure of God's design. "Crazy Horse wanted to keep the Bible, but I'm sure there was no one to translate it to him. But Big Tree said he wanted to *keep* it! He obviously learned something from Jack. Oh, something good will come of Jack's words, I just know it."

On what should have been a mournful occasion, that night they sat around the fire and talked about Jack joyfully — the man he was, a man chosen of God to exhibit His wonderful works — and when everyone was asleep but Reena, she stared up at the black canopy of God's sky and thanked Him for having the privilege of having known Jack Sheffield.

Chapter Twenty-Four

Ours for a Time

George Armstrong Custer looked around himself in disbelief. Everywhere was confusion, choking smoke, horses running here and there in total panic, the screams of dying men — his men, the Seventh Cavalry, the finest fighting force the West had ever seen — and he wondered how they had come to this.

He'd confidently taken over two hundred and fifty men of the Seventh into the valley of the Little Bighorn to attack a Sioux village. To his great surprise, he'd found more Indians than he'd ever seen in his life. In the Civil War he'd learned to gauge the force of an enemy, but that was when they were in formation. Before he knew it, the Sioux and Cheyenne were swarming around them like flies. He knew there were at least a thousand of them, probably more, with even more showing up by the minute.

Custer's men began shooting their own horses to use as barricades on the featureless plain. This didn't work, however, since there were no organized battle lines. The Indians were *everywhere.*

Bleeding from a gunshot wound to the side, Custer took a quick survey of the land and knew that if they didn't make the top of a rise to his west, all would be lost. There they could form a line of resistance with their repeating carbines that could withstand any charge. Shouting to make himself heard, the beleaguered troop around him began fighting their way to the rise, firing and dying on the way.

They were closing in on the hilltop, and Custer was beginning to feel better about their situation. His wound was seeping badly, and they had already lost many men, but he felt his confidence rise. Firing his pistol, he saw a brave go down from the back of his horse. *This battle will be won!*

He heard someone shouting his name and turned to find a sergeant gesturing frantically to the hill behind him. Turning, he felt his heart skip a beat and surge downward to his belly.

Over the rise rode more Indians — many more. In the lead was a handsome, light-skinned Sioux with a fierce countenance. Their eyes met over the rolling smoke and mayhem. Custer saw a determination such as he'd never encountered and an unmistakable look of triumph in the Indian's eyes.

The hill would not be gained. His command was doomed. All this Custer realized in the fraction of an instant.

The boy general had been outwitted, and now he would pay for it with his life, and the life of more than two hundred and fifty soldiers of the Seventh Cavalry.

Hunter's little band reached Fort Benton on June 28, three days after the Battle of the Little Bighorn. They had no knowledge of the news, having just traveled over barren prairie and rolling hills, and it wasn't until they were restocking their supplies for the final leg home that Del happened to see a newspaper with shouting headlines announcing the event. After standing at the counter and gazing at it in stunned silence for a moment, he turned to Reena and Hunter. "You two have a look at this."

They were putting rolls of fresh bandages in a basket and turned to face him. The headline read:

MASSACRE AT LITTLE BIGHORN!!
CUSTER DETAIL WIPED OUT!!
BOY GENERAL DEAD!!

Reena and Hunter froze in what they were doing. The large print of the blaring

441

headline seemed to magnify the event even more, which was undoubtedly the intent of the editor.

Hunter dropped the bandage roll he was holding, strode over to Del, and unceremoniously snatched it out of his hand.

"You gonna read dat, you gonna buy it," the proprietor warned. He was about fifty, with a round belly, bushy eyebrows that grew together, and a pronounced German accent.

Del held up a hand. "You'll get your money, buddy, don't worry."

The proprietor definitely liked that and became garrulous. "Bad business, dat battle. Killed everyone, including der horses. Mutilation, scalping . . ."

Reena half listened to him drone on about the battle, but her mind was still numb. All those boys she'd seen and been around were dead. Gone. What had happened? They'd been so confident and seemed so capable of handling any force that could come their way.

Hunter grunted while reading the article, and Reena asked, "What is it?"

"The list of names on the casualty list. The Norton boy is on it."

Reena felt a deep sadness. Josh Norton had cared for Faron, and she dreaded having to tell her uncle the bad news. "What about Denny Simms, Josh's friend?"

Hunter's eyes ran down the list. His look told her the answer.

They paid for their bill, loaded the wagon, and left in a somber mood. At first no one took it upon themselves to tell Faron of the battle, but he sensed their mood and asked from the back of the wagon, "What's happened?"

Reluctantly, Reena told him. Faron's face didn't change, but she noticed that he swallowed hard and his hand automatically went to the breast pocket of his coat where he'd placed the buttons belonging to the boys, wrapped in addresses of unsuspecting parents. "Well," he said in a quiet, scratchy voice, "I suppose I look a bit foolish whining over me arm, when those young boys lost their whole future. What a shame."

That night the campfire sizzled and popped, providing the only noise to be heard. None of them felt like talking. Del half-heartedly tried to start a conversation twice, but his efforts went nowhere.

Finally, Hunter asked Reena, "Could you tell me what God's plan is in all that death? I don't understand."

Reena sighed. "We can't know God's complete plan, of course. There *is* the fact that there could have been that many

443

Sioux women and children killed on that day as there were soldiers. It's happened before." She shrugged her shoulders and felt more tired than she ever had in her life. "I don't know the answer, Hunter."

Del said, "Maybe that army learned a little lesson about respect of other people and nations. Maybe that'll happen."

Hunter nodded. "Maybe so."

After a long silence Faron said, "I think we ought to write those boys' parents."

"We will, Uncle," Reena assured him.

"No, I mean right now — tonight. Deal with the feelings we're havin'."

They talked it over and decided that it was a good idea. Reena had purchased paper and ink in Fort Benton for just that purpose, but she hadn't expected to be using it so soon. Earlier that afternoon, after hearing the terrible news, it had seemed to her that the chore of writing relatives of dead boys would be something to postpone and dread. But as they all four added their thoughts and sorrows over the deaths, and poured their feelings down on paper to people they would never know, it seemed to heal their own private wounds and make the night more bearable.

"You know," Hunter said, after they'd finished and read through both letters aloud, "those boys are gone, and this news will hit the parents hard, but . . . it makes all the difference in the world when you have trust in the Lord. God has given me a peace now about the whole journey that earlier I didn't think was possible. Despite this tragedy, despite Jack Sheffield losing his life, I still know that God is in control and will always be in control no matter what happens."

"I know what you mean, Hunter," Reena murmured. "I feel the same way."

Del and Faron, both having never given their lives to Christ, listened to them carefully and thought about their words.

"Those boys," Hunter continued, "all of them — they walked beneath God's heaven on His earth, and for a time they were ours. I couldn't get the thought out of my head as we rode along today that somewhere, in small towns and big cities all over this country, somebody still remembers their smiles, their touches, their lives. It's as if they'll live on in the people who loved them." He paused and shifted the logs in the fire, looking embarrassed. "I suppose I'm just rambling now."

Faron was watching him closely while he spoke and now said, "You just keep on talkin', lad. You're about the first man I've ever met who knew what he was talkin' about when he opened his mouth. I heard you pray over us the other day. You thought I was asleep, but I wasn't. I see you pray with me niece every evenin', and I'm right proud that she's found herself a man with integrity. So you just talk all you want to."

Hunter smiled. "Thank you for that, sir."

"Hunter," Del said, clearing his raspy voice, "could you . . . um . . . would you mind . . . ?"

"What is it, old friend?"

He looked at them helplessly for a moment, then blurted, "Well, I sure do like to hear you pray. Would you mind sayin' one now, for those boys' families you was talkin' about? I bet they sure need it tonight."

Over the fire, Hunter and Reena locked gazes. Del had never shown any interest in God, and this was a definite breakthrough. Secretly they grinned at each other out of pure joy.

Hunter turned to Del and said, "I'd be glad to."

They prayed beneath God's sky, with the stars winking and flickering their majesty.

The next day the sun was warm but not unpleasantly hot. Reena felt better than she had in a month. The tiredness seemed to have melted from her bones, and she felt an energy that had been lacking for some time. To take a break from the hard wagon seat, she saddled Del's horse and rode along with Hunter ahead of Del and Faron, chatting with him and enjoying his company. Occasionally, she would throw her head back and feel the warm rays on her face that seemed to spread to her whole body.

After a while, the urge humming through her became irresistible, and she grabbed the reins of Hunter's horse and summoned a dead run from her own.

Hunter gave a yelp of surprise, and it made her laugh merrily as the wind tore through her ebony hair. When she turned to look at him she saw him laughing, too. Over his shoulder she caught a glimpse of Del and Faron staring after them from the wagon, their mouths tiny black holes of surprise.

Reena led them almost a mile before stopping abruptly at the crest of a hill. The sight below made her gasp even more than she already was. Spread out before her was the land, rich and deep and glorious. Rolling hills studded the landscape, with a deep river cutting through the area that shone impossibly blue. She'd startled a herd of deer as they'd grazed and watched as they bounded away in their distinct, graceful manner.

Jumping down from the horse, Reena tied both sets of reins to a nearby tree and said, "Come with me, my darling!"

"Where?"

"Down there!" she cried, not waiting for Hunter, but taking off at a run down the gentle slope. When she reached the bottom, she turned and found him near, panting for breath, watching her with amused uncertainty.

"Reena, have you lost your mind?"

"Do this." She extended her arms straight out from her sides.

"What?"

"Do like this, silly! But you can only think of wonderful things — that's the rule."

His eyes were on her, eyes that were clear and radiated with his own unique passion that was all hers.

Reena giggled. "Look, I've got goosebumps!"

"I love you, Reena."

He joined her and together they walked through the waist-high prairie grass, arms extended, fingertips brushing red, yellow and blue wildflowers that tickled their palms when blown by the wind.